FROM THE FRONT OF THE CANTINA SOMEONE SHOUTED, "LET HIM GO AND BEG IT FROM HIS OLD LADY!"

Morgan knew without looking that it was Jesse Bruton. Now came an instant not unfamiliar to him, the split second when everything around him seemed to stop: the moment of decision.

In that frozen bit of eternity he assayed Bruton's slouching stance, the pair of pistols slung from belts that crisscrossed at a level where Bruton's belly button would be. The X the straps formed would be an ideal target to aim for. Rising easily, his gun hand curled comfortably next to his holster, Morgan said, "That's a mighty offensive familiarity, sir. I await your apology."

"Wordy bastard, ain'tcha," Bruton said and his arms twitched upward.

Drawing his Colt and leveling it with the X, Morgan said flatly, *"Don't lift 'em another inch, Bruton!"*

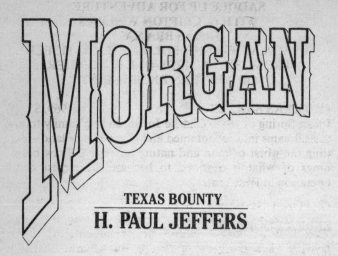

MORGAN

TEXAS BOUNTY

H. PAUL JEFFERS

ZEBRA BOOKS
KENSINGTON PUBLISHING CORP.

ZEBRA BOOKS

are published by

Kensington Publishing Corp.
475 Park Avenue South
New York, NY 10016

First printing: September, 1989

Printed in the United States of America

To Elaine Rose

"I'll sell my horse and I'll sell my saddle;
You can go to hell with your longhorn
cattle."

— *The Old Chisholm Trail*

Part One
Miss Rebecca Colter

Chapter One

Spurring his gray horse, Morgan darted up a gentle slope toward a rider waiting as still and rigid as an equestrian statue, silhouetted against a barely risen sun on the lip of the low red clay bluff above the brown muddy meander known as the San Antonio River. Cresting the hill, he felt the soggy kiss of the warm, muggy, and sluggish wind that blew perpetually across sixty miles of brush and scrub from the sun-flaked green waters of the Gulf of Mexico to hardscrabble land around the South Texas town of Goliad that was good for nothing except the raising of longhorn cattle.

West and south of the bluff had been gathered nearly ten thousand of the ungainly creatures. Rounded up over the past month under the watchful eyes of Morgan and his *caporal*, a savvy Mexican called Dalgo, they were branded with the B-C of the Colter ranch and doggedly collected by half a hundred cowboys and vaqueros into the restless tawny sprawl that filled a wide hollow a mile behind him. Reining up, he twisted slightly to peer back at them from the saddle of the able Mexican pony which got its name from the Spanish for its gray color—Grulla—and that was his choice from the corral when it came to trucking with longhorns.

"Good morning, Mr Morgan," said the shadowy and

sun-halo'd figure at the crest of the hill — Rebecca Colter, smiling for him at the crack of dawn and dressed in a buckskin skirt, dark blue woolen shirt, red bandana knotted loosely around her neck and, dangling against her back, a straw sombrero with the brim bent up almost to a point at the front that she favored for wild sunset gallops atop these same bluffs. "It appears to be a fine day for commencing a cattle drive."

"Sure is," he said with a grin, adjusting the tilt of his head and the brim of his weathered hat to block the blinding sun directly behind her.

"It's an impressive herd," she declared, nodding toward the cattle with her green eyes as wide open as those of a hungry bird of prey about to swoop down on them from her lofty perch.

"Three thousand or so more than went up the trail last year," he said, glancing back. "With two thousand more from the Anderson ranch to be joining us up at Cuero," he added with a frown.

Her smile faded. "I know you don't approve of the arrangement, Mr. Morgan," she said in a scolding schoolmarmish tone that was not unfamiliar to him. "You've made your objections quite plain. But I gave my word to Mr. Anderson. The deal is done. So let's not go over it again."

"No, ma'am," he said stiffly. "You're the boss."

The green eyes shifted past him to the herd, lingered for a moment — lovingly, he observed — then came back decisively to him. "You may take them to market, Mr. Morgan."

"Yes, boss," he said with a dimpling smile, saluting her as smartly as if he were back in the Seventh Cavalry and she were George Armstrong Custer himself, then wheeling away from her and the painful sun and spurring Grulla toward the herd.

Impatiently, Dalgo sped out to meet him, the moon

10

face and drooping black mustache of the caporal beaded with sweat already. "Do we have the señorita's blessing to proceed?"

"We do," cried Morgan, whipping off his hat, waving it exultantly above his head and bringing it down with a soft slap on Dalgo's shoulder.

"*Bueno*," he beamed.

"So let's get a move on, *amigo!*" laughed Morgan. "It's a mighty long hike to Kansas!"

Moments later as Dalgo yelped joyfully and waved his sombrero to signal them, the dozen cowboys Morgan and he had picked for the drive began to goad reluctant and sullen cattle across the first of the many rivers, great and small, between them and their fateful appointment with the weighing pen, loading chutes, and cattle cars of a railway in Kansas, Illinois slaughter houses and packing plants and dinner tables even farther east.

They would be half the day passing the spot where the woman on the dun horse on the red clay bluff watched.

When she could no longer see the young man on the gray horse at the point of the herd, knowing she would not see him again for six months, she spurred the horse, quickly descended the bluff and rode fast through the brush and scrub with the ascendant sun burning her tear-dampened face.

Chapter Two

"Thursday's child has far to go," went the nursery rhyme.

Her mother died birthing her.

She'd been born on a Thursday, a day full of storms raging westward from the Gulf and howling angrily against the sturdy adobe western walls of her father's sheltering house.

Soon after he had put baby Rebecca's mother in the ground, Buck Colter had been advised by the respectful and considerate citizens of Goliad to get himself another woman. As soon as his proper period of mourning for his wife was over, he must marry again, he was warned; not for himself, of course, but for the sake of the girl. Rebecca would be needing the guiding hand of a woman, they counseled. South Texas was no country for a girl to grow absent the taming example of a woman.

And, of course, Buck would want a son to inherit all that he had built.

He'd not heeded their advice and when he'd died these persons of long memory hastened to point out to one another in the hushed conversations that attended his funeral that their most dire predictions had come true. Look what had happened! All of the grim forecasts concerning Rebecca had come to pass. Because she was allowed to grow up unfettered, she was precisely the wild and willful young woman they had foretold.

Anyone could see how she was by the manner in which she conducted herself every Saturday when she rode alone into town supposedly for the purpose of fetching supplies—snobbish and brazenly flirtatious! Having lunch alone, she sat by the front window of the Case Hotel dining room where she could not be overlooked, yet as she invited attention from the men of the town, she conducted herself as though the men were beneath her station, as if somehow she were better than anyone in Goliad and equal to any man.

In these snoopy people who felt it was their place to speculate, there was no doubt that she would have to marry. She had become the richest woman in Texas and, therefore, a prize for the man who married her. As independent as she was, she was still a woman and, they believed, running the Colter ranch was something beyond her capabilities—beyond those of any woman! Why, even her father had needed the assistance of a man called Novillero and his right-hand man, the capable vaquero named Felipe Hidalgo but called Dalgo, in managing a vast enterprise spread over thousands of acres of the Nueces Strip and employing hundreds of men in the spring and summer when the herd had to be rounded up and driven to the market at the railhead at the terminus of the Chisholm trail in Abilene.

Years earlier they'd believed she might marry Jesse Bruton until Buck drove him off the ranch with a bullwhip, for reasons no one ever could discern.

Next, they supposed she might choose Novillero.

Then came this mysterious fellow by the name of Morgan who had risen in prominence on the Colter ranch since the death of her father.

13

Certainly Morgan was closer to her age and considerably better looking than Novillero. Tall, slender, and lithesome, he moved amiably through Goliad but with the sure bearing of a soldier and the confidence of a young man who seemed to be at ease with the Colt six-gun slung from his right hip and tied to his thigh with rawhide thongs.

Glancing at him as he passed and peering down at him from their windows whenever he rode into town, they wondered, "Who is this Morgan?"

He was a Yankee. That was for sure. All anybody had to do was hear him talk to see that. He'd hailed from Pennsylvania, someone had heard, and had landed in Kansas for some reason no one could quite pin down. He definitely had been in the army. A captain in Custer's cavalry, he was, it was stated for a fact. He was the youngest captain in the entire Union Army, it was said, given his epaulets by Custer himself at the age of fifteen at the Battle of Gettysburg. Later, he served as chief of scouts for Custer at Fort Riley and had scalped at least ten Indians in several battles. For some reason he had a falling out with Custer, possibly over the affections of a woman in Junction City, Kansas, and wound up in Abilene as a saloon owner and gunfighter. Someone who had cause to visit Chicago a couple of years back seemed to recall reading a magazine article about his exploits as a gunman. Killed at least twenty men, the article said, although never without provocation. Whether Morgan was his first or last name, no one knew except him — and he wasn't saying anything to confirm or lay to rest any of the stories about him.

When Rebecca Colter chose "Mr. Morgan," as she always called him when referring to him in conversation with others, to be her new trail boss and her business rep at the cattle markets following the untimely death of Novillero, the story that swept the town like prairie fire was that she had taken Morgan as her lover.

So rampant was it that he couldn't ride into Goliad on ranch business or just to relax with a bottle of mescal at the El Dorado cantina without feeling the scorch of lascivious eyes on his back and hearing the gossips' whispers as he passed, like the hiss of snakes.

Yet the rumor was as baseless as the one that had held she was about to up and sell the ranch and move to Kansas City or San Francisco.

However, the speculation that she was not up to running a ranch and would soon abandon the enterprise had been easily laid to rest. To do so, she'd taken charge of a drive, making the journey up the Chisholm Trail and commanding top dollar for a herd of eight thousand longhorns in hard bargaining at Abilene, demonstrating beyond any semblance of doubt to the skeptical folks of Goliad that she could be as good as a man in the cattle business and that the daughter of Buck Colter was the match of her father when it came to having a head for business.

Burying the gossip and rumors that flourished after the death of her father that she couldn't cut the mustard and that she would soon give up and sell the ranch had been easy; stilling the stories concerning her taking Morgan as a lover would not be so easy—if she cared to.

Chapter Three

For years, it had been speculated that she would marry Andrew Stoner, known far and wide by the monicker Novillero, because he'd made a reputation by fighting in the bullrings of Mexico when he was only fourteen years old and was still talked about with admiration and awe in the cantinas across the Rio Grande. As a youth he might have become Prince of the Corrida de Toros had he not been discovered making love to the beautiful wife of the owner of a bullring in Mexico City and killed the jealous husband in a ferocious struggle by stabbing him in the heart with a *banderilla*.

Fleeing to Texas and eventually finding sanctuary on the Colter Ranch, first as a cowboy and then as Buck's trusted foreman and trail boss, he'd been top hand for more than a year when the tomboyish 14-year-old everyone referred to affectionately as Little Miss Becky sauntered into the tack room he used as an office in a wooden shed built against the bunk house and said, "Teach me roping."

Looking up from his paperwork, he regarded the boyish girl with amusement. "Now why on earth does a pretty girl like you want to know about ropin'? Where's the call for a girl to use a rope?"

16

"If I'm to run this ranch someday," she said confidently, tossing her long chestnut hair, "I believe I ought to know something about every job on the place. Roping is a good way to start."

"Yeah, ropin's as good a way as any," he said cautiously, adding, "Does your daddy know about this?"

"No."

Shaking his head, he said, "Don't you think he ought to?"

"I'll tell him," she asserted. "When the time comes. You just let me handle my father."

"Well, your daddy pays me, darlin', so I think I'd better check with him before I let you go dallyin'."

With the resignation of a man often defeated and who long ago had learned the futility of resisting his daughter once her mind was made up, Buck Colter responded, "If that's what she wants to do, she'll do it one way or another, so rather than have her going around to every half-assed hand on the ranch, she'd better learn from the best, and that's you, Novillero."

"She's a spoiled brat and a pain in the ass," was the disdainful opinion voiced by Colter hands at the news that she would be among them on the range. But soon, having observed her at work, grudgingly they admitted that she could hold her own and she was accepted as one of their kind with the only concessions to her sex being the guardedness of their language in her presence and the laying out of their bedrolls at night so that they faced away from hers.

By her third roundup when she was seventeen and no longer a flat-chested and hipless tomboy but a shapely young woman, ignoring her sex was decidedly more difficult, so that Novillero made sure each night that he was positioned protectively between her and the men.

That she rode the range and slept amidst cowboys

was not something that could be kept from the residents of Goliad. They saw her come to town on Saturdays and among them the opinion of her was divided, depending on views held regarding her father; his detractors expressing shock concerning her and his friends stating with outraged righteousness that there was no way the daughter of Buck Colter could ever be anything but proper and upright, even among randy cowboys riding the wide-open range.

For years to the people of Goliad she had been Buck Colter's freckle-faced, pigtailed tomboy and then with dazzling suddenness she had become a beautiful young woman who was well aware that she was the attention of all eyes when she sashayed past a group of ranchers in front of the general store or the cowboys hanging around the saloon adjacent to the Case Hotel. Nor did she go unnoticed by businessmen and traders staying at Taylor's Hotel and seated in a row of chairs on the porch sunning themselves, smoking cigars and letting their breakfasts settle as they surveyed the passing parade on the main street of a town that was on a boom.

Her purpose in being in Goliad on Saturday was not to be noticed, although she enjoyed the experience, but to do the buying of whatever staples or supplies the Colter household and ranch required. At the Maetze Brothers store she was respected for her knowledge of everything from barnyard hardware to the packets of English teas which she preferred over coffee. At the Neyland and Sanderfur livery she knew her way around wagons and wagon equipment and was as conversant as the owners with the trappings required by horses and men who rode them.

When she had a lot of shopping to do she came into town in a buggy, but if she had little to purchase she arrived upon a handsome chestnut. Wearing a buckskin shirt and glove-soft blue denims with the legs

18

tucked into knee-high tan boots with the Colter B—C brand carved in them, she invariably ate lunch alone by the front window of the Case Hotel while all the items she bought during the morning were being loaded into the buggy.

This was viewed by the women of Goliad as her putting on a shameless display and the opinions they voiced of her often included the word "hussy."

Of all the opinions of her which Novillero overheard during his occasional visits to town, the one that made the most sense, he thought, came from Migdalia Coffee, the widowed and independent-minded owner of the El Dorado and the mother of Sarah, a sixteen-year-old beauty with the same fierce individuality as Rebecca. When catching disapproving remarks about Rebecca, Migdalia would stamp her tiny foot on the smooth-worn planks of the floor of her establishment, jam her big balled fists against her ample hips and with an excoriating look in the direction of Rebecca's detractor exclaim, "Why should a woman not do the things she wishes to do? A woman is as good as a man. This is a woman who one day will own her father's ranch. How can she be a success if she does not known anything? It is right for her to learn, to know. This is her *right*."

Though never within earshot of Migdalia, it had been said for years by the same people who were critical of Rebecca that Migdalia's child, Sarah, who seemed so much like Rebecca, was Buck Colter's other daughter. A year younger than Rebecca, they pointed out in whispered amusement, Sarah was obviously the spawn of a feverish union of a lonely man who'd recently lost his wife and a vulnerable, lonesome, and hot-blooded Mexican woman whose husband had died within weeks of the passing of Colter's wife while giving birth to Rebecca. Except for the year's difference and the darker tone of Sarah's skin and hair, they said, the girls could have been twins!

This was a ludicrous slander against Buck Colter, Novillero insisted loudly, but in moments of quiet thought as he rode the seemingly boundless expanse of Colter range he could not honestly deny that in the two girls there were striking similarities, not only in looks but in their temperaments — strong-willed and defiant, self-confident, bold, brave, and daring — even brazen.

The speculation that she had a half-breed half-sister whose mother was the owner of a saloon Rebecca supposed she ought to have denounced as a calumny and those who spread them as a pack of slanderous and scurrilous scoundrels. Instead, she pretended ignorance and went about Saturday business in Goliad secretly relishing the scandalized stares of the women and imagining what was being whispered behind the upraised hands shielding their gossip-dripping lips.

Except for a mumbled "Howdy, Miss Colter" and tipped hats as she went by, the men she passed were tight-lipped, although in their eyes she readily recognized what they were thinking. If she knew men — and she was certain that she did — her liberal stands on the issues of negro emancipation and the vote for women were far from their thoughts regarding her. It wasn't her ideas they were interested in. It was her body. Lust was written all over them, the old as well as the young among them. And not just because of her youth and good looks, either, she believed.

In these hungry-eyed men of Goliad and the men who were simply passing through boiled more than the natural sexual instinct. In their hot eyes she detected a burning frustration of men who were being denied their needs by those same women who looked with disdain upon her. Enslaved in their kitchens and encumbered with the wifely labors imposed upon them, they had found ways to exercise the only power they possessed over men not granted to them by men, bestowing or withholding their sexual favors in the same way they could rule their children by granting treats to express approval and denying them to show displeasure.

She would never be like them, she vowed.

She would never let their gossip become her reality.

Especially after the death of her father, when they went wild with speculation about her, she set her mind to showing them that she was not the person they believed her to be. To prove to them she was not like them, to show that she was not going to sell out and to demonstrate that she didn't care what they said about her keeping the company of men, she'd led that season's drive to Abilene.

Novillero would be the trail boss, she decreed. Dalgo would come along as caporal. "Mr. Morgan will serve as our scout," she said, "especially through the Indian Territory and, of course, once we are across the Arkansas River, into Kansas to Abilene."

In Kansas, their luck turned bad.

On the second afternoon past the Arkansas the wind whipped up sharply from a suddenly blackening western sky streaked with lightning bolts and thunderclaps rolling at them with the hollow thuds of distant cannon.

"As if these cows didn't have a bad case of the jitters already," groaned Novillero.

"It's comin' at us mighty fast," said Morgan.

"Maybe it'll pass quick," said Dalgo, hopefully.

Novillero shook his head. "It'll be an all-nighter; ain't that right, Morgan?"

"Afraid so. I'd say it'll be a day blowing over and then we can expect a blast of cold. Maybe even a little snow."

"Snow! God, how I hate Kansas."

Anxiously, Dalgo asked, "Shall we bed down the critters?"

"No, keep em movin'. Better to maintain the pace while the storm's ragin' and it's still light. And hope the thunder and the lightnin' passes over quick. I'd rather have a herd on the move durin' a storm than have it hit when they're sleepin'."

At last, when bedding the cattle was unavoidable, Novillero chose wide open and flat ground that in his estimation would be best for coping with a stampede should one occur, ordering the riders to close in on all sides, crowding the cattle until they were so compact and solid a man might walk from one end of the herd to the other without setting boot to ground.

"Not a very hospitable welcome to Kansas, Mr. Morgan," said Rebecca Colter, teasingly, when he rode back to the wagons for a cup of coffee. "I trust things will improve?"

"It's rain that makes the grass grow, ma'am," he retorted. "And it's grass that fattens cattle, you know."

Ten minutes later, back with the herd, he grumbled, "What the hell's she expect, sunshine and dryness forever?"

Circling cattle numbered in the thousands while cold rain drummed his hat and Grulla's head in a torrent, Morgan reckoned the weather was a match for anything Noah had encountered.

"The Good Lord must love cattle, Grulla," he whispered into the horse's ear, "to have made so many of 'em."

Turning aside and tilting down his head to let the water run out of the brim of his hat, he chuckled, "And He must like rain quite a bit, too, to keep such an ample supply on hand."

The only relief he found from the blackness was the blinding flashing of lightning turning the darkness into a moment of instant daylight and revealing the herd standing in shoulder to shoulder uneasiness with the higher figures of cowboys as black as cutout-paper silhouettes on horses prancing anxiously at the edges, the men praying silently that the bolts and the bangs of thunder wouldn't spark a skittish cow to scare and start them all running.

Novillero had divided the night riding into two watches of six hours, the change being made at midnight.

Promptly at twelve, he rode out as Morgan's relief. "How's it been?" he whispered.

Morgan whispered back. "Antsy."

"Them or you?"

"Both."

"Cussed rain."

"If it was dry you'd be cussin' the drought."

"Life's a cussed bitch."

" 'Specially if you marry her," Morgan laughed.

"What the devil's a shorthorn named Morgan know about marryin'?"

"Enough to know I don't plan to."

"What about that cute señorita at the El Dorado?"

"She's a child. And as long as the female sex is on our minds, what about you and you-know-who?"

"Don't know who you're talkin' about."

"You don't? Does the name Rebecca Colter sound familiar?"

"Don't start up."

"Sooner or later she's gonna need a man."

"I expect so."

"You oughta be him."

Pulling with such suddenness on the reins that his horse reared a little, Novillero snapped, "Hell, boy, are you blind? You're the one she fancies!"

"That's . . ." In the corner of his eye Morgan saw a flash — not lighting. ". . . crazy!"

23

An unmistakable bang.

A pistol shot—no question about it.

From the other side of the herd.

Then Novillero's cry. "Oh, Christ."

Grulla quickened between Morgan's legs, tossing his mane impatiently, prancing anxiously, pawing the ground, his ears pricked up, nostrils smelling the sudden danger crashing to life somewhere out there in the impenetrable darkness of the pouring-down rain. Somehow, above and through the storm of sounds raised by the cattle, cowboy voices were heard yelling, "Stampede!"

Nothing in Morgan's experience matched it; not a wild ride beside a herd of buffalo running for their lives while he was gunning for one from a saddle on his first buffalo hunt, not being in cavalry charges in the war, not during raids on Indian villages along the Platte and the Washita.

Suddenly out of the roar came Novillero's voice. "Ride to the lead, Morg. Git ahead of 'em! Turn 'em back on themselves."

Carried forward on Grulla's back and the horse's instincts, Morgan quickly reached the front of the thundering mass of shapes that looked like a torrent of ink-black water rolling toward him and sweeping along with it a tangled forest of skeleton-like tree limbs and branches—their horns glistening wetly in the momentary flashes of the unrelenting lightning.

They're unstoppable, he thought, as Grulla raced them.

In a flash of lightning he caught a glimpse of Novillero speeding ahead of the herd itself, as if he were leading them in their mad dash—the last he saw of him until an hour after sunrise when Dalgo found Novillero's broken body pinned under his dead horse.

"Looks like the horse spilled," Dalgo said, kneeling

24

and making the sign of the cross. "The herd ran right over them." Bowing his head, he prayed in Spanish.

When he was finished he looked up at Morgan, still on Grulla, and said, "I'll get help bringing him to camp. You're the one who ought to go tell Miss Colter."

"Yeah, I guess so," Morgan said grimly. "Then I suppose we'd better find out what we've lost of the herd and see how many we can round up."

"Sure thing, boss," said Dalgo. "Whatever you say."

"How did this happen?" she demanded angrily. "What caused it? Was it the lightning? I was told that there'd been a shot fired. How could anyone have been that stupid?"

"I questioned the men about the gunshot but none would admit to being the one who fired it," he lied.

He'd asked no one.

Who the hell really cared now, anyway?

Whoever fired it, whether accidentally or on purpose, maybe in a misguided notion that a shot would control a rambunctious cow, that man would spend the rest of his life regretting it.

Novillero had been a good man—straight and honest.

Responsibility for his death would be a heavy burden on the conscience of whoever did it, which was punishment enough.

"There's no telling exactly what set 'em off," he said.

"So how did we fare? Besides Novillero, I mean. How are the men? Serious injuries? Have we lost the herd?"

"Nobody's hurt that bad. Lots of bumps and bruises and cuts. No broken bones have been reported. As far as the men go, we got off good. The herd? It appears that we've lost about a couple of hundred. A dozen or so got trampled. The rest are scattered. We could round 'em up but that'd take a good deal of time. Right

25

now I think we'd better keep the rest of the herd on the move. Press on to Abilene."

"We'll move tomorrow," she said firmly. "The men need rest after what they've been through. And we must have a service, as best we can, for Novillero. You'll say a few words, won't you," she said, not asking but stating it, the matter settled just like that.

After a day and night of drizzle, the next morning broke clear and so cold that the last of the rain had frozen into a sparkling veneer that cracked and crumbled on the blankets as the men flung them aside, the ice tumbling into piles like shattered glass and glittering like diamonds.

Shivering as they walked to the grave that Dalgo had had dug, they drifted into a circle, each man taking a position in it that matched the place in the circle they made of themselves when driving a herd.

Morgan stood at the head of the grave—the point man.

His words for Novillero would not be from the Bible, he had decided. For the man who'd dreamed of being a prince of the Corrida de Toros, he recited a line from *Hamlet*. "Good night, sweet prince, and flights of angels sing thee to thy rest."

After the burial she said, "I never knew a young man who had such a store of pretty words in his head as you."

"It's on account of my mother, ma'am. She put a high value on me learning the Holy Scriptures and Mr. Shakespeare."

"You did well."

"I just wish I was called on to recite the words in happier circumstances."

"The death of Mr. Stoner—Novillero—is a tragic loss," she said, touching his sleeve. "I wish we had more time to mourn him, but the hard fact is, we don't.

26

We've still got several thousand cattle remaining to be taken to market. Somebody's got to take charge, to take over as trail boss. And to do that, I'm picking you."

Chapter Four

Romantic thoughts about Morgan had blossomed at the first moment she'd seen him, a surprise guest of her father's at supper on a balmy afternoon late in the winter of 1867. At the age of sixteen after being raised in a womanless house, she had deemed herself quite accustomed to men and therefore was surprised to be left breathless by the sight of him.

He'd come to Goliad with a letter from Joseph McCoy, a cattle trader soliciting Texas ranchers to drive their herds one thousand miles north to the livestock market and railway shipping depot McCoy had built in Abilene, Kansas.

In addition to being a businessman who was always willing to listen to a possibly profitable enterprise, her father was a hospitable man, inviting Morgan to share their evening meal.

Mexican food that was so hot it felt as if it would leave blisters on the tongue caused Morgan's eyes to water, but even more fiery a revelation to him was this girl's willingness to argue with her father and his willingness to tolerate it.

In reply to his assertion that he could not leave his daughter alone while he led a six-month cattle drive to Abilene, she chided, "I'm not a child, daddy." Tossing long silky hair that was the same chestnut color as her father's but laced with flashes of red, she declared, "It's silly of you to think I can't get along on my own for a few weeks."

"Months," he corrected.

With a jittery glimpse at their handsome visitor, she said sharply, "So, months. So what?"

"My daughter has a mind of her own," said her father, turning to Morgan with a patient smile, "but I'm afraid she has very few manners. I apologize."

"If you can get better prices in Kansas," she persisted, her green eyes flashing, "I don't think you should miss the chance. If this were my ranch, I wouldn't lose such a good opportunity."

She expected a rebuke, but her father laughed. "Think you're quite the businesswoman, eh?"

"It's just common sense, daddy," she said in a softer and more appealing tone as she turned her gaze to Morgan again. "After all, this gentleman has come all the way down here to solicit you. It would not be right, either to him or to yourself, if you were to reject his idea simply because of me when I am perfectly able to take care of myself. I do recall you saying, often, that business is business and must not be influenced by personal feelings or emotion. Yet I find you proceeding solely from the basis of how you feel instead of what your head for business must be telling you."

Frowning, her father threw up his hands as he turned to Morgan. "If you have children or plan to, Mr. Morgan, be warned by what you've just witnessed. Sooner or later, they will turn on you!"

"I have no children, sir," he smiled shyly, fixing smokey blue eyes on her, "but when I do—if I find the right woman to marry—I'll remember your words."

Self-conscious under his steady, searching gaze, she teased. "So handsome and not married. My, my, my

29

aren't you going to be some lucky girl's catch!"

"Becky," her father chastised, "now you are out of place."

"Think nothing of it," said Morgan, reddening in the face as she grinned with pleasure at embarrassing him.

After supper, while her father served brandy and passed around cigars in the trophy room where he conducted business, she went out of her way to be seen by him through doors opened to admit cooling evening breezes. Dressed in a loose shirt, tight britches and knee-high boots, she strode from the house to a barn, then appeared a few moments later leading out a bareback dun horse, swung onto it and galloped toward the river with her chestnut hair flying and burnished by the setting sun, knowing he was watching her.

Later, lying awake thinking about him, she whispered to the secret-keeping darkness of her bedroom, "He is good-looking, isn't he? Very serious! Acts much older than he looks!"

At breakfast, her father announced, "Very well, Mr. Morgan, this spring, Colter cattle will move up the trail to Abilene."

"That's great, Mr. Colter," Morgan beamed with boyish enthusiasm. "You won't regret it!"

"There's one condition, however."

"Name it, sir."

"You ride with us."

"Well, I'll be happy to accompany you, sir, but I'm not exactly a cowboy."

"That don't matter. I just want you on hand in case the deal isn't as sweet as you say, so I can wring your neck."

"If all I promised don't come true, Mr. Colter," Morgan said, his eyes turning sidelong toward Rebecca, "I'll buy you the rope to hang me with!"

She giggled, perversely enjoying the idea of him being hanged.

"I'm going riding, Mr. Morgan," she announced, "and you're welcome to accompany me. If you think you can keep up."

The same dun from the previous evening was already saddled and she waited patiently upon it while Morgan readied his horse, but the moment he was up, she let out a whoop, flicked the dun's shoulder with the reins, and left him and horse behind in a spray of gravel.

Approaching a steep rise that crested in a bluff high above the valley of the San Antonio, the dun slowed, its racing ride of the night before taking its toll. Rested for days and barely winded, the horse Morgan called Strawberry scaled the slope easily and quickly, flying past the striving dun half-way up and rearing exultantly at the top. "That's quite a horse you have," she said, reining-in her stressed and foam-flecked horse.

"Cavalry-trained," he boasted, stroking the strawberry roan's neck lovingly.

"You were cavalry, too, I heard."

"Custer," he said, as though the name were enough.

"I met him once," she said, crinkling her nose as if she smelled something offensive. "Once was enough. Horrid person!"

Jerking upright, he snapped, "Where'd you ever meet General Custer?"

"In Houston. I accompanied my father there on business soon after the war. We were at dinner at our hotel and during the course of the meal a business associate of my father introduced us to Custer and his wife. I thought he strutted like a peacock."

"It sounds to me like your Rebel sympathies were coloring your judgment."

"On the other hand, I found Elizabeth Custer quite charming. Far superior to him in breeding, style, and

31

class."

Sneering, he said, "The men of the Seventh Cavalry call her the Queen of Sheba."

"I'm not surprised, they being soldiers and of a very low class themselves."

"I was a soldier."

"A Yankee, obviously."

"Need I point out that we Yankees won?"

"Due entirely to the simple fact that your side had more men. In war, the side with the most soldiers generally wins. I believe that if you were a truly fair and honest person you would concede that all through the war your side was outwitted, outmaneuvered and outsmarted by General Robert E. Lee."

"Then how come Lee was the one who surrendered at Appomattox?"

"I can see why you admire Custer. You're as arrogant as he is. In a rather cute, boyish way."

"Something of a snob, aren't you? Smart-alec, too. And a tease. You think you know it all. All about war. All about Custer. All about men."

"I don't know everything, but I can spot a . . . *maverick*."

"What in consternation is that?"

"Among cattle, mavericks are ones that have not been branded. They wind up being owned by whoever rounds them up. You're of the human variety, although I can't imagine anyone who'd want to put a brand on you. In my estimation, you would turn out to be nothing but trouble."

"Well, you needn't fret, 'cause marrying is the farthest thing from my mind. And if the notion ever did get into my head I'd recite these lines:

I thought if only I could marry,
I'd sing and dance and live so gaily;

32

But all the wedded bliss I see
Is rock the cradle, hush the baby."

Blushing, she turned her head.

He exploded with delight. "Ha! You're as bright red as a beet. Miss Sophistication embarrassed by a racy little poem!"

"Nonsense. What could possibly embarrass me in that ridiculous verse?"

" 'Rock the cradle, hush the baby!' Sex rears its ugly head! You can't have a marriage without a baby and, the last I heard, you can't have a baby without . . ."

Suddenly, the hand that had been gently stroking the dun's neck rose and lashed out like a whip, slapping his face with a force that sent him hurtling out of the saddle sideways.

Why she had slapped him remained a puzzle to her.

Desperately, she had wanted to kiss him.

Soon he was gone, keeping his promise by riding with her father at the point of the herd to Abiliene — out of sight but never completely out of mind.

Two years later, as she returned home from an excursion to Goliad for provisions, she'd rounded the corner of the big house heading for the barn with the happy prospect of a meal for just her father and herself when she saw him in the yard, stripped to the waist and briskly currying his strawberry roan.

As he turned abruptly at the sound behind him, he said, "Howdy, Miss Colter," as a tentative smile danced at the corners of his mouth.

"Oh," she gasped. "It's you."

"Yep, I'm back," he said, scooping his shirt from the ground and quickly putting it on.

Turning away so that he could not see her delighted

smile, she said, "Like a bad penny!"

In the following weeks she'd watched him at a distance, discreetly and safely, as he was painstakingly transformed from greenhorn into cowboy by the ever-patient Dalgo, whose exasperated curses gave way so readily to encouragement and praise.

From his first halting attempt at plaiting a rawhide lariat and an initial miserable failure at bringing down a tame cow by its tail to the triumphal day when Morgan roped, threw, and hobbled a steer and Dalgo declared that he was born to do battle against *el toro* armed only with a cape and bandillero, she watched him, pretending that she didn't want to be seen while he pretended not to have noticed her.

But Dalgo had seen her and teased her about him. "That boy has eyes for you," he said, "and you for him."

With a scornful laugh she retorted, "That's pure bull!"

They were at the horse corral on a muggy Saturday morning in early August, three weeks after Morgan had arrived at the ranch. While Dalgo was hitching a horse to the carriage for her weekly shopping in Goliad, she glanced Morgan's way often, slyly, as he threw a saddle on a sleek coal-black mustang, one of half a dozen wild horses waiting to be broken.

"That is a horse with a bad heart, *amigo*," warned Dalgo as he walked away from her toward the corral. "It has a mean spirit. I do not think you should try to ride this, this . . . *diablo*."

With a furtive glance at her, Morgan sneered. "Is that so? He doesn't look tough to me. I've seen plenty of contrary horses! Don't forget, I was in the cavalry during the war. And not just any cavalry, either! I rode

34

with Custer." His voice rose as he spoke until, at last, he was almost shouting. Certain that she couldn't miss hearing him, he boasted, "I can handle any horse."

With a shrug, Dalgo said, "Very well, *amigo*. It's your neck," and stepped aside as Morgan thrust the toe of his boot into the stirrup.

"Diablo," he muttered as he vaulted into the saddle. "Is that your name, hoss?" As if he understood, the horse snorted defiantly, reared and threw him off backward.

Worse than the sickening thud his body made as he slammed to the ground was Rebecca's burst of shrieking laughter.

Burning with humiliation, Morgan leapt to his feet, caught the dragging reins of the hellish horse that was prancing around the corral like a boxer who'd just won the first round of a prize fight and sprang into the saddle again. To his surprise, the horse stood still, gentle as a lamb. "There, that's much better," he said softly, smiling as he leaned forward to stroke its neck.

Suddenly, the horse shook its head and lurched forward in a series of leaps straight off the ground.

How he stuck to the beast, she had no idea, but he smiled confidently at her as the horse settled again, standing as still as a statue.

Cautiously, he waited, then said, "Is that it? Got it all out of your system?"

The horse jerked its head up and down.

"What's that s'posed to mean?"

Like a statue, the horse stood motionless.

"Thinkin' things over, ain'tcha? Thinkin' of some new trick to unseat me. Well, think all you want. I'm not gettin' . . ."

Cut off in mid-sentence, he rose and pitched forward as the horse kicked up his hind legs and catapulted him over his head in a cartwheel that ended with him flat on his face five yards in front.

Spitting dust speckled with blood, he sat up. Before he recognized pain, he was agonizingly aware of her girlish laughter pealing louder than the bells that seemed to be ringing in his ears.

Pushing himself to his feet, he felt aches as bad as a hundred knife points coursing from his hair to his toenails. Bending over to retrieve his hat, he thought he was going to faint, so he came up slowly — eyes darting toward her — and used the hat to dust his clothing. Although he fixed his eyes on the horse's as he advanced toward it, at the edges of his vision he still was able to see her standing beside the buggy, waiting and watching, grinning from ear to ear with exquisite pleasure at the humbling he was taking from this hellish horse before her voracious, mocking eyes.

Although he was certain that he'd cracked some ribs and despite the trickling of blood from his nose — possibly broken, too — he mounted again, defiantly.

With scratched skin peeking through ripped denim, he clamped his knees to the animal's sides like jaws of a steel trap, wrapped the reins tightly around his right hand and with every screamingly pained sinew drawn taut, whispered, "Go for it, Diablo," and waited for an eruption.

It came immediately as the horse ducked its head and bolted forward. Pitching violently, snorting and wheezing, it whirled in the middle of the corral kicking up dust and dirt like a cyclone, trying to throw him. Jerked forward and back, pitched up and to both sides, flung this way and that, his head whipsawing and his whole body flopping as if it were a limp rag doll in the hands of a child throwing a tantrum, he held. Somehow, he held.

Madly and meanly, the horse danced dangerously close to the corral fence.

"Get off, *amigo*," cried Dalgo.

"Jump," she yelled.

"Jump hell," he grunted, pulling the loop of the reins even tighter, so tight his fingers tingled.

Crashing sidewise into the fence, the horse slid forward.

As pants ripped and peeled back to expose his right leg and hundreds of splinters knifed into him, he screamed in pain and jerked the reins viciously to the left, straining the horse's rawhide hackamore and savagely forcing its head to twist left and its body to lurch away from the fence and to the center of the corral where it continued to whirl madly, head down and rump up. Finally, winded, exhausted, and discouraged, it settled into sulking, loping circles until it gave up to him, utterly defeated.

"*Loco, loco, loco,*" cried Dalgo as he vaulted the fence and dashed across the corral. Throwing his arms around Morgan, he cackled a laugh. "You are crazy, boy! Crazy! But I love you for it."

Grinning, Morgan said, "*Muchas gracias,*" as his eyes peered past him toward her.

Caught looking, she shrugged haughtily, tilted back her head, settled into the buggy, snapped the reins and rattled away without looking back. But as Morgan limped from the corral, she heard him say, "What a nosy bitch she is."

The heat that summer was just starting to build when he'd arrived as a greenhorn but by the time of the coming of the first autumn tempest whipping off the distant Gulf he was working the ranch as capably as the best of the hands and often as well as Dalgo and Novillero.

In fall and winter he was strong, dauntless, and tireless and seemed blissful whether it was at the crack of dawn when she heard him speaking gently to the horses as he fed them their breakfasts, or at midnight when she listened for him through her open bedroom window as he was whistling a tune or singing one or exploding with a laugh at some joke Dalgo or Novillero had cracked.

Before long, Novillero had inducted him into the management of ranch affairs, teaching him how to do the accounts and all the other paperwork that the livestock business required, leading her father to credit him with a real head for business and, only once, to declare with a wistful admiration, "He's a youngster any man would be proud to call his son."

Little by little from Novillero and Dalgo she learned what Morgan did when, work and pay permitting, he spent from Friday to Sunday in Goliad; taking a room at the Case Hotel, getting barbered, drinking mescal at the El Dorado cantina and flirting innocently with Sarah Coffee.

Though she tried various ways of eliciting the facts from Dalgo, she had not been able to discover whether Morgan spent any of his hard-earned wages at a house of ill repute at the edge of town.

She assumed that he did—being a young man at his lusty prime—but having made the assumption, she found herself trying to imagine what sort of women he might favor and if that kind of women would vie with one another for his attention, handsome as he was.

He was the handsomest young man she'd ever seen, surpassing by far the best looking one before he'd arrived in her life—the despicable Jesse Bruton. He'd gone too far with her one day in the barn when she was barely fourteen so that she'd had to cry out for help, summoning her father, who drove Jesse off with a bullwhip, but had wanted to slay him on the spot.

The thrashing given to him and the truth of the matter notwithstanding, Jesse, being a thorough scoundrel, had boasted to his friends at the El Dorado that he'd had his way with her completely until Novillero marched in on a Saturday night and gave him a second thrashing.

Having her honor saved and then championed had been a thrill, although it was evident later on from the looks that were directed at her that there were some people in Goliad who still believed Jesse's scurrilous lies.

These were the same gossips who now attributed the oldest sin of all to her in the person of the new hand on the Colter ranch.

Perhaps, they said hopefully, this soft-spoken, polite, good-looking, mysterious, and possibly quite dangerous Yankee known only as Morgan might prove to be strong enough to tame her.

Chapter Five

The strength which she had sensed instinctively in him at their first meeting at the dinner table, when she'd taken his side against her father on the question of driving cattle to Abilene, asserted itself in events surrounding the death of her father.

Beholden to cattle for their livelihoods, Buck Colter and others traveled to a desolate spot a few miles across the Rio Grande River because the time had come to punish those who would slaughter cattle that did not belong to them.

Forty such dastardly thieves and their leader, notorious Juan Flores, made their headquarters in a box canyon with three narrow entrances due west of Piedras Negras.

Except for the noises of the horses, it was a silent march of grim but determined men who had followed Morgan at the head of their column through the brushland, across the Rio Grande and into Mexico where the land rose slowly but steadily from easy foothills of scrubby red earth to sharply uplifting and ragged brown bluffs gouged with shadowy crevices and cliffs split by the mouths of meandering canyons until, at last, at nightfall they reached the one they had been seeking.

Dividing the posse into thirds under the cover of darkness, Morgan took them to three openings in the sheer rocks from which, come dawn, they would attack. Novillero would lead one group. Shanghai Pierce would lead the second. Morgan and Buck Colter would lead the rest.

"All because of cattle," Morgan whispered to himself as he got to his feet and climbed into Strawberry's saddle, a signal to his men to mount their horses.

Pointing his six-gun skyward, he fired two shots.

Instantly, gunfire erupted everywhere.

"Total surprise," he yelled triumphantly to Buck Colter riding at his side as they pounded through the easternmost narrow neck of the canyon. From the west and south blazed the others. Like three pent-up rivers suddenly bursting their bounds, they flooded the canyon.

"*Venceremos!*" cried Colter, waving his six-gun joyfully as he advanced into the camp and fired at the men of the Flores gang. To him they seemed like the cattle they preyed upon, as they scrambled and ran. Startled, bewildered, and confused, they were at the mercy of the men on horses. Mercy? Never! "Show no mercy, men!"

Racing behind him, Morgan thought fleetingly of the great warriors of history who had fought from horseback — Alexander the Great, Caesar, Napoleon, Washington, Lee, Custer. Daring men armed with a cause they believed in, whether history had judged them right or not, or men whose sense of righteousness and justice demanded they take up arms and slay those who did wrong. Admirable men, all. But none more so than Buck Colter as he galloped through this narrow Mexican canyon firing left and right with a Colt six-gun at a rapidly dwindling number of bandits — "Damned bandidos," he called them — who deserved only the severest punishment for their deeds. For stealing cows. For slaughtering them for their hides. For impeding the flourishing of the livestock business in Texas. For standing in the way of the progress of Texas itself! These were the lessons being spoken by the bark of Buck Colter's pistol. One of the oldest lessons of all: Thou shalt not steal. And that other far more readily obeyed preachment of the Old Testament — an eye for an eye!

Exultantly, Colter thundered across the canyon floor, spun the gray around and began thundering back the way he'd come. But he'd covered only half the distance when a Mexican with a pistol in each hand bolted from behind a boulder and fired twice at point blank range.

With a prolonged scream and spurring Strawberry viciously, Morgan raced into the Mexican and sent him cartwheeling to the ground, then, leaping from the saddle, threw himself upon the stunned Mexican, drew a Bowie knife and plunged it to the hilt into the center of the Mexican's heaving chest again and again and again.

Only a sudden silence stopped the savage stabbing as the shooting ended as abruptly as it began.

Gasping for breath, he wiped the bloody blade of the Bowie on the shirt of the dead man he was straddling. Standing, he gaped in stunned relief as the remaining members of the gang recognized that they could not win and that if they fought on they had no hope of survival. Throwing away their guns, they cautiously raised their hands and waited.

Twenty-six had been killed.

Seven surrendered, two of them with superficial wounds.

Novillero asked, "What do we do with 'em?"

Morgan turned.

In the distance behind the line of prisoners he saw the body of Buck Colter. One more hero in the annals of Texas history, he thought. A good man. A good boss.

A good father.

Then he thought of Rebecca, now fatherless.

Anxiously, Novillero demanded, "Do I hang 'em?"

Behind him in the slashing heat of a high sun lay Buck Colter's body and as Morgan stared at it, an anger he had never known before rose in him like bile, bitter and burning. "No," he snapped. "Don't hang 'em. Make them kneel. Right here in front of me. Get them down on their goddamned knees!"

Dragged forward and shoved to the ground, the prisoners peered up at him with begging eyes, chattering beseechingly, *"Por favor, señor!"* their hands clasped as if in prayer.

Nodding, Morgan growled, "That's right, bastards! Pray! *Dios! Dios! Dios!*"

Sobbing, the men lowered their heads and mumbled prayers in Spanish.

"This is like *Hamlet,*" Morgan said with a smile as he turned to Novillero. "Do you know your Shakespeare?"

Novillero shook his head.

"Too bad," Morgan laughed. "If you did you'd know the scene where Prince Hamlet observes a murderer praying. 'Shall I kill him now?' he asked himself. 'If I kill him when he's praying, won't his soul go straight to heaven?' Hamlet's trouble was that he couldn't make up his mind. Well I'm no Hamlet."

Drawing his Colt, he pressed the muzzle into the forehead of the first Mexican.

"Please don't, *señor,*" sobbed the prisoner.

Blind with a need to avenge, Morgan cocked the Colt.

"Por favor! Mercy!"

"My friend Buck didn't get any mercy from you! *Vaya con dios, bandito.*"

Sidestepping down the line of kneeling prisoners, he fired six times point-blank between their terrified eyes.

Holstering the Colt, he turned to Novillero and re-called another line from the play: " 'And so I am re-venged.' "

Standing over Colter's body, it was as much for Re-becca's sake that he said, "We can't bury him here. Buck deserves to lie in the ground he loved. He belongs in the land along the San Antonio and that's where we'll take him."

A coffin had been acquired in Piedras Negras along with a wagon and team.

Seeing them coming slowly up the road to the house with the coffin on the back of the wagon, Rebecca waited quietly on the porch until it drew to a stop, then descended tearlessly and, placing a hand on the box, turned to Morgan. "I hope his death was not in vain. Have you wiped out the Flores gang?"

Her question posed to him was a surprise and a puz-zle and left him momentarily speechless. "Those band-its won't be bothering Colter cattle any more."

Stroking the rough wood of the coffin, she nodded and said, "Good." Leaving it, she ascended the steps to the porch then turned and smiled at him. "It was good of you to bring him home. Very decent of you. Very considerate. We'll have the service in the morning. There is a family cemetery by the river. I'd be beholden to you, if you would speak."

Startled, he blurted. "Me? You'll be wanting a man of the cloth, surely."

"Buck Colter owned to being a Christian," she said, "but he was not a member of any church. Daddy be-lieved in men far more than in churches and he ad-mired men who admired words. You're such a man. I'm sure you'll find appropriate ones to say over him."

That night Morgan came to the house to borrow a Bible. "My mother got me to recite a lot of this great book by rote," he explained self-consciously, "but I thought I'd look through the Good Book for something that might be more fitting than the verses she had me learn."

"Whatever you choose will be right, I'm sure," she said.

Her name was written in the front of the Bible.

It was the last of the Colters that would be listed there, he realized. Staring at it, he wondered if she would keep the tradition by inscribing in it the names of the children she would bear; not the name of Colter, of course, but the family name of their father.

Turning the pages of Exodus, he remembered a passage that might serve in his eulogy for Buck Colter.

And God said, 'Let the earth bring forth the living creature after his kind, cattle and creeping thing, and beast of the earth after his kind;' and it was so.

And God made the beast of the earth after his kind and cattle after their kind, and every thing that creepeth upon the earth after his kind: and God saw that it was good.

In the morning at the side of the grave he held his hat against his chest, stood straight and declared, "We who work with cattle are likely to forget what a noble creature the cow is."

Suddenly lifting her head, she peered across the grave with a quizzical upturn of the corners of her mouth.

The look unnerved him but he continued, noting that cattle had been singled out for mention by God Himself in the Bible.

As sudden as she'd looked up at him, her eyes turned down.

Had he erred in going to the Bible to find words to fit her father?

Was she shocked?

45

Had he offended her?

If so, he told himself, the deed was done. All he could do now, he said to himself, was press on.

"Now it may not seem as if cattle are God's creatures," he said, forcing himself to look at the others gathered around the grave—Shanghai Pierce, Novillero, Dalgo, the house servants and as much of the populace of Goliad as had heard the news of Buck Colter's death and had come to pay their respects. "To those of us who live with cows," he continued, "they sure don't seem divine! Hellish is more like it. They seem more like demons of the devil when they're contrary, when we're roping 'em and throwing 'em down and earmarking them and burnin' our brands into them, pushing them a thousand miles up to Kansas. But where would we be without 'em?"

His eyes drifted back to her as she stood as motionless as a statue, the green eyes appearing closed as she stared into the grave with its broad-shouldered Mexican coffin.

"Without cattle," he said, looking to the mourners, "how could any of us have come to know Buck Colter? And if we all didn't know Buck, how much poorer of spirit would we be?"

Her eyes opened to him—tearful and wondering.

"When they write the history of Texas," he continued, his tearful eyes fixed on hers, "they'll need more than a few lines or even a few paragraphs to tell his story. They'll need a chapter, at least, and, I expect, an entire book devoted just to him. And I'm sure the day will come soon when the place where we're standing now will bear a memorial stone marking this grave. If it were left to me to say what that stone should be, I'd say without hesitation that it ought to be a carving of a longhorn."

Turning abruptly, she said nothing as she strode to

46

her horse, the racing-hearted dun she favored for her wild and solitary rides, and galloped away.

After Las Cuevas, the people of Goliad looked differently upon this slender, unobtrusive, quiet-spoken, and gentlemanly visitor, taking new notice of things about him that they had all seen before: the Colt six-gun slung low on his hip, the Bowie knife in its Indian bead sheath flapping against his thigh, the eyes that once were seen as curious and inquisitive now appearing wary and on guard. Finding himself the object of quick glances and outright stares from the men sunning themselves on the galleries and the women who came to town to shop, he again heard their whispers linking his name with Rebecca Colter.

Sara, the devil-tongued daughter of Migdalia Coffee, could be relied on to tell him everything that was being said.

"They say you are sleeping in the big house with her!"

"They say you will soon marry her."

Then, one sultry Saturday night at the cantina, she said teasingly, "They say she is going to sell off the stock and the property and go to live in California . . . with you."

"Well, whoever *they* are, tell 'em they are full of bull manure," he shouted, his voice booming across the cantina and stunning the patrons into silence as surely as if he'd fired a six-gun.

A year later, in the spring of 1872, he was on the trail again pushing cattle to Kansas—her cattle—and she missed him terribly.

Part Two
The Trail Boss

Chapter Six

Riding point beside Dalgo, Morgan twisted in his saddle and gazed back at the slow river of cattle, their horns and bodies half obscured by their own dust, then tilted his head to study the sky. "Another two hours of good sun left," he judged. Turning forward, he added, "The Guadalupe's prob'ly another four."

Lighting a cheroot, Dalgo said, "You figurin' on pushin' up to the river before we make camp?"

"Novillero never liked the idea of moving a herd in the twilight," said Morgan thoughtfully, "and neither do I. On the other hand, it'd be nice to take them across first thing in the morning when they're wide-eyed and bushy tailed."

"Your call, boss," smiled Dalgo, breathing smoke.

Assaying the herd again, Morgan said, "Well, let's drive 'em to the river and the darkness be damned. Meantime, I'll dash ahead for a palaver with Mr. Anderson of the Double A ranch about the details of adding his herd to ours. That'll take me an hour, more or less. I'll be back by sundown."

"Sounds good to me, boss," said Dalgo in a cloud of smoke.

"Pass the word, *amigo*."

In the first three days covering the thirty miles between Goliad and the Guadalupe with the Anderson ranch just beyond it at Cuero, the pattern for the entire drive had been set as cowboys and cows had become accustomed to him and one another and to the rhythm he'd set for the drive. Guided by the position of the sun in the daytime and the North Star at night, he headed them up at daybreak, strung them out for the morning, rested them so they could graze while the drovers ate their midday meal at high noon and then drove through the afternoon to the spot he'd chosen for bedding them for the night where there was good water.

"The art of the trail is grazin' and waterin' the cattle, but the waterin' is the most important of the two," Novillero had taught him.

Startled by the notion that driving cattle to market was a form of art, he'd quickly learned that getting cattle to take water called for patience and a great deal of practice, exactly the requirements for success in any art.

From that moment on he'd discerned art — and beauty — in every aspect of driving cattle and found himself wishing he possessed the talents for capturing that beauty in sketches on paper, oil paint on canvas or, like his friend Hank Kidder, with words printed in a newspaper.

Once upon a time, he remembered as he watched Dalgo traveling back through the herd, he'd had a chance to try to be like Kidder.

Years ago when he was a bewildered boy caught in the sudden stillness that followed the Battle of Gettysburg and the utter loneliness and fury of learning that his father had been killed, Kidder had read his spirit and pleaded with him not to join the army to slake his thirst for revenge for the death of his father. "You've got an inquisitive nature," Kidder had told him. "You've got a flair for words. And you've got something else every good newspaperman happens to need."

Dubious, Morgan asked, "What'd that be?"

"Curiosity," exclaimed Kidder, his eyes alight. "A need to find out what's going on. If you didn't have that, you'd've never traipsed off into the middle of a war the way you did."

"I didn't exactly expect to get into the fight myself," he said, as much an apology to his father's memory as to Kidder.

"That's my point," Kidder said. "You weren't looking for trouble. You were just interested in seeing the war up close! I've watched you over these past few days, wandering around camp asking questions, poking your nose here and there like a hound dog. You've got the natural curiosity it takes to go after the news, so if you were to ask me for advice—and you haven't—I'd say that what you ought to do during this war is not soldier in it but report about it."

"Wouldn't know where to start."

"You could start as my assistant. It wouldn't pay much, but you'd eat and you'd be learning. I think you have the makings of a newspaperman. And maybe even a writer. What do you say?"

"I'd have to ponder that a while, Mr. Kidder."

"Sure," Kidder said with an understanding smile and a manly slap on the back. "You think about it. Sleep on it."

That evening, dusty and worn and with his eyes ablaze with the light of purpose and the glory of victory and astride his prancing black horse, Major Ward Kimball of the U.S. Cavalry rode proudly into the camp.

Remembering that night nine years later from the back of a horse called Grulla at the point of a herd of ten thousand Colter cattle on their way to Kansas, Morgan saw that there came moments in a person's life that when looked back upon were seen as forks in a road and, perhaps, the wrong road taken, but which at the moment did not seem to be an instant of choosing at all. For him, such a moment had come at dawn the next day as the Union Army stirred from its camps around Gettysburg and rose to march south. It had been a flawless Pennsylvania summer's morn when the air was clear and clean after a thundershower, the grassy hills smelled fresh and life to a boy of fifteen promised to go on forever.

The two roads before him that morning had pointed eastward to New York with Mr. Henry Kidder and maybe a newspaperman's life or southerly with the army and Major Kimball — a very simple choice, it seemed to him on that brilliant morning.

Now, looking back years from a place that was a lifetime's distance from Pennsylvania, he recognized that on that splendid morning in July by electing to take a road that was not the one Kidder had hoped he would pick, he was choosing one that would lead to other forks with no turning back and bringing him to this moment as Rebecca Colter's trail boss on his way to Kansas.

Behind him were cowboys carrying out his orders to push ten thousand plodding cattle an extra two hours through dwindling light and darkness to the Guadalupe — lean men with skin weathered by the sun until it was tough as rawhide, tight lips and terse tongues, jaws set proudly, searching eyes as keen as sky-wheeling hawks and hearts as open as the country that had nurtured them and the animals in their keeping.

Not a man among them did not understand that taking a herd to market was a serious business. For three months they would be a world unto themselves, their survival depending on their instincts, skills they'd learned and the tools they packed on their horses and into the supply wagons or which they carried with them: six-guns, sheath knives, rawhide ropes and hobbles, saddles, bridles, blankets, boots, slickers, hats, kerchiefs, and whatever else they deemed vital.

More than these, however, their well-being and that of the cattle would rest upon the man on the next horse, from the two point drivers to the swing riders on opposite sides of the herd to those at the drag end. From start to finish they had to be a team working for the good of the herd and the boss who owned it because, they all understood, if they were to reap the rewards of their labors when they came to the end of the trail, their boss, Rebecca Colter, would have to prosper.

Nor was there one among these men who did not appreciate that their success and their well-being depended upon the man she'd chosen to lead them.

Looking back at them from his gray horse, Morgan marveled at them and tried to fathom what sustained these game men and boys, whether on a hot and dusty day such as today or on drenching days when they had to endure rain-sopped hats, dripping slickers, soggy boots and slippery-backed horses.

He'd found it easy to understand how men could put up with such hardships and privations during the war when they'd been fired by a patriotic spirit, but what goaded these flinty Texans to keep going? Money? Good wages awaited them when the stock was sold, of course, although most if not all of it would be squandered in a few days in Texas Street saloons, gambling dens, dance halls, and whorehouses of Abilene's notorious Devil's Half Acre.

Was that all of it?

Were those short days of their being carefree, footloose and happy ample reason to endure three or four or six months of the rigors of the long drive to Kansas when danger could take the shapes of savage Indians, snowstorms, rain, hail, thunder, lightning, and the ever-present possibility of stampedes?

Perhaps it was the danger that motivated them.

Or was it for them, as it as for him, the allure of the quiet and solitary moonlit nights circling the resting herd, singing softly to himself as much as to the cows and coming to grips with himself and his past and wondering what forks might lie in the road ahead that, like the one he'd chosen years ago at Gettysburg, allowed no turning back.

"Shoot, what am I doing daydreaming when I got work to do?" he said abruptly, shaking his head, jerking Grulla's reins and urging the horse into a gallop northward, reckoning that he had plenty of time before sundown to reach the Anderson ranch, confer with its owner about the combining of the Double A herd with Rebecca Colter's B—C brand and return in time to take charge of the night-drive to the river and the bedding down of the herd.

"Hello, Morgan," shouted Able Anderson as he emerged onto the porch when Morgan reached the fieldstone and oak house atop a rise overlooking a bend of the Guadalupe already shadowed by the deepening dusk. Dressed in faded blue bib overalls and gray cotton shirt, a man of modest stature and sunny temperament whom Morgan had seen occasionally in Goliad, Anderson had inherited the Double A ranch from his pioneering grandfather and father. It was a few hundred acres of well-watered land along the river south of Cuero and thirty miles north of Goliad. But his cattle business had never recovered from the hard times that hit the Texas livestock industry during the war and he had been struggling for survival. On top of these woes,

56

he'd been stricken by a heart attack in the winter of 1870 and had been unable to send any stock to market in 1871. Now in the spring of 1872, he had been warned by his doctor that any attempt to lead a cattle drive would almost certainly kill him.

Hearing of his plight, Rebecca Colter had suggested that the Double A brand be combined with hers. "What's a few more head when I'll be sending so many up to Kansas? What are Texans for if not to help one another?"

Now, here was her trail boss come to arrange for the coupling of the herds.

"You're nothing less than a godsend," exclaimed Anderson, extending his hand as Morgan stepped up to the porch. "Come in and have a glass of whiskey and then a little supper!"

"The drink I'll take gladly," said Morgan, "but I'll have to skip the supper, sir. Got to get back to the herd, y'know."

"Of course you must," said Anderson with a shrug and smile. "The cattle always come first, eh?"

"Yes, sir," said Morgan, following him into the cool and dusk-dim sitting room cluttered by big stuffed chairs and a couch with thick arms and backs.

Bringing Morgan a glass of bourbon, Anderson chuckled, "Time and a herd wait for no man, eh?"

"You know how it is, sir," said Morgan. "I just rode ahead to let you know that we're here and that we'll be crossing the river in the morning."

At that moment came the bang of the door closing and a shout: "Pa? Whose hoss is that out front?"

Then, a suddenly looming shadow in the doorway, the voice took the shape of Anderson's son.

"Oh, it's you, Mr. Morgan," he said, stepping into the light. "Long time, no see."

"Six months or so," said Morgan, remembering it

had been on a Saturday night at the El Dorado cantina in Goliad when Migdalia Coffee had the boy thrown out for drunkenness, a fact that Morgan would not mention out of sympathetic consideration for the father.

A hellion even by frontier standards, Hugh Anderson had been raised motherless because his had died at his birth, leaving the raising of the boy to his father, already striving to save his ranch.

Now seventeen years old, the boy was a shade over six feet tall, lean and hard but still possessed of the coltish awkwardness and unfinished appearance of a fourteen-year-old. Normally, for the handsome and fair-haired only son of Able Anderson, these could have been winning traits, but the boy insisted on demonstrating a maddening attitude of bragging and boastfulness, a cocksure overbearing manner, a general contrariness, belligerence and quarrelsomeness that were part of an overall contentiousness. That was the result of the boy's hanging around the El Dorado cantina with the worst elements, including Jesse Bruton, one of the worst of the sorriest branch of the Bruton family tree!

Joyfully, the boy's father declared to his son, "Mr. Morgan has arrived with the Colter herd, so it appears that you'll be departing in the morning for Abilene!"

Shifting dark eyes to Morgan, the boy said, "Is that so?"

"Indeed it is," said Morgan, although if it had been left to him to decide, rather than Rebecca Colter making the decision to let the boy accompany his father's herd, the boy would be staying at home.

"Taking the son along will serve to allay any doubts from any quarter concerning whether Mr. Anderson got a fair shake and a square deal," she'd stated emphatically, although Morgan could not imagine anyone, especially Hugh Anderson, not accepting her word on anything. "It may also be of benefit to the boy and his dear father if the kid were to learn about the cattle business from you, Mr. Morgan," she added.

Respectfully, he replied, "You know, Miss Colter, a trail boss has plenty to do without adding tutoring greenhorns to the list."

"If my memory serves me correctly," she responded tartly, "You learned in just that fashion, tutored by Novillero."

"Just so," he said sheepishly—defeated by the truth.

"By the way, Mr. Morgan," said the Anderson boy. "I've invited a couple of friends of mine from Cuero to come along. I hope you don't mind."

"Hugh, you ought to have consulted with me first," objected his father.

"It's all right, pa," the boy said cheerfully. "They're not gettin' paid. They're just for company."

Dubiously, Anderson asked, "Who are they?"

"Will Garrett and Henry Kearnes. Swell fellas!"

Morgan knew of them.

A pair of no-accounts, he would have said of them if asked. But they might serve to keep the boy out of his hair, he reasoned. "They're welcome," he said generously. "But everybody on a drive has to pull his weight, paid or not."

Chapter Seven

Like a line of railway cars hooking up with the main train from a siding, three thousand Anderson head attached themselves to the Colter herd as the last longhorns struggled up the muddy north bank of the Guadalupe at mid-morning.

"Keep the herds a couple of miles apart," Morgan said to Dalgo. "As much as you can."

Aiming for the North Star from the Guadalupe at Cuero the herd would march to the Colorado River of Texas and then on to the Brazos at Waco, continuing straight to the Trinity at Fort Worth and beyond the Red River into Indian Territory where the waters they were to encounter were the Washita, where Morgan had accompanied Custer in a slaughter of the innocent Indians of Chief Black Kettle's village, the twin branches of the Canadian, the Cimarron and, at last, the Arkansas.

The idea was to drive as fast as possible the first few days, he explained to the Anderson boy, as Novillero had once explained it to him, pushing the cattle hard to get them as far from their home range as possible to minimize strays and homesick runaways—both cattle and cowboys.

The first days were also for taking the measure of the

men, he asserted, leaving Anderson with no doubt that he would be watched, along with Garrett and Kearnes — a warning if Anderson ever heard one.

Amusement at being put on notice gave way, however, to a rising curiosity about Morgan, so that Morgan was also being watched, although he appeared to Anderson to be too busy to notice.

Usually he started each day riding the point with Dalgo, Anderson noted, until he was sure the caporal had the direction right and understood all his instructions for the day. Then he'd drift back along the line checking with the flank riders until he'd reached the greenest hands riding drag ahead of the wagons and behind the cattle where the view was longhorn-rump and the dust was thick enough to choke on. Assured that everything was as it should be, he'd charge forward again and leave the herd behind, becoming a solitary figure exploring the territory ahead and looking for hazards, water and the next spot to settle down for the night. Returning to lead them to the bed ground he'd chosen and spending twilight making last rounds checking on men and livestock as the cattle began to lie down, he always ended up the last to squat by the campfire to eat.

Admirable, Anderson concluded. A man of purpose much like his father, but scary in his quietness and in a way he had of sneaking quick sidelong glances or occasionally staring across the mass of cattle or through the smoke of a campfire — the kind of a look a man gives another when there's a grudge between them or he just doesn't like the looks of what he sees, a feeling in the gut that no matter what, the other man is one he could never warm to.

After a week of it, he'd had enough.

Waiting until Morgan had finished his morning routine and was riding forward of the herd alone, he dashed after him shouting. "Hold up there, Morgan! Hold up!"

Halting Grulla, Morgan turned and waited.

Drawing up beside him, Anderson blurted, "I'd like to ride a ways with you if I can. Got somethin' to get off my chest."

Booting Grulla into movement again, Morgan said, guardedly, "Very well. Unload it."

"You don't care much for me, do you?"

"Not much."

"Why not?"

"You're a spoiled brat; that's why."

"That's a pretty strong opinion, seein' as how you hardly know me."

"I know your reputation. And the stripe of people you truck with."

"Ha! That's somethin' comin' from you! Morgan, the Gunman of Abilene! That's you, ain't it? Don't deny it!"

Morgan nodded slowly. "Was me."

"How many men did you kill?"

"The first one was one too many."

"At least I never killed nobody."

"Pray you never have to."

"Ah, I see! Those men you killed, you had to!"

"I never drew first."

"You expect me to believe that?"

"Believe anything you want; it doesn't matter to me."

"Just what does matter to you?"

"Getting my cattle to market."

"*Your* cattle? Last I heard, they belong to Rebecca Colter and my old man."

Stopping again, Morgan seized the collar of Anderson's shirt. "Don't refer to your father that way in front of me ever again. Show some respect to him. He deserves it." Lowering his hand and riding again, he said softly, "You only get one father and you should prize him."

"I do prize him!"

"Is that so? Are you prizin' him when you hang around gettin' drunk at the El Dorado cantina with the likes of Jess Bruton? And what about this pair of galoots you've invited along on this drive?"

"Will and Henry are fun!"

"With the sad shape your father's in, it's time you stopped thinkin' about fun."

"My old, uh, my father's never voiced objections about me havin' good times, so why in tarnation should I care what you say about it?"

"No reason at all, save for it being the truth. Now, if you've gotten everything off your chest, I've got work to do. Or is there more you'd like to say?"

"Nope. I just wanted to know where I stood on this here drive, is all."

"Where you stand is as I stated. I think you're a spoiled brat and that you'd do better for yourself and your father if you'd mend your ways and . . . start growin' up. Now you know."

Riding off, he felt the boy's eyes like a pair of daggers at his back and hoped that his harsh words would spell a change in the boy's attitude.

Smiling, he remembered a confrontation of his own of a similar nature with his first trail boss, Novillero. Rangy, flat-bellied, slim-hipped, eagle-eyed, tight-lipped, and abrim with the qualities that made for good army officers and superb leaders on the trail, Novillero had been hard-boiled and firm but fair, diplomatic in handling quarrels, honest, fearless, willing to do anything he asked one of his men to do and better at doing any of the jobs on the drive than anyone under him.

After a week of accompanying Buck Colter on the first drive of Colter cattle to Abilene, Morgan declared to his friend California Joe Milner, "I don't think the trail boss cottons much to me. It's a feelin' I have from the way he looks at me. Like he doesn't trust me."

"That's the look he gives to every *niño*."

"*Niño*? What's that?"

"It's Spanish for a kid."

"Well, I'm not a kid. I was in the war and got a wound to prove it. I've tangled with Cheyennes. *Niño!* Bull!"

"All that's true, but for a man like Novillero, it's provin' yourself on the trail that counts. Till a man does, he's a *niño*."

"So what the devil do I have to do?"

"Mebbe on account a your relationship with Buck Colter he thinks you're a kind of a boss. That'd make a man standoffish."

"I'm nobody's boss. Never have been, never want to be."

"If that's so and if what Novillero think of you's so damned almighty important to you, then do somethin' about it."

"Like what?"

"Like astin' Novillero fer a job to do. Let 'im know you'd like to carry some a the weight on this here drive. He won't ast you."

Determined to give it a try, at first light as Novillero was cutting the day's horse from his remuda, Morgan hailed him. "Mr. Stoner, I'd like to have a word with you," he said, purposefully. Suddenly dry in the mouth, Morgan stammered, "It's about, about . . . me. It's about, uh, me not, uh, carryin' my weight on this here cattle drive."

"Not carryin' your weight?" Novillero said, throwing a saddle onto the big mustard-colored horse he used when he planned to range far ahead of the herd that day. "I don't get your meanin', Mr. Morgan."

64

"First-off, there's no cause to be callin' me mister. Morgan'll do just fine."

"And second-off?" Novillero said, reaching under the horse's belly for the far end of the double-rigged cinch.

"I want to be useful."

"Doin' what?" Novillero said, coming up straight with half a smile.

"You're the boss. You tell me."

With narrowed eyes surveying him sideways as he finished saddling the horse, Novillero said, "Well, *niño mio,* suppose you start by tellin' me somethin'. You ever been on a drive?"

"Once," Morgan said proudly, remembering Jim Thompson's cattle the previous fall. "Part of the way," he added, figuring to be honest. "From the Arkansas on into Abilene last September with a herd owned by a Mr. Thompson."

"So Big Jim sold in Abilene, eh?" said Novillero, swinging into the saddle. "I'd like to hear about it, so git your hoss, Morgan, and tell me about it whilst I make my mornin' rounds."

"See what I mean?" observed California Joe boastfully that night as Morgan returned from a full day's riding with Novillero. It had been as vigorous an experience as any with Custer's cavalry. Morgan moaned, dropping to the ground, aching and weary, and spreading a blanket beside the campfire. "All it takes is one to break the ice," said Joe, mouthing a spoonful of syrupy beans that soon dribbled down his beard. "Now that you've done it, ain'tcha glad?"

"Delighted," grunted Morgan, lying back with his head cradled in his hands.

Like his first weeks at Fort Riley as an attentive student in California Joe Milner's School for Scouts, Morgan's next few weeks beside Novillero had been a hard tutoring in what Novillero laughingly called "Cow College" where the lessons were riddled like buckshot with the colorful words and phrases of a lingo that was half-Spanish, half-American and all about cattle.

He'd learned to keep his eyes skinned for anything and everything going on around him and came to understand that if a cowboy appeared to be staring, it was nothing personal, just a built-in wariness from living on the range or on the trail where anything or anyone could prove to be a hazard.

Feeling as if he were one of them at last, he shouldered his part of the workload from eating dust with the greenhorns on the drag to lonely two-hour shifts on the nightwatch keeping company with three thousand cows and marking the time by the Big Dipper until a sleepy-eyed relief rode out.

Riding beside Novillero at the point of the herd as they plodded the last miles of flat prairie turned lushly green with sweet-smelling spring grasses to the edge of Abilene, he'd felt a rising awareness of manhood that had nothing to do with any of his abilities on a horse or how he handled himself on a cattle drive, nothing to do with how easily women took a fancy to him nor his being 21. And certainly not because of his reputation for handling a six-gun. Rather, it was a realization that he was respected by other men for what they found within him as a person—loyalty, dependability, honesty, steadiness. The things his mother taught from her books and called virtues and what his father had shown him in the fields and in his own demeanor and called character.

Exactly the lessons young Anderson needed to learn, he said to himself as he scouted ahead for a place to bed the herds.

That evening, wide-eyed, he stared into a black sky sprinkled with a thousand flecks of light and for an instant believed he was still in the army, expecting that if he turned his head he would discover Major Ward Kimball sleeping nearby. Then he became aware of the cold hard ground, the smell of saddle leather cushioning his head, the scent of cows and horses and sleeping men and the muted far-off sound of loneliness given voice by a cowboy's lullaby to a herd already sensing the dawn showing itself as a sliver of gray light cracking the sky low in the east.

Throwing off his blanket and peering past the campfire, he saw Anderson sleeping peacefully, curled up like a child, and hoped that all he'd said to the boy would sink in and that this drive would change him . . . for the better.

"Time to get 'em up," he shouted, startling cowboys awake. "Time to move out these beasts that the Good Lord has given us!"

Hopefully he watched Anderson throughout the day, seeking some sign that what he'd had to say might be having a positive effect, but in vain.

On the next day he was encouraged when Dalgo informed him that the boy and his pair of companions had ridden off on a hunting expedition, expecting their quarry to help feed the hands. But although they claimed to have killed three buffalo, they came back with no game.

Furious, Morgan shouted, "You don't shoot buffalo on a cattle drive just for the fun of it!"

With nothing but a smirk in reply, the boy swaggered away.

Catching up with Morgan, Dalgo said quietly and reasonably, "Forget about that kid, boss. He ain't worth frettin' over."

With a sigh, Morgan said, "You're right, *amigo*. Only I just despise waste, you see."

"The buffalo? There's lots of buffalo, boss!"

"Nah, it's not just the waste of buffalos that gets me,

although what they did is a sin, sure as God made little green apples! What I hate to see is the waste that kid's making of his life. And knowing how he's going to break his father's heart someday."

"It's them other two, Garrett and Kearnes, that's leadin' him astray. They're kids and so's he. There's nothin' you can do, boss. No use you actin' as if you're his pop, 'cause you ain't. So you might's well leave him be."

Slowly nodding his head, Morgan broke into a lop-sided smile. "As usual, *amigo,* you're right." Tapping a fist lovingly against the caporal's shoulder, he asked, "How'd you get to be so wise, hombre?"

How wise Dalgo was, indeed, he realized many times in the following weeks of watching the Anderson boy—hopelessly and sadly—until, three months, nearly a thousand miles and seven big rivers later with the Indian Territory behind them, they approached the Arkansas River with Kansas on the other side.

Ten miles south of the water looking for a bedding ground, he spotted the two riders.

Three miles in advance of the herd and a quarter of a mile in front of him, they were white men, not Indians, which was a relief.

They were coming toward him fast.

Thinking they might be bandits, he let his right hand slip down to his Colt Army pistol, but suddenly the riders were waving their hats and whooping joy-ously, indicating friendliness.

Twins possibly, brothers certainly, they were a lean and lanky pair grinning through sunburned faces. "How do, mister," said the one who, seen up close, was obviously the older, "I'm Johnny Lee and this is my brother James. We're from the town of Newton and we're here to invite you to bring your cattle to market there. You'll get top prices. Best in Kansas."

"What makes you think I've got cattle to sell?"

The boy's eyes peered past Morgan and his chin came up, pointing. "The dust cloud yonder."

Twisting in his saddle, Morgan looked at the pale yellow smudge against the blue sky. "You've got sharp eyes, Mr. Lee," he said, turning to the boy.

"Must be quite a sizeable herd to raise that much of a cloud," said James Lee, his cornflower blue eyes fixed on the horizon.

"More than twelve thousand head," said Morgan.

"Wow! That'll be the biggest herd Newton's seen so far," said Johnny Lee.

"Sorry to disappoint you, but Abilene's our objective," said Morgan.

"Since the railroad's reached Newton," asserted James, "nobody's goin' all the way to Abilene no more."

"Newton's sixty miles closer," exclaimed Johnny.

"Maybe so, but Abilene's got all the necessary amenities and . . ."

"Shucks, sir, so does Newton! There's nothin' in Abilene Newton don't have. I'm authorized by Joseph McCoy to . . ."

"Hold on! Did you say 'McCoy?' "

"Yes, sir," said Johnny. "He's the gentleman who hired James and me to ride out this way lookin' for herds and to . . ."

With a laugh, Morgan slapped the boy's shoulder. "No need to explain, boy! I did the same job for Mr. McCoy and for Abilene years ago! So, Joe McCoy's doing business in Newton, is he? Well, you hightail it back to town and tell him that his old pal Morgan of the Colter Ranch of Goliad accepts his kind invitation and will be heading his way with twelve thousand head of the best beef Texas has to offer."

Turning his horse, Johnny exclaimed, "Will do, sir!"

Grasping the horse's bridle, Morgan said, "Before

you go, don't you think you'd better tell me where to find this town of Newton?"

"Straight ahead, sir! Just follow your nose!"

"How far?"

"About forty miles as the crow flies."

"Well, a longhorn's no crow," Morgan chuckled delightedly, "so I reckon we'll have to manage it on foot."

Chapter Eight

"We'll bed 'em on this side," said Morgan, his steel-blue eyes fixed on the river. It was the Little Arkansas brimming with water compared to the trickling Red River they'd crossed on the fourth of July. Now, on August 16, stretching behind him for more than ten miles were twelve thousand head of cattle, the combined herds of the Colter Ranch at Goliad and the Anderson ranch at Cuero.

"We'll let 'em drink their fill tonight and tomorrow morning and cross 'em over in the afternoon," he declared, turning to the sweaty and dust-covered caporal beside him. "Pass back the word, Dalgo."

With a snaggle-toothed sunburst of a smile, the short, thick-bodied Mexican wheeled his yellow-speckled brown horse back toward the herd. "Right away, boss!"

"And tell young Mr. Anderson to ride forward," Morgan shouted after him, gruffly.

"This is the first and last time that I'll be mixing herds on a drive, believe me," he said, more to himself than for Dalgo's benefit as he lifted his weathered old cavalry hat and ran his fingers through a mane of damped-down and sweat-matted yellow hair and then swabbed his lean, angular, sun-leathered face with a blue and white wipe.

Replacing the hat, he jammed all but a small corner of the kerchief into the back pocket of his trail-broken Levi Strauss jeans and stood in the stirrups. Hooking his thumbs together and stretching his arms above his head, he flexed the muscles of thighs and calves and swiveled forward, back and to the sides from the waist with his hands clamped on hips above a black gunbelt cinched tightly around them and the holster anchored to the cone of his thigh with a rawhide tie.

"Cussed heat," he grumbled, picking at his faded blue cotton workshirt and the seat of his pants, ungluing them from his sweat-slicked chest, back and rump. Easing down into the saddle, he stroked a thumb across a sweat-beaded mustache as fine as new cornsilk and looking as if he'd only recently decided to grow it instead of having nurtured it for nearly six years. He'd decided to let the hair grow on his upper lip while lying in an army hospital in Washington during a convalescence from the effects of a Rebel minnie ball fired into his left chest while he rode into a battle at Jetersville, Virginia, behind General George Armstrong Custer only a few days before General Lee surrendered his sword to General Grant.

Turning in the saddle, he gazed back at the herd, judging it. Slimmed considerably from their long walk up from Texas, they were in good enough condition to bring a decent price but if they were to command the best money, they were going to require a few weeks of fattening on Kansas grass, meaning a further delay for him in making a deal and that much longer before the hands could be paid. Letting his mind dwell for a moment on that unsettling thought, he imagined the havoc that unpaid cowboys could cause. If they griped at being asked to wait for their money he would have to go to a bank for a loan secured by the herd, meaning paying interest. Or he could sell the stock in their present condition, taking a loss and having to explain it to the owners—Able Anderson and Rebecca Colter.

Of the pair, she would be the harder to deal with.

"Without a doubt," he grunted as he spied a rooster tail of dust at the edge of the herd—the Anderson kid riding hell bent for leather.

Reining up, he said, "Dalgo says you wanted to see me, Mr. Morgan."

"I do," said Morgan, concealing his anger at being referred to as "mister" by someone only four years younger than himself. "I wanted to inform you personally that we'll be making camp here tonight."

"Is that so?"

"Any objection?"

Craning his neck and squinting into a cloudless sky, the boy said, "Kind of early to be beddin' down, ain't it?"

"It's not the hour," said Morgan stiffly, "it's the water."

"Is there none farther?"

"All I know is that there's plenty of it here and now. And the here and now is all I care to think about at this time."

Lowering his head, Anderson forced a tight smile. "Well, if it was up to me, we'd push on a ways, but my pop said I was to follow your orders, so it ain't up to me."

"Exactly."

"Then why bother to explain why we're haltin' so early?"

"My mother raised me to always be polite."

"How nice."

"You should also know that instead of heading for Abilene we'll be taking the herd to market in Newton, which is sixty miles closer and where, I'm assured, we'll get top dollar."

"Whatever you say, Mr. Morgan," said Anderson with more sarcasm than surprise.

"We're now close enough to the railhead that you could, if you wanted to, cut out your herd and proceed on your own the rest of the way. There's nothing between here and Newton to stop you. Or you could drive on to Abilene if the idea of Newton doesn't suit you."

"Come this far together, might's well stay that way. How far do you reckon we have left?"

"Thirty miles, give or take a few."

"Five days?"

"In my estimation we ought to let the herd feed its way to Newton. These animals are worn out and weary. I'd allow a week."

"Are you askin' me my opinion? Or is that your polite way of telling me the way it's gonna be?"

"Like I said, you can always cut out your herd and proceed alone."

"I'll be heedin' my pa and stickin' with you, Mr. Morgan. Pa says there's nobody he'd trust more'n you with his herd, except for that fella they called Novillero. And Novillero's dead. 'You stick with Mr. Morgan,' my old man said to me, 'and you'll learn somethin'.' Well, I've never gone agin my pa yet."

"That's good of you."

"Goodness got nothin' to do with it."

"No?"

"Shoot, if I was to go agin you and my pa found out, he'd whale the bejesus out of me."

Morgan smiled, a picture forming in his head of Able Anderson, a gentle, soft-spoken and slightly built man, taking a stick to his strapping son. "You'll be keeping your herd with the rest, then?"

"That is so, but since we are so close to our objective and you'll be keeping such a slow pace, I may just ride

74

ahead into town. You know, to reconnoiter the place, scout out the buyers?"

Head for the saloons and whorehouses, you mean, Morgan thought. "An excellent idea," he said, glad to be rid of him.

The boy's tight smile ignited into a grin. "Great! And I think I'll take my pals Will and Henry with me."

"They're part of your outfit," Morgan said, "so if you want to take 'em along into town, it suits me just fine."

"That's what I'll be doin'," said Anderson, departing at sudden gallop.

"And good riddance to more bad rubbish," muttered Morgan, turning his eyes from him to the herd as Colter cowboys buzzed around them like insects, blunting the point, milling the lead cows and dispersing them into a widening brownish black stain upon the rolling pasture of the lush and life-giving grass of a pretty valley watered by the Little Arkansas.

Since they'd set out from the valley of the San Antonio, he figured, it had been more than a hundred days.

Chapter Nine

In the annals of American frontiers, Newton's heyday as the Wickedest Town in Kansas would be short-lived, lasting only as much time as it took the Atchison, Topeka and Santa Fe railway to stretch farther across the plains. Enterprising individuals would erect cattle pens and loading chutes and build a new town to meet the needs, cater to the whims and quench the thirsts of elegantly tailored livestock buyers and sun-scorched and trail-stained cowmen and cowboys in a patch of sin called Hide Park.

But when Morgan rode in on Sunday, August 20, 1871, Newton did not look a bit like a flash in the pan.

Although he knew that almost all of the structures flanking Main Street were brand new, they had the stolid look of permanence.

Proceeding through the town, he came to the railhead stockyards. Smaller than those at Abilene but with ample room to expand, the corrals would hold upwards of four thousand head, he estimated as he rode slowly past six loading chutes that were rattling from the tread of the cattle being goaded onto half a dozen railway cars.

Pausing to watch, he noticed someone else with his eyes on the cattle and intently observing the loading activities from a black-dyed silver-studded saddle on a handsome sorrel. "Well, hoot and holler," he cried, galloping forward, "if it isn't Mr. McCoy!"

Wearing a black bowler hat, black suit, white shirt and bow tie, Joseph McCoy was dressed in exactly the outfit he had on the first time Morgan laid eyes on him in an unknown drinkwater hamlet called Abilene — sixty miles north and five years back!

The sign over the door said: Bratton Hotel.

To call it a hotel was generous, its looking nothing more than a large log house as he tethered his horse to a hitching post in front. He walked through an open door into a combined dining room and lobby which he found to be deserted except for a man in a black suit hunched over one of the tables reading a St. Louis newspaper spread out like a tablecloth.

"Excuse me," said Morgan, "would you be the owner of this hotel?"

The man did not look up. "I am not," he said, disgruntled at being disturbed. In his late twenties by Morgan's estimate he had neither the appearance of farmer nor soldier. Not a man of the prairie in his black outfit of fine cloth and cut possibly acquired in New York or Philadelphia. His face was adorned with an ample drooping black mustache and could not be mistaken for anything but that of Scottish heritage, there having been plenty of Scotsmen around Gettysburg to instill a familiarity with the breed. "The proprietor is John P. Simpson," he said quietly, looking up at last from his newspaper, "and he's in the back. If you'll wait, I'm sure he'll return presently."

"Thanks."

"Not at all," the man said, returning attention to the newspaper but looking up again when Simpson came in. "You've got a customer, John," he said with a nod toward Morgan, adding, "I presume."

"A room with a bath," Morgan announced.

"The room's upstairs," said Simpson, a large man with muttonchops that only served to exaggerate his round-as-a-pumpkin face. "The bath's out back. Dollar for both."

"A dollar *each?*"

The man in the suit coughed a laugh but did not look up from his paper.

"A dollar *total,*" said Simpson.

"Can I get a proper meal in this establishment?"

The paper-reader uttered another small sound, possibly a stifled laugh.

"Mrs. Simpson serves supper at five o'clock."

"Is the meal extra?"

"Twenty-five cents."

Drawing a sealskin purse from beneath his shirt, Morgan said, "Well, for a bed, bath and a proper meal, I guess a buck and a quarter is fair."

"Fair or not," said Simpson, "it's the tariff."

"I've got a horse. Have you got a stable?"

"Out back."

"Is that extra?"

"No charge for stablin' but the feed'll cost."

"Naturally, I'll want to feed Strawberry."

"Bag of oats is a dime."

"I'll take care of the horse first, then the bath and then the room, only I'd appreciate it if you don't see me here by suppertime if you'd come and get me 'cause I might be asleep and I sure don't want to miss my supper. It's been a long while since I had a proper meal cooked by a woman."

"Don't worry a bit, son," the proprietor said as Morgan headed toward the door, "I'll see that you don't miss it."

"There's a true westerner," the man at the table said as Morgan left. "First thing on his mind is the welfare of his horse. If it comes down to a choice between supper for himself and oats for his horse, you know who'll get the meal!"

Two hours later, the food was ready.

"My name's Joe McCoy," the man in black said, standing and extending a hand, "and I'd be pleased if you'd sit at my table for the meal. No sense in us sitting alone, is there? Nothing makes a meal more satisfying than conversation, eh?"

"That's friendly of you, sir," said Morgan, shaking McCoy's hand. "My name's Morgan."

"What brings you to Abilene, Mr. Morgan?"

"Just passing through. Aimin' for California. And you, sir?"

"I'm here on behalf of the cattle business."

"I didn't know there were cattle in these parts."

"Soon will be," McCoy exclaimed.

"Here you are, gentlemen," said Mrs. Simpson, a large, happy woman in an apron, setting the table with their meal of buffalo steaks, boiled potatoes, cabbage and onions. "Plenty more in the kitchen," she said cheerily, "so don't you be shy about askin' for seconds."

"I won't," Morgan laughed.

"One day you'll be able to dine everyday on Texas beefsteak instead of buffalo. Thanks to the railroads."

"You've got a lot of confidence in the future of the railroads. Is that your business? Are you employed by the Kansas Pacific?"

"Not exactly."

"You are or you aren't, seems to me."

"I've got a contract with the railroad. It's my intention to make the town of Abilene the main shipping point for Texas cattle."

"Shipping the cattle where?"

"Back east."

"That's an ambitious scheme."

"It has been my waking thought and sleeping dream for quite some time."

"Well, I wish you luck."

With a chunk of buffalo speared with a fork and halfway to his mouth, McCoy winked and smiled. "Luck will have nothing to do with it. But planning will. And I've been doing a good deal of planning, believe me." With a quick flash of a prideful smile, he drew a pair of cheroots from a pocket. "If you'd care to join me in a post-prandial smoke and a stroll while the daylight lasts, I'll show you where this extravagant enterprise is going to be established."

"Sounds fine to me," Morgan said, hankering for tobacco.

The last lingering glow of the setting sun cast golden light across the land as McCoy led him toward the railroad tracks in the flatland east of Mud Creek and north of the town.

"There's not much to say about Abilene at the moment," said McCoy, stabbing the air with the unlit cheroot, "but it won't be long before it's an important name on the map. Like almost everything in these parts, Abilene is new. It wasn't settled until 1857 and not laid out until four years later and given a name."

"Abilene," said Morgan, puffing the fine cheroot with its sweet aroma, unlike the manure-smell of Ward Kimball's smokes. "It's a pretty name."

"Biblical, of course," said McCoy, coming to an abrupt halt just short of the tracks. "Loosely translated it means 'city of the plains.' It's not exactly a city but it's certainly on the plains!" Stamping his foot on the still-hard ground, standing knee-deep in grass, he declared, "This is the spot. Here is where pens and loading chutes will be built. And a scale, of course. I've bought a ten-ton Fairbanks that has the capacity to weigh a carload at a time." Pointing back toward the cluster of structures that was Abilene, he said, "Between here and the town I'll be putting up a hotel, as fine as any in Kansas City or St. Louis, so the men who come to trade in the cattle will have proper accommodations. All this building supply, equipment and material will be coming in by train or overland freight any day now. The pine is coming from St. Louis and the hard wood from Lenape. From Junction City I've hired a contractor to do all the finishing. I plan to spend the summer building and begin shipping in the autumn at the latest."

"Sounds fine," said Morgan, trying to visualize the result as clearly as McCoy obviously could.

"There's work to be had, if you're interested."

"Thanks, Mr. McCoy, but my heart's set on reachin' California. I do wish you luck, however, but one thing about your idea does puzzle me."

"And what would that be?"

"How do these cattlemen in Texas find out about all this and how do they get their cattle up here?"

"I've already written to several owners of large ranches—friends of Sugg's and mine—telling them of this undertaking and inviting them to drive their herds to Abilene."

"Do you reckon they'll come?"

McCoy lit his cheroot at last, savored the tasty smoke, puffed it into the gentle April air and said, "Son, if they don't, I'll wind up flat broke and a damn fool, won't I?"

He'd not been a fool and he did not wind up broke. Now, here McCoy was, in Newton, Kansas. Riding toward him, waving his hat, Morgan shouted, "Hey, Mr. McCoy!"

Turning in his saddle, McCoy gasped, "Morgan!"

Reining up, Morgan grinned, "I might have known that if there's cattle around, so's Joseph Geiting McCoy! Lordy! Have you given up on Abilene?"

"Hell no," chuckled McCoy, "I'm now mayor of the place!"

"Congratulations! When did all that happen?"

"This past April."

"Well, they couldn't've picked a better man for the job. But if you're mayor, how come you're here and not there?"

"Cattle business, of course. The fellas who are behind this new enterprise here in Newton hired me to help them get started, considering all the experience I gained in starting up the cattle market at Abilene."

Gazing at the cattle thundering up the loading chutes onto the cars, Morgan said, "Looks like you've got things thriving already."

Drawing a gold watch from his vest pocket, McCoy said, "It's very near my dinner hour. Will you join me? Be my guest? There's a hotel that has a decent menu, though not as fine as the one at the Drover's Cottage! Come on! We'll have a meal and I'll fill you in on all that's happened since I last saw you. When? A year ago?"

"More or less," said Morgan. "Things had changed a good bit even then. It came as quite a shock when the marshal . . ."

"Tom Smith."

"Right! 'Bear River' Tom Smith! Well, as I was saying, it came as quite a shock to me when I walked into Long Charlie's last year and was told by Marshal Smith that I had to hand over my gun. That wasn't the Abilene I remembered! I guess his job's a lot easier these days, what with the herds coming here to Newton

82

. . . and all those rowdy, trouble-making cowhands, too!"

Abruptly somber, McCoy said, "Regrettably, Tom Smith was killed in the line of duty."

"Is that so? How?"

"About five or six months after you'd sold your cattle and headed back to Texas. November! Yes, it was in November. He'd gotten a call for assistance from the sheriff of Dickinson County in arresting a settler by the name of Andrew McConnell on a murder warrant. McConnell was holed up with another hard case, Moses Miles. Poor Tom Smith never got within range of those nesters. They got him with rifles and as he lay dying, they finished him off with an ax."

"Gosh, that's awful. Even though his rule about checking guns in the saloons made me a mite nervous, I still took him to be an able fella."

"Tom was first rate, no doubt."

"So, who's got the bridle on the old town these days?"

McCoy's eyes glinted and a smile quickly overspread his lips. "James Butler Hickok, better known as . . ."

Morgan grunted a laugh. "Wild Bill!"

Beaming, McCoy said, "You've heard of him."

Morgan shrugged. "Who hasn't?"

"I hired him to police Abilene in April, soon as I became mayor."

"That must have made my old pal Henry Kidder happy. He was always strong for law and order. How is Hank? Is his newspaper prospering?"

"He's doing quite well. He endorsed me for mayor."

"I imagine so. One law and order man backing another! Makes sense."

"Your other pal, Charlie Carew, didn't."

Morgan barked a laugh. "Long Charlie's definitely not what you'd call a strict law and order man. I assume that Marshal Hickok has put the kibosh on the antics along Texas Street?"

McCoy eased into a sly smile. "He's done a good job of taming the denizens of the Devil's Half Acre, yes."

"I've been told that the same cannot be said of Newton's counterpart of the Half Acre, however."

McCoy laughed. "Hide Park!"

"Seems like the devil will get his due no matter where and never mind the name."

"Men will be men."

"And cowboys, cowboys. Is there a marshal in Newton?"

"Indeed so. A fine young man, name of Thomas Carson. He's got the toughness required to handle trouble in any way, shape or form . . . or from anyone looking for it . . . or for anyone who finds trouble is looking for him."

Morgan chuckled. "Is that last a reference to me?"

"There were times when trouble came your way. I recall."

"That was Abilene. This is Newton. That was then. That was when I had a certain reputation. Nobody knows me here."

"The name and memory of Morgan's still fresh," said McCoy, suddenly solemn once more. "Be careful, my friend. Now, let me introduce you to Tom Carson."

"If it'll make you happy."

"It will."

Chapter Ten

Across Main Street from the hotel, the marshal's office was little more than a wooden shed with one room outfitted with an oak desk, three chairs and a pair of metal cages no bigger than a privy; unoccupied at the moment.

Rising behind the desk as Morgan and McCoy entered, Carson was lean and rangy and moved with the alertness required of anyone who wore a badge and the quickness of a man who knew how to make effective use of the Colt six-gun slung low on his right hip.

"Tom, I want you to meet a friend of mine," declared McCoy. "His first name's Hugh but he only answers to his last — Morgan."

The marshal came around to the front of his desk. "Morgan? *The* Morgan?" He extended his hand. "The one I read about in the newspapers and the one people have told me so much about all over Kansas?"

Grasping the outstretched hand, Morgan said, "My late father used to tell me, 'Believe little of what people tell you and nothing you read in the newspapers.' "

"Morgan's here as the trail boss and rep for the Colter herd," said McCoy.

Sitting on the corner of his desk, the marshal nodded his head slowly. "You've got cowhands by the name of

Anderson, Garrett and Kearnes?"

"They're with the Anderson herd. They combined with the Colters for the purpose of the drive. How is it you know about them?"

"A friend of this Anderson got himself shot and killed last night by a hard case called Mike McCluskie. It was a ruckus at Tuttle's Dance Hall and Saloon in Hide Park. Now, Anderson and the other two are vowing revenge on McCluskie. Since you know the three, I'm thinking that maybe you could round them up and haul their butts out of town . . . 'cause McCluskie's not a man that amateurs should be messing with. I'm a man who's in favor of heading off trouble if I possibly can."

"Why don't you just round up the three of 'em yourself and run 'em out of town?"

"On account of the fact that I don't know them. Never laid eyes on them. Wouldn't know them if I tripped over them."

Morgan cracked a smile. "I'm not a lawman."

"Let's just say that you'd be doing your friends a favor."

"Well, they're not exactly my friends but I'll do what I can."

Hide Park lay south of the railroad. Like the rest of Newton on the better side of the tracks, it had the look of permanence. Rather than appearing to have been recently constructed, its parallel strings of saloons, dance halls, gambling rooms, and bordellos flanking its wide dirt thoroughfare seemed to have been standing there for years and business appeared to be as brisk as any Saturday night on Texas Street in Abilene. In the midst stood Tuttle's Dance Hall and Saloon, the logical place to start, he supposed.

86

When he pushed through unpainted batwing doors and crossed the sawdust-covered floor to a long and crowded mahogany bar, it was every drink emporium he'd ever entered, but through the tobacco smoke and among the rambunctious cowboys, the available women, the card players, and the drinkers at the bar he did not find young Anderson and his two nettlesome saddle buddies.

"Name your poison, fella," declared a burly, balding bartender with the same handlebar mustache and beer belly Morgan had found on saloon keepers everywhere, excepting skinny Long Charlie Carew. "If we ain't got what you want," he said, advancing on Morgan's spot at the end of the bar near the batwings, "it don't exist."

Seeing a half-empty bottle of it on a shelf behind the bar, Morgan nodded at it and said, "Mescal."

With arching eyebrows, the bartender reached behind himself toward the shelf forested with liquor bottles, picked out the mescal and brought it and a glass to the bar. "You really like this stuff?"

Morgan shrugged. "It's an acquired taste."

Setting down the bottle, the bartender grunted, "It's your gut," and began to pour.

Judging by the care he took, Morgan concluded he was being served by the proprietor. "Are you Mr. Tuttle?"

"I am."

"Well, sir, I'd appreciate it if you'd just leave the bottle."

Lurching back, Tuttle grumbled, "I don't fancy havin' to pick you off the floor drunk and then havin' to toss you out."

"Don't fret, Mr. Tuttle," Morgan said, stroking his own mustache, a pale whisper compared to the roaring assertion of Tuttle's handlebar. Drawing coins from his pocket to pay for the bottle and plunking them on the bar, he said, smiling, "Never been carried out of a saloon yet and I sure don't plan on beginnin' now."

He was not a falling-down drunkard and he never would be, he'd vowed to the memory of his mother somewhere along the way. Looking down at the coins on the bar, he remembered her asking, "After all, is it not written in *Proverbs* that the drunkard and the glutton shall come to poverty?" "Yes, ma," he'd replied dutifully, though he could have cited *Ecclesiastes 8:15:* "A man hath no better thing under the sun, than to eat, and to drink, and to be merry."

Rather than becoming a boisterous presence when he drank, he turned quietly inward and when he spoke it was not a testy outburst but the soft and gentle expression of what he was thinking—a nostalgia for the crisp nose-biting winds of a Pennsylvania woods with crusted snow crunching underfoot as he and his father tracked deer; the slumber-bringing voice of his mother reading passages from the Holy Bible, William Shakespeare or Charles Dickens; the comradeship of barracks and tent which bound him to any man who'd soldiered whether for North or South; the skirl of bagpipes playing the "Garry Owen" as the Seventh Cavalry paraded past in salute to their commander—George Armstrong Custer; hunting buffalo on the grasslands of Kansas with a wizened old frontier character who called himself California Joe and was always spinning yarns about far-away places such as the Pacific coast and Texas where, he'd said to Morgan's utter disbelief, cows had horns stretching wider than a man's arms.

When drinking, he also turned his thoughts to the Morgan who had come unexpectedly to the Colter Ranch at Goliad not so long ago and received askance looks and been regarded by the people of Goliad as just another wandering stranger with a peculiar way of talking but who soon became a familiar and friendly figure to the townsfolk and to patrons of Migdalia Coffee's El Dorado cantina—lanky, likeable, and laconic, except when Mexican mescal loosened his tongue.

Nothing of the more recent Morgan passed his lips when he drank, however. No matter how much mescal he consumed, he never let slip any clue to the existence of another Morgan, the one who had blazed a fearful reputation with a Colt six-gun that still echoed in the streets and the saloons of Abilene and, judging by what Marshal Tom Carson of Newton knew of him, all over the frontier.

Unlike Marshal Smith of Abilene, Morgan noted gratefully as he scanned Tuttle's saloon, Carson had not imposed a ban on carrying guns in drinking emporiums. Peering into the mirror behind the bar, he noticed that Mr. Tuttle, like Charlie Carew in Abilene, kept a shotgun in a sling and a pair of six-guns with long and heavy barrels suitable for braining any rambunctious cowboy who might get it into his head to make trouble. For some reason—the knowledge of the presence of these weapons under the bar, a natural peacefulness of nature among the patrons or simply the earliness of the hour—Tuttle's saloon was quiet; so quiet he could hear the clicking of the gambling chips at the poker tables at the back of the room and the clinking of the bottles against the rims of glasses as Tuttle worked his way along the bar topping off drinks.

Presently reaching Morgan, he asked, "How you doin' with that Mexican cow piss?"

With half the half-bottle remaining, Morgan smiled. "Doin' just fine, sir." Sensing that Mr. Tuttle was of the talkative variety of the saloon-owner species, he scanned the room quickly and said, "Business appears to be thriving."

"Fair to middlin'," said Tuttle guardedly.

"It's early. In my experience, things tend to liven up later."

"You got experience, hunh?"

"I had an interest in a saloon in Abilene once."

"Is that so?"

"Long Charlie Carew's. Ever hear of it?"

"I did. Didn't know Charlie had a partner, though."

"I was a silent partner. Eventually I sold out to Charlie."

"How come? Didn't care for the trade?"

"Oh, I guess I just got the wanderlust. Found my way to Texas. Now I'm in the cattle business."

"An owner?"

"Shoot, no. I'm just a lowly trail boss."

"That's quite a switch, from saloon owner to Texas trail boss."

"Life's full of twists. And filled with new things. Like mescal."

Tuttle chuckled and topped Morgan's glass. "I was wonderin' why you were drinkin' this stuff. It's mostly Mexicans who ask for it, although the Mex business mostly goes to a place at the end of the street where they got a Mexican band. You know, all that cook-a-rat-cha noise. My place has American music."

"I haven't heard any evidence of it so far."

"The band starts at ten. That's when the girls show up, too; in case you were wonderin'. Till then, the only excitement's at the card tables."

"I heard you had some trouble the other night. A shooting?"

Easing back, Tuttle turned wary. "What's that to you?"

"It's nothing to me personally, except the man who got shot was a friend of one of the hands that came up the trail with me and Marshal Carson asked me to see what I could do to head off any trouble. There's been talk that my man may come gunning for the shooter, a gentleman by the name of McCluskie?"

"If you want my advice, sir, you'll not be getting mixed up in anything like that. McCluskie's a dangerous man."

Scanning the room again, Morgan said, "Is he here now?"

Slowly, Tuttle shook his head.

"What about any friends of his? Any of them here?"

"Nope."

Morgan smiled. "Well, maybe none of 'em will show up. But if my man shows up, rest assured that I'll do my best to keep him roped in. And maybe you'd do the same regarding McCluskie, since you know him and I don't."

"Seems to me that's the marshal's job. Or are you his deputy?"

"Not at all. My only interest is in getting my man back to his father down in Texas all in one piece."

"That's mighty decent of you. Most men I know wouldn't get mixed up in a fight that wasn't theirs."

Morgan's eyes drifted through the room again. "Well, I've seen a lot of shooting in saloons and I guess I've gotten to the point where if I can prevent one, I'm willing to give it a try." He looked back at Tuttle, grinning. "Besides, you've got a nice place here and I'd hate to see it damaged by a lot of flying lead."

"And what makes you think your man will come lookin' for McCluskie in my place? They could run into each other anywhere in town."

"True enough," said Morgan, helping himself to more mescal, "but since it was here that McCluskie shot the boy the other night, it seems likely that my man will start looking for him here. Anyway, I have to start somewhere, don't I?"

Tuttle pondered this for a moment, then leaned

across the bar, whispering. "You're right, I do know McCluskie. And he is a reg'lar here. But you should know that he's got a pal that's always with him—a weasel-faced runt named Riley. A kid who's not complete upstairs. He follows McCluskie around like a faithful dog and looks harmless, but he packs a pair of Colts in holsters under his armpits beneath a vest. He's fast. So watch out for him."

"Appreciate the advice."

"I'll let you know if McCluskie and his pal come in," said Tuttle, drifting down the bar.

Promptly at ten, the band took places on a small stage—a piano player, a fiddler and a drummer—and women appeared as if from nowhere, available for dancing and other diversions. In paint and pretty dresses, they looked used, but they proved sprightly partners as women-starved cowboys left their drinks on the bar and losers at the card tables folded their holdings to try their luck in a different kind of gamble.

Near eleven, McCluskie barged in.

Identifiable instantly because he was accompanied by a frail and consumptive-looking youth who could have been none other than McCluskie's faithful dog Riley, Morgan edged past the dancers to the opposite end of the bar.

Immediately, Tuttle headed toward them intending to pass along Morgan's warning that they were hunted men, but before he reached them, the batwing doors flew open again and Anderson strode in. At his side were Garrett and Kearnes and a third youth Morgan did not know.

"McCluskie," shouted Anderson, the name a challenge and a threat, cutting off the music and silencing the poker chips.

Rearing upright, McCluskie went instantly for his gun but was not fast enough, barely clearing the holster before Anderson had his pistol out and fired twice. Spinning around, McCluskie dropped to the floor with his neck gushing blood.

In the same instant, Morgan saw Riley's rising hands but before he could warn Anderson or draw his own Colt, Riley's guns were in his hands and blazing.

Screaming unintelligibly, he advanced the length of the bar while startled and terrorized patrons ducked for cover.

By the time he passed through the batwings, he had stepped over the bleeding bodies of Anderson, Garrett, Kearnes, their friend and two cowboys who'd had nothing to do with any of them.

Bending over Anderson, Morgan examined a tiny hole in his chest but from the river of blood flowing from under the boy's back he judged that it was a killing wound.

Garrett and Kearnes would survive, he expected.

The third youth was dead, shot through an eye. Also dead were the two cowboys whose names no one knew at the time.

Immediately, Marshal Carson formed a search party to pursue Riley. "I'd be pleased to have you along, Morgan," he said. "I hear you're the best when it comes to tracking."

"That's mighty flattering, marshal," said Morgan, slowly shaking his head as he gazed down at Anderson's corpse, "but as we say in Texas, I ain't got no dog in that fight."

With a puzzled glance at the body of the boy, Carson said, "I just supposed you'd want to come along, seein' as how this fella was one of your cowboys."

"Well, you supposed wrong."

Chapter Eleven

"What will you be tellin' the kid's father about how it happened?"

It was not until they were nearly a week out of Newton on their way back to Texas that Dalgo posed the question that Morgan had asked himself immediately when he realized that there was nothing that could be done and that Hugh Anderson was going to bleed to death on the sawdust-covered plank floor of Perry Tuttle's Dance Hall and Saloon.

He'd answered himself then as he answered Dalgo now: "I'm going to lie."

The boy and his friends Will and Henry had been having a peaceable game of cards when this hardcase troublemaker by the name of McCluskie just started shooting up the place, he would say. As bad luck would have it, they got hit. It was an unfortunate instance of the boy being in the wrong place at the wrong time. Rest assured, Mr. Anderson, your son had been innocent of any wrong-doing. As a matter of fact, Mr. Anderson, you'd have been mighty proud of how your boy changed! The experience of being on the drive did him a world of good, believe me. Made him into a man you'd've been pleased to call your son! Don't know how we could have made it to Kansas without him.

On an overcast, unseasonably cool and breezy day after the shooting that already was going into the lore of Kansas as "The Tuttle Dance Hall Massacre" while Marshal Carson's posse was beginning its search for Riley, at a burial ground that was as new as the town of Newton he'd spoken Shakespeare alongside the boy's shallow grave. "Present mirth hath present laughter. What's to come is still unsure. Youth's a stuff will not endure."

Gone was the chill of that day as Morgan rode beside Dalgo, their pace set not by the plodding of a herd of cattle but by the speed of wagons loaded only with the needs of themselves and a half-dozen returning Texas cowboys who'd gone broke lavishing their trail wages on women, cards, and drink in Hide Park.

But they were still alive, he said to himself.

Although well intentioned, Dalgo had twisted Morgan's thoughts from the glories of the present day with its hard July sun and summer warmth and the whisper of a soft wind across the high prairie grass to past days when Death had ranged over the plains and across his trail on a pale horse — a galloping grim reaper with a bloodied scythe as his weapon.

Just as sharp, Dalgo's question pricked Morgan's brain to set loose a flood of memories of funerals.

Grizzle old California Joe Milner came to mind, tenderly preparing young Daniel Lonetree, a peaceable Kaw Indian killed by a Cheyenne in the carnage of a village beside the Platte because Daniel wore the blue of the U.S. Cavalry. Painting the placid face, Joe had draped the boy's body in a buffalo robe and sat for nearly an hour speaking Kaw as if Daniel could hear him, then lifted the body in his strong arms and carried him from the ruined and smoldering village to a slope shaded by cottonwoods where he scooped a shallow grave from the pliant earth and laid the body in it with the head facing the life-giving east.

After arranging rocks and stones upon the slight mound, Joe rose, standing straight with his face to the sky and his lips forming silent words.

"I'm really sorry, Joe," said Morgan, seeking to console.

"Dan'l walked the good path in this life," Joe said with the joy of it glowing in his eyes, "and he'll come back someday, somewhere. Mebbe to the Neosho valley ag'in. Mebbe someplace else. His is a young soul, so he's not done his journey yet."

Not long after, it was California Joe offering Morgan consolation and comfort in the face of senseless death along the Washita.

Morgan had barely entered the village when he saw Major Ward Kimball sway suddenly in his saddle and then pitch sideways to the hard ground, the left side of his head shot away, his tongue lolling from the gaping mouth.

At the same time, he saw the Indian who'd done it — young, grinning, proud, the gun in his hand still smoking, exactly as the day when Daniel Lonetree had died at the Platte. "You heathen bastard," he screamed, leveling his Colt and firing again and again, the bullets slamming into the Indian's chest, spinning him, and then in the back, spinning him again, turning him into a whirling dervish until the six chambers of the gun were empty.

Nearly blind with hate and tears, he'd leapt from his horse onto the dead Indian and, as he'd done with the Indian who'd killed Daniel Lonetree beside the Platte, slashed away his scalp.

By mid-morning, the shooting was over and wagons descended into the shallow Washita valley in search of the wounded, dying, and dead of George Armstrong Custer's cavalry. Leading one of them, Morgan picked his way through the carnage. When they came to the body he had been looking for he dismounted and stood at attention like an honor guard. "It's Major Kimball," said the shocked corporal in charge of the wagon and four privates who had the duty of gathering up the dead. "He was a damned good man." Just before noon, Custer rode triumphantly through the ruins. When he saw Morgan, he reined his prancing black horse to a stop. "I'm sorry about Major Kimball. He was a damn fine soldier. I'll miss him. The nation will miss him. We'll be needing more men like him if we're to make this country safe."

Yet Kimball had not died in such a noble cause. An error had been made. "These weren't hostiles at all. This was Chief Black Kettle's village," grumbled California Joe. "He's always been a friend of the whites. He kept many of the chiefs from going to war. Talked 'em into signing peace treaties. We done lost a powerful friend amongst the tribes. And I doubt that there'll be another. I'm afraid that instead of guaranteein' peace by this, we're just gonna stir up more trouble. All-out war, prob'ly. That's the trouble, you see, when you think that all Indians is alike and everyone is better off dead. That's a truth that Custer ain't ever gonna larn . . . and one day it'll be the ruin of 'im."

"And the stupid son of a bitch will deserve it," mumbled Morgan bitterly.

After that, he'd had enough of the army.

After that he'd headed to Texas.

But Death followed him to Goliad, swinging his scythe to cut down the fatherly Buck Colter and the next year reaped Novillero in the midst of a stampede.

"You sure are quiet, *amigo*," said Dalgo, his soft and songlike Mexican cadences drawing Morgan back to the present. "You ain't said a word for five miles. Must be somethin' heavy on your mind."

Forcing a smile, Morgan said, "Not at all. Day dreamin' is all. Such a pretty day! When a day's this nice, I just go wool gatherin' in my head. My mom and dad used to take me to task for it."

"Well," said Dalgo dubiously, "you sure had a sad look on your face."

"I guess I'm just tired," Morgan said. "And a trifle saddle sore," he added, rising in the stirrups and rubbing a hand against his rump rather than explain that he'd been quiet because Death had been dancing around his head for the past five miles. "Besides," he went on brightly, "how could I be sad when I've got a check in my saddle bag for upwards of two hundred thousand dollars—twenty bucks a head—payable to Miss Rebecca Colter?"

"Amigo," said Dalgo as his round face broadened into a grin, "I bet when she sees that check she's gonna throw her arms around your neck and give you a big wet kiss right on the lips!"

"You crazy Mex," Morgan sneered. "You've sure got a wild imagination."

"Oh yeah? I ain't imaginin' nothin'. I knows what I see. And what I see is the way that woman looks at you."

"How's that, pray tell?"

"With longin' in her eyes!"

"That's bull."

"No, it ain't," Dalgo giggled.

"The sun's gettin' to you, hombre," Morgan laughed, reaching between their walking horses and tugging the brim of the Mexican's sombrero down to his broad nose.

Sliding back the hat, Dalgo said, "It's none of my business, of course, but I think the time's come for you to throw a rope on that woman."

"Is that so?"

"Yep," said Dalgo, circling a hand in the air. "Lasso her and hog tie her," he added, mimicking the roping and throwing of a cow. Clenching a fist and plunging it toward the ground as if he held a branding iron, he cackled, "And then put your mark on her — hisssssss!"

Laughing, Morgan said, "That's very good, *amigo*, only take my word for it, Rebecca Colter's not for branding. Not by me, that is."

"Why not you?"

"Because I'm way, way below her station. I'm nothin' but a no-account . . . cowboy."

"Now who's talkin' bull?"

Abruptly impatient with the conversation and jerking his horse to a halt, Morgan thundered, "Look, *amigo*, it's a long way to Texas, so do me a favor, will you, and not bring up this subject again?"

Shrinking back, Dalgo muttered, "Anythin' you say, boss."

A sullenly silent mile later, Morgan said, "Hey, I'm sorry for getting so cross back there. I was out of line."

"Nah, it was me that was," said Dalgo, his dark eyes shining with relief and pleasure at the passing of the storm.

Unimpeded by ten thousand cattle, the weather, or hostile Indians and in less than half the time required to go up the Chisholm Trail, they crossed the Red River into Texas on the first of September.

A week later, they reached Cuero where after a night's rest Dalgo and the hands proceeded with the wagons to cross the Guadalupe while Morgan rode eastward to the Double A ranch carrying a Bank of Newton check in the amount of sixty thousand dollars for the sale of Able Anderson's herd and the lie that he had been rehearsing since the senseless shootings in Perry Tuttle's saloon.

"Your boy was strictly an innocent bystander," he said, sensing intuitively that Able Anderson was pretending to believe what he was hearing but accepting none of it.

As he sat reserved and guarded in the big overstuffed chair with its crocheted coverings by the window in the sunny parlor of the mournful house, Anderson said it was good of Morgan to come and tell him. Kind of him. Decent. "Bringing the proceeds of the sale of the herd is deeply appreciated," he went on as he poured bourbon for Morgan. "You obtained an excellent price!"

"No more than the herd deserved, sir! They were excellent cattle. A damned fine herd!"

Handing Morgan the whiskey, Anderson sighed, "And the last. I'm through with it."

"Oh, you don't mean that," said Morgan urgently, although he could read the contrary in the old man's face.

"All this was to be my boy's," Anderson said, stretching out his arms as if to encompass the land. "With him gone, what's the point? I'll sell the place now."

"Don't make that kind of decision immediately, sir," Morgan pleaded. "Give yourself some time. Think it over. This is a fine ranch you've built."

Anderson smiled wanly. "I built it for him."

"Well, do me the favor of thinking it over," said Morgan, finishing the whiskey and rising from the corner of the heavy couch. "Promise?"

Anderson nodded slowly. "Sure."

"Good," said Morgan, smiling.

As he opened the door to leave, Anderson asked, "Are you a married man, Mr. Morgan?"

"No, sir."

"Ah," sighed Anderson. "Then you have no sons."

"Uh, no, sir. No sons," Morgan whispered as he stepped from a vestibule onto the porch.

Closing the door, Anderson muttered, "That's . . . good."

That evening for the first time in nearly six months Morgan and Dalgo ate a Mexican supper prepared by Rebecca Colter and served at the gleamingly polished long table of her spacious dining room aglow with silver plates and glittering candlesticks in the rambling adobe house built and expanded by three generations of Colter men who had passed to her their shared vision of a prosperous future built upon longhorn cattle.

"It's a personal triumph for both of you," she said, raising a delicately stemmed glass of red wine in salute, first to Morgan and then to Dalgo for the success of their drive. "I assure you that as soon as I deposit the check for the sale of the herd you'll be rewarded with a handsome bonus."

"*Muchas gracias,*" beamed Dalgo as his mischievous eyes darted from her to Morgan with a look of romantic expectation Morgan had last seen on the trail from Newton.

"How very sad that is," she said when Morgan told her of Able Anderson's grief-driven but impetuous declaration of his intention to sell his ranch.

"Please don't take this wrong," said Morgan. "I know it will sound heartless of me, but I think Mr. Anderson's tragedy can be an opportunity for you if you were to buy him out."

"It's not much of a ranch now that he's sold his stock,"

101

she said thoughtfully. "Except for the house and the furnishings, what's left that'd be worth the price?"

Lifting his wine, Morgan whispered, "The land."

Chapter Twelve

Feeding slivers of kindling into a wood-burning stove, Dalgo declared, "There's no boredom like bein' at a line camp in winter."

"You said it," said Morgan, spreading his bedroll atop the bare wooden slats of an iron cot as memories ignited of winter nights in Pennsylvania that were snug gatherings with his parents, his mother darning or mending or sewing or reading a book and his father cleaning hunting rifles, tying flies for fishing or mulling over the farm's accounts in front of the hearth while wind-driven snow frosted windows and drifted against the door.

Winter in South Texas was hot and dry days in a saddle and chilly nights in ramshackle places like this, one of a hundred camps dotting the Colter territory of the Nueces Strip.

"We'll soon have some heat in this little hacienda," said Dalgo optimistically, striking a match and dipping it into a mass of dried scrub and crumpled paper, "and then some coffee, sowbelly and fried beans."

Sitting cross-legged on the creaking bed and rolling a cigarette, Morgan moaned, "Lord, what I'd give for a decent meal again."

They'd been two weeks riding the circuit of camps checking on the men and the cattle. He estimated as he stretched out on his side on the bed facing Dalgo that it was going to be another week of cold nights and miserable meals in similar cabins and huts, some occupied and some deserted like this one, before they returned to the ranch, their inspections done.

Besides the stove, his bed and an identical one heaped with Dalgo's belongings, the shack was outfitted with a square pine table with a faded and coffee-spotted checkerboard cover and four rickety straight back chairs with cowhide seats. Studded with nails supporting half a dozen well-used tin cups, a cupboard against the wall near the stove had been slapped together from raw pine boards and now sagged from the effects of years of storing fire-blacked pots and skillets and a wooden box piled with utensils. That none of this had been used in the year since their last rounds of camps was evidenced by a veneer of dust so thick on the floor that Morgan could make out his boot prints to the bed and Dalgo's to the stove where, satisfied with his fire, Dalgo turned and dropped onto a rickety chair and propped his feet atop the pine table, his spurs hooking the checkerboard cover and drawing it up at one corner—like the skirt of a flirtatious whore.

"Concerning this decent meal you've got your heart set on, boss," said Dalgo, "can I ask who you'd like to share it with?"

Lurching up with the cigarette slanting from the right side of his mouth and the smoke curling up into his eye, making him squint, Morgan thundered, "No, you may not."

Cackling a laugh, Dalgo said, "The *señorita* at the El Dorado? Or—dare I say her name—Rebecca Colter?"

"Stay off that topic, *amigo*," snapped Morgan, snorting smoke and flicking a burnt match at the Mexican. "Just get that bee out from under your sombrero . . . *pronto*."

"All I'm sayin', boss," said Dalgo, swinging his feet to the floor, "is that, in my opinion, such as it is, the time is ripe for you to start thinkin' about settlin' down and raisin' a family."

Groaning and hanging his head, Morgan studied the glow at the tip of his cigarette. "You sound like a priest." Looking up, frowning, he asked, "When did you become a *padre?*"

Rising, Dalgo moved to the stove to study the progress of his fire. "Don't need to be no priest to see that the right thing for you to do now is to declare yourself to the lady in question, marry her, and give her some babies."

"Is that so?"

"That's so, boss. For her sake, for your sake and for the sake of the future of this here ranch."

"For the sake of the ranch?"

"I've lived here most of my life and I happen to care about what's goin' to happen to the place. Now I know that Miss Colter is a capable lady and that she means it when she says she intends to run the place and make it better, but sooner or later she's goin' to have to marry."

"So?"

"So, who she marries is goin' to have a lot to say about runnin' this place, isn't he?"

"Reckon so," said Morgan.

"Once I believed that the man she married ought to be Novillero. But he was shy about makin' himself available. And I guess she was not too keen on him. Anyways, now he's dead. So in my way of seein' things, that leaves you. And I'm not the only one who sees it that way. Practically the whole town of Goliad expects the two of you to get hitched. Most of the hands, too. In fact, the only people who don't seem to see a wedding in the cards for you two is you and the lady."

"Holy thunderation," exclaimed Morgan, flinging

105

the butt of his cigarette to the floor and grinding it under the heel of his boot, "that takes the cake! What the devil are we, the main topic for discussion all over Texas?"

"Maybe not all over Texas," said Dalgo with a broad grin peeping out mischievously from under his flowing black mustache as he drew down a battered coffee pot from the sagging cupboard, "but you're sure as hell the main gossip between San Antone and Shanghai Pierce's El Rancho Grande over at Matagorda!"

"Shanghai's been putting his two cents in about this?"

"So I've been told."

"By who?"

"People who seen old Shang a few weeks ago."

"Just what's that old boar's head been sayin'?"

"That Rebecca Colter needs some sons and that he can't think of anyone better suited to provide 'em than you."

"Sons!"

The word exploded like a six-gun fired too close.

"Sons!"

It ricocheted in Morgan's head and lodged there like a bullet.

Sons.

His sons.

Rebecca Colter's sons.

Their sons.

" 'Tis a happy thing to be the father unto many sons," said William Shakespeare's King Henry VI, he recalled. But at the same moment the mournful voice of Able Anderson came back to him out of the dim light of a dusty parlor where Death had wielded his leveling scythe. "Are you a married man, Mr. Morgan?"

"No, sir," he'd replied.

"Ah," the old man had sighed, "then you have no sons."

"No."

"That's . . . good," Anderson had said, meaning what?

That sons can break a man's heart by getting shot to death in meaningless moments in saloons in Kansas.

How many fathers' hearts had he broken, Morgan wondered, by the killing of their sons? A trio of hard cases by the name of Dowd. The first to die at his hands outside the army, they had a father. There'd been a downy-cheeked and sensitive-featured youth with hair as blond as drought-parched prairie grass going for his gun in Long Charlie's saloon and dying from his foolhardiness; somebody's son.

Before them into the sights of his gun had ventured the sons of other fathers—a boy in a Rebel uniform dying unkissed by his father in a Pennsylvania woodland, a Cheyenne's son in a village on the Platte and another son of an Indian when Custer blundered into Black Kettle's camp along the Washita.

Of course, Morgan was someone's son, too, wasn't he?

The son of Thomas and Catherine Morgan of Gettysburg, a tousle-haired kid who had stumbled into a war and met Death and followed him barefoot around Union Army headquarters with cornflower-blue eyes wide in wonder, the fifteen-year-old farmboy who quoted Shakespeare. And then the heartbroken son with tear-streaked cheeks dutifully burying his fallen father.

Now he was glad that his father hadn't lived to know that his son had become a flinty twenty-year-old famous for killing the Dowds and others and as a result had come to view the world through on-guard steel-blue eyes while keeping his gunhand ready as he leaned against a bar with a Colt six-shooter slung low on his hip and its holster lashed to his thigh in case he had to make a fast draw.

That he'd relied on his Colt Army six-shooter did not set him apart from the other men of the frontier for whom there had been no law save that of self-preservation.

"Morgan is not a bad man," Hank Kidder had written for a New York newspaper, "and when he resorted to his gun it was to defend himself or others. Unfortunately, his skill at handling a Colt and stories of the men he has shot to death with it have made him vulnerable to challenges by the more daring rowdies amongst the cowboys who arrive in Abilene with the herds."

Walking slowly toward the opposite end of Texas Street, dodging and weaving cowboys on horses and those stumbling to and from the saloons, the card parlors and the bordellos, he'd learned that he had to be increasingly aware of the possibility that at any moment a man or boy with Morgan on his mind and a gun in his hand might emerge from the mob, a doorway or an alley.

"I always feel sort of sad when I see all this," he'd once explained to Hank Kidder as they observed the brash cowboys carousing in Abilene. "On the surface it seems like nothing but well-deserved fun, but believe me, the fun of Saturday night on Texas Street turns into the hard reality of morning when most of these men will wake up with aching in their heads and nothing in their pockets."

Of those who'd died in the pursuit of their fun, Hank Kidder had written, "On such occasions there are few tears shed, or even inquiries made, by the respectable people, but an expression of sorrow is common that active hostilities did not continue until every rough stone was dead."

Had there been no one to mourn them? Of course there'd been! Their mothers and fathers! Once loved, probably still loved, each had been someone's son.

As surely as if he'd drunk an entire bottle of mescal in one evening at the El Dorado cantina, Morgan became intoxicated with the notion of sons—fathering them, raising them, teaching them, molding them. Soon, he was able to see them. Two sons. Strong, capable and worthy, they accompanied him. No matter where he was nor what he was doing, they were at his side. So real were they that he half-believed that if he spoke to them they would answer—respectfully, of course; no son of his would ever show disrespect for his elders, especially not for his father!

As to their mother, his imagination fixed upon the memory of his own, the sainted Catherine Thomas Morgan who had cherished books and tried to instill her love of them in her son, but in all his travels he'd encountered no woman like her of marrying age.

Whores and dance hall girls! They were the company he'd kept. Pretty and fun and satisfying to be with they were. But trollops.

As he went about the boring chores of maintaining the Colter ranch in wintertime so that come spring all would be in readiness for another roundup of cattle and then the long, arduous, and never boring trail to Kansas, he harkened back to the few women who had crossed his path since Gettysburg, women who were not the sort men took as wives with the objective of bearing sons.

Save one.

Sue Cantrell!

"There is one partikler daughter of joy at Sally Magruder's bawdy house name of Sue—Sweet Sue Cantrell," California Joe Milner had declared at Fort Riley in the summer of 1866. "Jest about your age and speed. She'll take to you like honeysuckle to a front porch."

Where a wide and rutted dirt street and the town of Junction City came to an abrupt end and the prairie began stood the gaudy, yellow clapboard, three-story house whose only sign that it was more than a residence was a row of horses tethered to two hitching rails flanking the two steps that led to a porch and a brown-painted door with one large window made of squares of stained glass. Next to the door with folded arms and a wary look leaned a bear of a man with a brace of six-guns holstered backward so that drawing them would have been a crossed-arm action which to Morgan seemed to be a foolish and possibly fatal idea. "Hey, Joe," he said as they ascended the steps, "long time no see. Who's that with you? One of your bastard sons?"

"This is Morgan," said Joe as the man laughed, "and I'd be proud to have him as a son."

"You could do worse than Joe as your pap, Morgan," the man said, turning the knob and opening the door for them. "Welcome to Sally's. Check your gun at the bar."

From a dark vestibule they passed into a parlor brightly lighted by lamps on walls of red wallpaper and the glimmer of candles in a sparkling glass chandelier shaped like a bowl and hanging from the middle of the high ceiling. The effect was a soft glow cast on the faces, necks, arms, shoulders, and bosoms of six women clothed enticingly in pink, red, yellow, and blue chemises and arranged decoratively on chairs and couches faced to the doorway and the stout woman who stood next to it.

"Well, look what the wind blew in," she said, stabbing a finger into Joe's chest. "And who's this handsome galoot?" she said, stroking Morgan's arm. "My, my, my, they get younger every year, don't they?"

"This is Morgan," said Joe.

"Hi, cutie. Welcome to Sally's."

"It's a pleasure."

Squeezing his arm, she laughed, "That's the idea, darlin'."

The six women giggled.

"I was tellin' Morgan about sweet Sue," said Joe.

Jabbing an elbow into him, Sally said, "Joe, deep down inside you've got the makin's of a first-class pander!"

"Is Sue, uh, occupied, or what?"

"She's upstairs restin'. I'll send one of the girls up to fetch her but give her a minute to get presentable. It'll be worth the wait."

She was a lot younger and prettier than Morgan expected, with long brown hair that smelled like rosewater, cat-green eyes, high breasts, wide hips, long legs and fingers that felt like pussywillows stroking his damp clean-scrubbed skin.

"You're different," she said when they were finished and he was putting on his buckskins.

Standing with one leg in the pants and one out, he flashed an embarrassed smile. "Different?"

"Gentle," she said softly.

His smile changed to quizzical. "You mean, uh, others, aren't?"

She laughed; bitterly, he thought. "Hardly."

Dancing to get into the leather pants, because he didn't know what else to say, he said, "Sorry."

"You got nothin' to be sorry for."

"I meant, sorry on account of the others."

"Next time you come to Sally's," she said brightly,

"y'all be sure to ask for Sue again, hear?"

"Sweet Sue," he said with a smile as he sat and strained to pull on stiff new boots.

Beautiful she was. The most beautiful woman he'd ever seen, except for his mother.

Riding back to Riley, California Joe broke a long silence by spitting, wiping his mouth with a red handkerchief and turning a worried sidelong glance at Morgan. "I hope you didn't fall for that gal."

Feeling transparent, Morgan blushed. "What gave you that silly idea?"

"Boy, you got that look."

"What look?"

"The look of a fella that's been hornswoggled by a pretty face and an allurin' shape."

"Ah, that's horse manure!"

"I hope so, cause there's nothin' more pitiful than a fella that falls for a whore. Pretty soon a man who falls for a whore starts treatin' her like a lady. In all my experience there's nothin' that'll lead to a man's downfall quicker'n him thinkin' he can turn a whore into a lady."

"What if she was a lady before she became a whore?"

"There's no such creature, believe me."

He saw her on Saturday nights, sometimes having to wait until she was finished with customers, but when she welcomed him it was not in the bleak and businesslike cubicles where she greeted others.

With him she went to her own room. Large and airy and with the feel of permanence, frilled, curtained, cushioned, warm and welcoming, it was an expression of herself and going into it with him she felt as new and innocent as a girl for whom this would be the first time, sitting with him on an embroidered sofa with no sense of where they were and what she was and no urgency other than their desire to be together.

Blissfully he accepted the fantasy they had created, but on his third Saturday visit Sally Magruder met him at the door and announced, "Sue's not seeing anyone tonight."

Flinching as if she had slapped him, he exclaimed, "Why not?"

"Look, I'm not just one of her customers," he pleaded, pushing past her toward the stairway.

Seizing his sleeve, Sally said, "She especially doesn't want to see you."

"Well, she sure as hell is going to," he growled, pushing Sally aside.

Dashing up the steps, he reached her door, found it locked and pounded his fist on it. "Sue, it's me," he shouted. "Let me in."

"Not tonight, Hugh, please," she sobbed through the door. "Tonight I want to be alone."

Stunned, he shrank back. "What's the matter? Did I do something wrong?"

"No, you could never do wrong," she cried.

"Sue, I'm coming in. Either you open the door or I knock it down."

Slowly, tentatively, the door opened and he stepped into a room that was dark except for one lamp.

"Darling, what's going on? How come you're sitting here in the dark?"

A silhouette in the middle of the room, she was crying. "I don't want you to see me."

"Don't want me to see you?"

"Not like . . . this."

Striding to the lamp, he lifted it and carried it to the center of the room, holding it before her face.

"Oh Christ," he gasped as the flickering light danced upon her bruised and swollen features. With a growl rising from deep in his belly, he said, "Who did it?"

From behind him in the doorway, Sally Magruder

113

answered. "It was a man named Walters."

Turning and striding toward the door, Morgan snarled, "Where can I find the bastard?"

"Prob'ly at Farley's saloon just down the street," Sally replied, backing out of his way.

"What's he look like?"

"Big son of bitch," she said as Morgan paused at the top of the stairs. "He looks like a bear. A grizzly. And he's just as dangerous, too."

Farley's was one big room with a long bar to his right, tables to his left and a doorway to a kitchen at the back. The floor was hard dirt covered with sawdust. The roof was low and required customers to duck if they wanted to keep their heads from bumping hanging oil lamps. There were few men at the bar and fewer at the tables and all turned to look at him through an oily blue fog of cigar and lamp smoke as he came in.

"Which one of you is Walters?" he shouted across the silent and wary room.

At a poker table near the rear door, a bear-like man raised his head. "I am."

Advancing slowly, Morgan said, "Walters, you're going to have to answer for beating up a woman."

Laying his cards face-down, pushing back his chair and rising slowly with his right arm drifting toward a weighty Colt Walker too high on his thigh in a holster cut off at the end because it was too short for the nine-inch barrel, Walters squinted through the haze. "Whut woman? An' who the hell are you?"

"My name's Morgan and hers is Miss Susan Cantrell."

Walters blared a laugh. *"Miss* Susan Cantrell? That whore!"

"Whore or not, she didn't deserve what you did to her."

"She got paid her due."

"And now you're going to get paid yours."

Walters reached for the cumbersome Walker in its hindering holster, his arm jerking upward, bending awkwardly, wasting precious time while Morgan drew and formed a triangle with his arms, his Colt firm and steady at the point.

Two shots a split-second off from being simultaneous deafened the room.

First and true, Morgan's bullet slammed Walters in the center of his chest while the shot by Walter snapped past an inch amiss of Morgan's left ear.

A fair fight, all who were there to witness it agreed, although many of them thought the reason for it — the honor of a whore — was a bit far-fetched.

California would be the place to go, he decided, and he'd take Sue with him. Marry her. Settle out there by the Pacific Ocean, a place where he could have a farm like the one he'd grown up on, a decent patch of property where he and Sue could raise a family. "Up near Salinas is the place I'd choose if I were in your boots," said California Joe. "It's mighty fine cattle-raisin' country. The scenery's pretty. Weather's pleasant. No Indians to worry about either."

"Sounds mighty appetizin'," said Morgan, marking Salinas in his mind as the place to head for with Sue, if she'd have him. When to ask her was a problem. The summer was on the wane and the autumn snows were not far off, which was no time to head west, Joe attested, especially with a woman in tow.

But it was not to be.

The bearer of these bad tidings was Joe, returning from Junction City the week after the shooting of Walters with the news that Sue had gone back east. "I guess that trouble with Walters skeered her off," he said sympathetically as he walked with Morgan to the edge of the Riley quadrangle, " 'cause she packed her be-

115

longin's and collected her savin's that Sally was keepin' for her and left."

Morgan gulped for air. "What about me? Did she say anything about me?"

Joe shook his head. "If she did, Sally didn't mention it, and it wouldn't be Sally's way not to tell me if the girl had said somethin' about you."

Squaring his shoulders, Morgan said bravely, "Then I guess I'll just have to go after her."

"Shoot, boy, come to your senses," grumbled Joe. "You don't even know where she's gone to."

"You said she went east."

"The east is a mighty big place! You could spend your life lookin'. And life's too short to go chasin' after somethin' that was nothin' but a concoction in your head anyways. Face it, boy. Whatever there was between you and that girl was mostly in your head."

"She loved me. I know it."

Not since then had he let himself come under a woman's spell for more than a night of paid-for pleasure from a woman whose name he didn't care to ask in a whorehouse or in a convenient room over a saloon with nothing in it but a bed.

A wariness born of the bitter experience of Sue had stood guard on his heart as his six-gun protected his life.

Marry?

His answer to that question was an old Welsh poem he'd recited once to embarrass Rebecca Colter.

I thought if only I could marry,
I'd sing and dance and live so gaily;
But all the wedded bliss I see
Is rock the cradle, hush the baby.

But that was then and this was now, he said to himself as he addressed his daily chores, visited Goliad on Saturdays for the harmless pleasures of the El Dorado cantina where pretty Sarah Coffee was a tease to him but nothing more and made his bunk in cold and drafty ramshackle cabins when he rode the cattle ranges of the Nueces Strips with Dalgo while December of 1871 waned, snowless.

Chapter Thirteen

"Morgan!" called Rebecca from the back of her favorite dun horse as she turned the corner of the house and cantered toward the stable, fresh-faced and windblown from her customary Saturday visit to Goliad for provisions and the weekly mail. Waving an envelope frantically above her head as if it were a small white flag of surrender, she exclaimed, "There's a letter for you!"

Stepping from the tack room into the brilliant sun that made a halo around her, he raised a hand to shield his eyes and saw her in silhouette. "Who from?"

"The envelope doesn't say who from; only where from."

Striding to her with his hand out, he grunted, "Where then?"

Leaning down from the horse, she scraped the envelope under his bristle-bearded chin. "You need a shave!"

"I don't need a shave for fixing bridles," he said curtly, reaching for the envelope.

"It's from your old stomping ground," she said, whisking it away, teasingly. "Abilene!"

"From Hank Kidder, most likely," he said, grasping the letter.

Letting go of it, she said, "An old flame, probably."

"We're both wrong," he said, tearing open the envelope and unfolding its contents. "It's from Mr. Joseph McCoy."

"Oh, darn," she said, tossing her hair and sliding down from the saddle. "I was hoping so much that it was from one of your old girl friends!"

"Well, it isn't, is it?"

"How would I know? All I have is your word that it isn't," she said, leading the horse and disappearing into the dark of the barn.

Settling in the shade of an oak, he carefully opened the envelope and unfolded its contents.

The Drover's Cottage
Abilene, Kansas

January 1, 1872

My Dear Morgan,
I take up my pen to write you at the outset of a New Year because you have been much in my thoughts since last I saw you in Newton at the time of your very successful sale of your herd. In a few months you undoubtedly will be organizing another such enterprise, so I believe now is an appropriate time to inform you on recent developments concerning which you will surely demonstrate some interest as these events involve your friends, among whom I believe I am counted.

"Hell, yes, you're a friend," he mumbled, slouching comfortably with his back to the oak. "How could you ever doubt it?" he thought, "after all we've been through together?"

Distracted by the whinny of Rebecca's horse from the barn, he looked up from the letter and shouted,

"You need any help in there?"

"No," came her reply, like a shot.

"I was only askin'," he muttered, returning to the letter, which was a surprisingly long one — six pages, at least — lying in his lap.

First, I must say that I regret that we did not have more time to spend together on your visit to Newton and to renew our very special friendship. I will always remember you fondly and with a great deal of gratitude as the young man who was of such great help to me in organizing the cattle trade at Abilene, although you harbored grave doubts about the likelihood of that undertaking having any success.

She appeared suddenly from the shadowed barn, a vibrant figure in a loose white blouse, red neckerchief, a riding skirt as dark as the hide of a longhorn cow and rattlesnake-skin boots, striding purposefully toward the house as if she had no curiosity whatever concerning the letter he was reading, pausing only long enough before entering the house to declare, "Supper will be late today, served at seven, as I will be preparing it myself."

"Mouth-scorching Mexican grub, no doubt," he said to himself, lifting the letter directly over his eyes as he slid down to his back under the shady oak.

I must report regretfully to you that the year 1871 was the last one in which cattle business is likely to be done at Abilene. The trade has been driven away by the schemes and concerted actions of several individuals who took it upon themselves to take over the affairs of the town. Their purposes were not in keeping with the livestock business.

Rather, they desired to cater to the farmers who had suffered small grievances from the presence of the cattle trade and thus secure political strength. This resulted in the shifting of herds from Abilene to other locations along the railroad. I am sad to note that one of those who was instrumental in this sorry affair was Mr. Henry Kidder, whose newspaper became the leading voice of the doomsayers.

"Hank Kidder always was a reformer at heart," said Morgan, lowering McCoy's letter to is chest. From the first day he'd known him, he thought — way back in Gettysburg — Kidder had strong views on what was right.

"Yep, a righteous man," he said, picking up McCoy's letter again.

Even at the time of your arrival in Newton last spring the suicidal effect of the steps taken by Kidder and the others was painfully visible in Abilene. Four-fifths of her business houses became vacant, rents fell to a trifle, many of the leading hotels and businesses were either closed or taken down and moved to other points. Property became unsaleable. The luxuriant sunflower sprang up thick and flourished in the main streets, while the inhabitants, such as could not get away, passed their time sadly contemplating their ruin. The whole village assumed a desolate, forsaken and deserted appearance.

"Jeepers," exclaimed Morgan, bolting upright with the letter clenched in his fist. Then, opening the sheets again, he asked, "What about Charlie Carew?"

121

Unhappily, one of the victims of this onslaught is your friend and former business associate, Mr. Carew, who has abandoned his establishment and transferred as much of its equipment as possible, and himself along with it, to the new boom town of Wichita where the Atchison, Topeka and Santa Fe Railroad is being extended and which will be in full service come this spring, with the first cattle expected in its pastures, pens and loading chutes by June 1872 at the latest. Doubtless, it is to Wichita that you will wish to drive Colter Ranch cattle in the coming season, as there is nothing to recommend in Abilene nor, I expect, will there be in Newton. As I did at Newton, I will be making my services available to traders in Wichita by way of advice and consultation and, should you come to Wichita, will be very glad to see you again.

Should we chance to meet in Wichita, I will want to discuss some ideas I have regarding the future of the cattle business in Texas and on the topic of improving the breed by introducing into Texas the short-horned Durham cattle raised and fed so extensively and profitably throughout the Northwest and West. This breed is in almost every respect more valuable and profitable stock to breed and handle than any other throughout the entire West. It is my view that Texas must improve its cattle in blood and quality if Texas is to continue to compete successfully and profitably in the beef markets of the nation. The Durham is the means by which this may be achieved, I believe, and I hope that I may persuade you to my view when next we meet. With Durham stock improving its herds, Colter Ranch cattle will lead the way, I am certain. Therefore, I trust I will be seeing you in Wichita later in the year.

"Wichita," said Morgan wonderingly as he put aside the letter once more and searched his memory for anything about the town. Up on the Arkansas River it stood, he recalled. "A pimple on the prairie," California Joe Milner had called it once. "Wichita is a no-account collection of grass-roofed hovels shaped like beehives," he declared, "that will never amount to nothin'."

"Apparently you're going to be proved wrong about that, Joe," he laughed, imagining already the splendors of Long Charlie Carew's new saloon with its Irish-green batwing doors swinging open to admit the cowboys that had made Long Charlie's place a landmark in Abilene. How long would Wichita last as the Queen of the Cowtowns, until Wichita, like Abilene and Newton, would have to hire a marshal to make the town safe for the "decent" folks, he wondered as he picked up McCoy's letter again. As if he had anticipated the question, McCoy had written,

In the event that you may have wondered if Marshal Carson was successful in tracking down that madman Riley, I regret to inform you that the murderous fugitive eluded his pursuers and has never been seen nor heard from again. When I hark back to that gruesome event I cannot help but wonder why the cattle business of Kansas has been sullied by lawlessness and if it is futile to hope that the kinder, gentler nature of man will one day prevail or if mankind is a cursed creature with no chance of rising above his base nature. However, when I harbor these dark ideas, I turn my thoughts to you, my dear friend, and how you have overcome that darkness within you that led you astray in those years you spent in Abilene. I

123

rejoice for you, young man! May your future be filled with success.

Until I see you in Wichita, I am,

Very truly yours,

Joseph Geiting McCoy

With the letter carefully returned to its envelope and placed in a drawer of his desk in the tack room, Morgan scrubbed himself clean and shaved close, arriving at the house precisely at seven o'clock but smelling the aroma of the tongue-scorching Mexican meal that awaited him long before he gave a sharp rap on the rear door, walked in unbidden and shouted, "Anybody home?"

Appearing from the dining room in her riding clothes, Rebecca gazed at him in a way that was at the same time stern and teasing. "You've finished reading the letter from your old flame?"

Exasperated, he said, "The 'old flame' thinks you should breed your longhorns with Durham beef. What's your opinion?"

After pausing and thinking but showing no sign as to whether she knew what Durham beef was, she asked, "Will it make money for the ranch?"

"The 'old flame,' Mr. McCoy, thinks so."

"Then by all means, we must look into it."

"I will, when I see Mr. McCoy in Wichita."

"Wichita? Are you driving the herd to Wichita this season?"

"It seems to be the best place, according to Mr. McCoy."

"Well, he was certainly right about Abilene, wasn't he?"

"Indeed so."

"Wichita it is then," she said, turning away, adding as she vanished into the dining room, "It's a Mexican

124

menu this evening. I'm sure that will be all right with you. After all, you must fancy Mexican . . . since you spend so much of your time with *that* girl in that cantina in Goliad!"

Annoyed by her tone, he snapped, "What do you mean by *that* girl?"

"You know exactly what I mean," she said, smirking as she reappeared in the doorway.

"No, I'm afraid I *don't*. S'pose you explain it to me."

"As your employer, I don't have to explain anything to you."

"You heard somethin' in town! That's it. What did you hear?"

"Nothing."

"You heard some gossip about me! Somethin' about me and Sarah Coffee, right?"

With a scornful laugh, she spun back into the kitchen. "Really! The whole town knows that you're stuck on Sarah Coffee. So why would that be of interest to me?"

Nettled, he followed her. "That's horseradish and you know it. Bald-faced lies. Nothin' but idle gossip."

"If it's gossip," she said, turning on him, "then how come you're so riled up about it?"

"Lies get me riled."

"The gentleman doth protest too much, me think," she said, grinning. "Which is from Shakespeare, whom you like to quote so much."

"If you're going to quote the Bard do it right. It's, 'The *lady* doth protest too much.' "

"Well, according to what I was told, Sarah Coffee sure isn't protesting. And she is no lady!"

Through a laugh, he taunted, "She's as much a lady as you are."

Like the heads of a pair of tormented snakes preparing to strike, her hands coiled into fists and rose before her. "You dare speak of me in the same breath as that, that . . . no-account half-breed?"

Serpentlike, he hissed, "Sister!"

"You bastard," she sighed, recoiling.

"Half-sister," he said tormentingly as he advanced toward her.

"Shut your filthy mouth."

"Sure, Sarah's a half-breed, but she's your half-sister."

"That's a lie," she growled, thumping her fists upon him.

Seizing the flailing hands, he pressed them against his chest and let out a laugh that felt like thunder in her helplessness. "She's your half-breed, half-sister! That's what they say in Goliad. That's what they say in the cantinas. That Sarah Coffee is Buck Colter's other daughter."

"Lies and slander," she cried, struggling against his tightening grasp.

" 'Look at Sarah's eyes,' they say. Look at her nose. The chin. The neck. Her shape. 'Just like Rebecca's,' they say. The spittin' image of Rebecca, they say."

"You are contemptible."

"Hey, I didn't say it. They said it. The people of Goliad said it."

"And you believed them!"

Remorseless in his grip upon her, he chuckled. "And you believed what they said about me!"

Wriggling against him, she demanded, "Let me go this minute!"

"As to the eyes," he said, grinning and pressing his face closer, "hers are brown. Yours are green. Prettiest shade of green I ever saw. Oh, your eyes are much more beautiful than Sarah's. As every part of you is more beautiful."

"I warn you, Morgan," she said, wrestling him. "Let

126

me loose or I'll . . ."

Abruptly, he kissed her, muttering, "You'll what?"

"Fire you," she murmured, breathing the words into him.

"That's a relief," he chuckled as he let her go. "I was thinking you had a mind to shoot me."

"Perhaps I will," she asserted, spinning away.

"That'd be a big disappointment," he laughed.

"Is that so?"

"Yep. You see, I've been shot at a lot but I never have been fired," he said, overwhelming her resistance and drawing her back to him.

As she fought him, a memory of scorpions filled her head.

As a child she'd looked on with deadly fascination at a pair of them struggling in the dry dirt of a sun-baked draw down by the Nueces and found it curious that scorpions would be fighting one another. Then her father explained that one was male and the other female and that what looked like a fight was their mating. "Although he'd better be careful," he went on with a big laugh, "because when they're done she is apt to sting and turn him into her wedding dinner."

Buck Colter had never been reticent with her concerning sex, figuring that to avoid the subject as it related to humans would be a ridiculous exercise, when she was smart enough to deduce from all the reproducing going on among the animals she witnessed everywhere, that it would have a counterpart in people. But accustomed as she was to the idea of her partaking of it eventually, she had not anticipated that she might be like the female scorpion.

In a blinding revelation like lightning instantly illuminating a stormy night sky on the range, she recognized that an enormous power as old as Creation had resided dormant in her and was being released and reflected in Morgan's wondering, beseeching, longing, and hungering eyes.

While he was making love to her in the belief that she had succumbed to him, she realized that, like the male scorpion, he was the one who had surrendered and was in danger. No longer feeling as if she were in a struggle for her life, she ached with a hunger to possess the savage and thrusting flesh curving above her. Clutching and clawing at him and raking his back with her fingernails, she experienced at the same time a perverse pleasure in seeing him wince with pain, and an overwhelming need to engulf him with her desire that for too long had been pent up.

She wanted him and had always wanted him, she realized, and now she had him!

Part Three
If Only I Would Marry

Chapter Fourteen

"Go ahead and yell, Rebecca darling," said Migdalia Coffee consolingly as she dabbed away the sweat with a cool damp cloth.

She'd been talking this way for hours, as if the lilt of her half-Spanish, half-English could magically draw the child from the womb painlessly and then shaking a verbal fist heavenward and at God for imposing the curse of Eve on womankind when the baby didn't come right away.

Railing against the suffocating July heat and the impudence of the mosquitoes and flies buzzing against the netting surrounding the large sweat-soaked bed and cursing men in general and Morgan in particular, she said, "It's just like a man to be a thousand miles away when his first child is struggling to be born," and remembered the birth of her own Sarah in the absence of the one who'd sired her.

"Dalia," gasped Rebecca, "I just know I'm going to die."

"No, you ain't, honey," Migdalia said emphatically. "I know it feels that way, but you're doin' fine. It hurts now but once you have the baby in your arms you'll forget all the pain and you'll be sheddin' tears of pure joy."

Clutching Migdalia's big, calloused but comfortable hand, Rebecca sobbed, "Things won't be the same, will they? Everything will be changed."

"For the better," said Migdalia brightly.

"Can't see how," said Rebecca, gulping for air.

"Never mind that now, darling. Tomorrow and the next day will take care of itself. You just think about today and birthin' your baby, girl."

What came to mind was her wedding.

It had been nothing like the one she'd dreamed about for so long; no frilled and flowing white gown, no ceremony in a flower-bedecked church, no glittery reception in a San Antonio hotel and no being escorted down the aisle and waltzed around the ballroom by her proud and beaming father. Instead, she had been presented to Morgan by Shanghai Pierce in the parlor of her house on a gray and wind-swept Saturday morning in February before a small gathering of her dearest friends from Goliad, a handful of her father's pals come from the ranches of the Nueces strip and a delegation of four duded and slicked Colter ranch hands headed by Dalgo, who wept when she'd uttered her vow to love, honor, and cherish Morgan.

There'd been a slight ripple among the people at the deletion of the traditional wife's vow to obey, although it was less over the omission than it was a whisper of recognition that an independent woman who openly espoused the ideas of Susan B. Anthony would never pledge obedience to anyone or anything save her own conscience, especially if she also happened to own one of the biggest cattle ranches in Texas.

As to Morgan's feelings on the matter?

"You say any blamed thing you want," he'd said, "as long as you say 'I do' at the proper time."

At the time of the wedding she'd been pregnant one month.

Forcing a laugh through the pain of birth, she said to Migdalia, "I suppose the gossips of Goliad are busy doing their arithmetic."

"The hell with them, child."

Trembling, she closed her eyes, squeezed Migdalia's hand and moaned, "Nobody told me it would hurt so much."

"There's no pleasure without pain, child."

"God's curse on woman!"

"A child's no curse. A child comes by way of pain but in the glory of that child the pain is soon forgotten. You may be thinkin' all sorts of mean things about your man right now, about how he's the one that brought on all this hurtin' and then left you by yourself, but when your baby's been born and is in your arms—his baby, too—you'll forgive him and love him even more."

"It's not his fault he's not here. He wanted to be!"

No lie.

"We sure won't take any prizes for timing," Morgan had said with a bitter laugh when it became clear that the baby would be born during the summer and that he, no doubt, would be herding longhorns to Wichita.

For a time he'd argued that he could skip the drive, leaving it to Dalgo to be the trail boss. She would have none of it, declaring, "You'd only get in the way. And you'd be moping around this place with your face clear to the floor and wondering what you were missing by not being with the herd and carousing for a night or two with the cowboys once you hit

133

town."

"Somebody's got to be here with you," he insisted.

"I'll ask Migdalia Coffee to come. She's helped more babies into the world than any doctor I know. So you just go about your business of being trail boss and rep. Having you on the premises when the baby's being born would prove as useless as tits on a man."

So, he'd given in to her and, as was her custom, she'd sat astride her dun horse on a bluff waving goodbye at him on a chilly April dawn as he departed at the point of a herd of seven thousand cattle bound for Wichita.

The next week, leaving her cantina to be run by her daughter Sarah, Migdalia had moved to the ranch and into the house.

That had been in May.

Now it was early July.

The pains were more frequent.

"What day is it, Dalia?"

"Tuesday."

She thought a moment, abiding the contracting pain, then smiled. "That's good. Tuesday's child is full of grace."

Fetching a fresh cloth to wipe Rebecca's forehead, Migdalia asked, "Have you picked out a name yet, for if it's a girl or a boy?"

"We compromised. A girl? Naomi! Which was my mother's name. And Catherine, which was Morgan's mother's name. Naomi Catherine Morgan! We'll call her Catherine."

Laying a cooling palm on Rebecca's feverish brow, Migdalia said, "And what if it's a boy?"

"Morgan wanted to name him Owen, for his father, but I wanted to call him for my daddy."

Migdalia rolled her eyes. "Arbuckle?"

"He'll have three names," she said triumphantly. "They'll be Arbuckle, Colter, and Owen, in that order. *Arbuckle Colter Owen Morgan.* But we'll call him Colter."

Showing sparkling eyes and an impish grin, Migdalia said, "Suppose you get twins?"

Half in tears from the pain and half in laughter, Rebecca gasped, "Hush your mischievous mouth!"

"Either way, boy or girl, this is goin' to be a lucky child. If it's a girl, she'll have your beauty. And if it's a boy he'll have his daddy's good looks."

"Yes, Morgan is handsome, isn't he? So damned handsome," she said dreamily.

Closing her eyes as he formed in her mind, she found him a powerful presence swamping and drowning all pain and lulling her into a shallow slumber in which imagining him turned into dreaming him. In this twilight slumber he turned into tumbling bits in the twirling kaleidoscope of her memories of him.

Part boy, part man, part demi-god, he was again staring at her across a candlelit table while talking with her father about a crazy idea of driving Texas cattle to market in Kansas; pursuing her like a demon on horseback to the lip of a bluff with a fire-streaked sky fringed by the indigo of impending night; surprising her two years later by suddenly appearing at the ranch, bare to the waist as he tended the horse he ridiculously named Strawberry; doing his work and coming and going as if she did not exist and always being so damned respectful and saying, "Yes, ma'am," or "Yes, Miss Colter," as if she were years older than he and she were blind to him except as a hired hand.

With these images of him she again heard him

speaking beautiful words at her father's funeral and Novillero's and the music of his voice floating from the tack room late at night when he and Novillero and Dalgo were working or playing cards or his laughter ringing through her open window. Then, as vivid as life, he was holding her, kissing her, and making love to her until tenderness became violence and she was certain she would die from the exquisite agony.

"Oh, oh, ahhhh," she screamed.

Waking with a jolt, she felt the baby coming.

"Just yell your head off if you want to," said Migdalia softly. "Go ahead and let it out. Yell so loud Morgan will hear you all the way up in Kansas."

Chapter Fifteen

EVERYTHING GOES
IN WICHITA
BE SURE TO VISIT
LONG CHARLIE'S SALOON

The sign was ten feet wide and six high with bright red letters against canary yellow.

Gaping in amazement, Dalgo said, "First I ever seen anythin' like it."

"That," laughed Morgan, "is what they call advertising."

The only object rising above the foot-high grass of the featureless plain between them and the northern horizon, it had been canted slightly rearward by wind.

Tilting back his sombrero and wiping the sweat from his brow, Dalgo said, "What do you figure it means?"

With a shake of his head, Morgan said, "Just what it says. They got everything in Wichita and in Wichita everything goes. Same as any cow town. Let's just hope that they've also got a bunch of buyers willing to pay good prices."

"They'll pay," said Dalgo, cocking his head to their rear, " 'cause this is the best herd I've seen in a long time."

"Yeah, they're mighty fine," said Morgan. "They've covered the drive very well—as fat and sassy as I've ever seen—but there's a lot of them and it's quantity that determines price, not quality."

Proceeding beyond the sign, he dimly remembered passing by the tiny settlement called Wichita in the autumn of 1868 on his way to Fort Harker to join Custer's cavalry for the campaign to chastise Indians that had ended in the massacre of Black Kettle's village. What he recalled was that Wichita had been long a dwelling spot for the Indians it was named for, a tribe that built grass houses shaped like beehives at the junction of the Arkansas and the Little Arkansas. By the time he'd skirted the place on the way to meet George Armstrong Custer and the grim reaper called Death in the valley of the Washita, a pair of traders by the name of James Mead and Jesse Chisholm, the half-breed who gave his name to the cattle trail, had established a post. Around it whites began to settle, although sparsely, until the Wichitas were forced out of Kansas and into the Indian Territory. Now, in the summer of '72, the Atchison, Topeka and Santa Fe Railroad had a branch line established even farther south of Abilene than Newton and cutting the Chisholm Trail yet another 20 miles.

The next afternoon, leaving Dalgo in charge of the herd on a sprawling grazing camp south of the Arkansas, he rode into Wichita to seek buyers. At a bridge over the river he encountered a sign declaring that the law required all persons entering the town to check their firearms, but because he found no one on hand to take his, he fell in behind a jostling stage coach of the Southern Kansas Company and proceeded into the town. Along a wide, thronged and evidently thriving business thoroughfare he counted two hardware stores, a druggist's, a pair of bootmakers, the New York Clothing Emporium, a saddlery and harness store, four real estate offices, a jewelry shop and two banks.

Assuming that at the railway stockyard he would either find Joe McCoy or someone who knew where he might be, he asked directions to the depot from a barefoot boy in bib overalls and a straw hat who reminded him of himself in the distant and hazy life he'd led in Pennsylvania before the Civil War came roaring at him straight down the Chambersburg Road. "Go to the end of the street," said the boy with his wide brown eyes staring in awe at Morgan's Colt pistol, "and turn right."

Perched on the top of a rail fence affording a view of bewildered cattle being prodded up a loading chute and into a gently rocking slat-sided box car, the sixth in a string of three already filled and four waiting to be, Joe McCoy was attired for business, as usual, in a black suit, white shirt, black necktie and derby hat that always made Morgan think of him as a preacher. Appearing unchanged in the year since they'd run into one another at the railroad siding in Newton and the same as he'd looked five years earlier when Morgan had mistaken him for the proprietor of Bratton's Hotel in Abilene, McCoy shifted his eyes only momentarily from the chute and said, "Welcome to Wichita," as Morgan rode up.

Stepping from his horse directly to the fence, Morgan said, "The place seems to be thriving."

"Boom now, bust tomorrow. That's the cattle business," said McCoy as Morgan settled beside him.

"I'm glad to see you."

"How's prices?"

"It's a seller's market at the moment. Your timing's right."

"Glad to hear it. I got eight thousand head."

"I've got you a buyer representing a Chicago syndicate if you can come by the Harris House Hotel tomorrow afternoon. Know where it is?"

"Shouldn't be hard to find, I reckon."

"I'll show you," said McCoy, slapping Morgan's back. "Let me treat you to supper. Are you hungry?"

"You know me, Joe," smiled Morgan as they descended from the fence. "I've never been one to pass up free eats. Is there a barn where I can stable and feed my horse?"

Enjoying a vivid memory of their first meeting in Abilene when Morgan had bargained with the owner of the Bratton Hotel over the cost of oats, McCoy responded with an arm thrown across Morgan's shoulders. "The horse still comes first, eh?"

"Without a good horse a man's nowhere."

"Yours has an unusual name, I recall."

"You're thinking of Strawberry," said Morgan.

"Yes! Strawberry!"

"Strawberry's not exactly suited as a cow horse and is sort of retired these days. This one's called Grulla," Morgan said, stroking the horse's gray nose as they stepped across the railroad tracks.

"You can feed the horse at Arnold's Stable. It's near the hotel."

Like the Drover's Cottage in Abilene's heyday, the Harris House's ornate lobby rang with the boisterous hail-fellow-well-met voices of eastern-suited cattlemen who were looking to buy and the dusty-throated shyness of reps in red neckerchiefs, cotton shirts and

140

denim pants while the dining room murmured with the quiet satisfaction of ironclad deals closed with steel-gripped handshakes and now being sealed and celebrated with beefsteak, coffee, brandy and cigars.

Through their own steaks and in the respite while they waited for their coffee and brandy to be brought, Morgan grew aware of McCoy's keen dark eyes measuring him. Troubled, he asked, "Is something wrong, Joe?"

Startled, McCoy said, "What makes you think something's wrong?"

"You just look as if you've got something on your mind, is all."

"Ah, was I staring?"

"Well, a little."

"I am sorry! I was just drinking in how you seem to be prospering in your new life and how glad I am that things are working out so well for you. They are, aren't they?"

"Can't complain," said Morgan, sliding his chair away from the table and flicking open the buttons of a supple leather vest strained because of too much dinner.

"I'm glad," said McCoy, drawing a pair of cheroots from a hard leather case and passing one to Morgan. "You deserve it."

Morgan took his time lighting the cigar and savoring the tang of the first draw, then said, "I was grateful for your recent letter but sorry to read about your troubles with Hank Kidder. It was a harsh disappointment to learn that two of my best friends were at odds with one another."

"A disappointment to me, as well," said McCoy on a plume of savory smoke.

"Does your being here mean you've given up on

Abilene?"

"The cattle business has given up on it," McCoy said with a shrug. "The cattle are coming here to Wichita. I'm in the cattle business. So I'm in Wichita."

"Simple as that," said Morgan, tapping a long gray cylinder of cigar ash into a silver tray. "Strictly business!"

"By the way," smiled McCoy, "I have regards for you from Shanghai Pierce."

"That old razorback? When did you see him?"

"April. He was here in Wichita with a few cattlemen who were scouting the area looking for a suitable shipping point. Naturally, Wichita's town fathers were eager to fill the bill. We had a meeting after which Old Shang and the others agreed that Wichita was ahead of other candidates in the competition because of the size and variety of the town's banks, hotels and social accommodations."

"Everything goes in Wichita!"

"Ah, you've seen your old friend Carew's sign!"

"Charlie always was a promoter," Morgan laughed.

"He's right at home here, believe me. I've never seen a community so set on making something of itself as Wichita. This makes Abilene pale by comparison!"

"That may be, but they were good times in Abilene, weren't they?"

With a labored sigh McCoy said, "For awhile."

Twirling his cigar slowly between the thumb and forefinger of his gun hand, Morgan studied his friend's troubled expression and discerned the pointlessness of continuing on the subject. "In your letter," he said cheerfully changing the subject, "you mentioned the outstanding qualities of Durhams and the

142

potential benefits in breeding them with Texas stock."

"Indeed so," said McCoy excitedly. "Believe me, my friend, there is nothing which holds out the hope and sure promise of so great reward for the investment to Texan ranchmen as the crossing of their cows with grade Durham bulls. Texans must improve their cattle and blood and quality," he declared with an urgency in his voice that carried Morgan back to the evening at the Bratton Hotel when he'd described his vision of Abilene as the shipping point for all the cattle of Texas. While it was well established that Texas cattle could be fattened upon corn, he went on, it was not done as successfully as with the shorthorned Durham. Why not enhance the corn fattening of longhorns by breeding them with Durham? If done, there would be an astonishing improvement in color, form and weight! "If the cattlemen of Texas would import one carload of yearling bulls of Durham blood for each one thousand head of cattle they export annually, they'd soon see a marked difference in the quality of their stock. And the prices they'd get at the railhead."

"All that may be true," answered Morgan, "but how would this cross-breed handle a three-month, thousand-mile walk up the ol' Chisholm?"

With a wave of a hand trailing cigar smoke, McCoy declared, "But the breed won't be trail-driven, you see! They'll be shipped by railroad!" Putting the cigar back in his mouth and talking around it, he said, "It's only a matter of time until the railroads come to the cattlemen instead of vice versa! The day is fast approaching, Morgan, when you'll be loading Colter stock directly onto railway cars right there on the Colter ranch!"

"That's what she said."

"Who?"

"Rebecca Colter. She once said the same thing to me. About the day when there'd be a railway spur right there on the ranch."

"That's a mighty smart woman. If I were you, I'd marry her."

Grinning, Morgan exclaimed, "I did."

"Well done, boy! When was this happy occurrence?"

"Last year."

"I wish I'd known! I should have liked to attend the ceremony."

"Well, it was no big deal. We just sort of upped and got hitched."

"Congratulations," said McCoy, thrusting his hand across the table.

Beaming as he shook it, Morgan muttered, "Fact is, we're expecting our first baby any day now."

"Well what a great thing that is! Your first child," bellowed McCoy, startling others and provoking them to look up sharply from their meals and causing Morgan to turn bright red from neck to forehead.

Chapter Sixteen

"You'll find Mr. Carew's nefarious business establishment in Wichita's red-light district, known as Delano," said Joe McCoy, the expression on his face matching the disgust that honed his words as he and Morgan paused on the porch of the Harris House with dusk descending. "This latest incarnation of Abilene's Devil's Half Acre and Newton's Hide Park is located west of the river," he continued scornfully. "It's all there. Just like Abilene a couple of years back and Newton last year, Delano resembles hell after sundown. Brass bands whooping it up. Harlots and hack drivers yelling and cursing. Dogs yelping. Pistols going off. Bullwhackers cracking their whips. Gambling dens, dance halls, faro and monte parlors, whorehouses. They're all here in earnest."

With a mischievous smile, Morgan teased, "Sounds enticing!"

"And Mr. Carew's emporium is smack in the heart of it, as you might expect," said McCoy. "You can't miss it, though I wish you would."

Putting on his hat, Morgan said, "Well I can't leave town without droppin' in on Charlie just for old times' sake. Haven't laid eyes on that long drink of water since I left Abilene. It's nigh onto three years now. Which I find hard to believe." Descending a step, he said, "Where does the time fly, Mr. Mc-Coy? Seems like Abilene was only yesterday."

"This is the frontier, Morgan! Here, it's all tomorrow," said McCoy, peering into the distance. "In these parts yesterday doesn't count."

Leaving him and walking to the stable to fetch his horse, Morgan calculated that it had been almost six years since McCoy had enthusiastically escorted him on a tour of land where McCoy was dreaming of building his livestock business. There, in the emptiness of prairie surrounding a spot nobody'd ever heard of except as a rest stop where westward bound hardy souls could wet their whistles under the sod-roof of the dugout cabin where an old man named Josiah Jones purveyed whiskey in Abilene's first saloon.

On that night, as Morgan had said goodnight to McCoy, four horses were tethered in front of Jones's place.

Three of these customers were playing cards at a round table in a corner at the back while the fourth was at the bar.

Leaning on his elbows and clasping a glass of whiskey in huge hands as if he expected someone to try to steal it, he had on a fringed buckskin shirt, denim pants tucked into high rawhide boots, a wide cartridge-studded gunbelt supporting nearly five pounds of brass and twisted iron that was a Confederate Army Griswold & Garrison copy of the Colt

and a broad-brimmed and high-crowned white hat
that served to exaggerate his exceptional height—
seven feet of him at least, Morgan guessed. Bent
down guarding his glass and jawing with old man
Jones, he paused only long enough to turn wary eyes
toward the door as Morgan came in.

"Howdy," Morgan said to him, unanswered.

Without being asked, Jones half-filled a tall glass
with whiskey and plunked it on the bar before Morgan and said, "Evenin'."

With a nod at the card players, Morgan said,
"Poker's my game. Do you think they'd mind if I
asked to join in?"

"You'll have to ask them, son."

Picking up his glass and ambling to the table at
the rear of the room he heard the ghostly voice of
his mother admonishing him that cards were the
Devil's play-things, but, he reasoned as he approached the players, Catherine Thomas Morgan
had never been in the cavalry nor had to find ways
to hurry-along the long dark nights of winter in
Kansas or faced the prospect of this being possibly
the last night before a long and companionless ride
as far as California, so that socializing even with this
scruffy trio was welcome. "Is this a private game," he
asked, "or can anybody be dealt in?"

"All it takes is money," said the scruffiest of the
three.

Pulling up a chair, Morgan waited until the end
of the hand they were playing, estimating as he observed them that they were not very good at it, in
addition to being barely sociable as they judged the
cards they were dealt with blank eyes that rarely
lifted from the table, as silent and mirthless as owls

147

except to open, pass, raise, or call.

Easy pickings, they were. Easy money. Never had he had such a run of luck! The first one cleaned out in an hour. The second folding fifteen minutes later. The last slapping down two pair in face of his full house an hour after that. Double the cash he'd sat down with, he figured as he pocketed the pot. He'd won enough foldin' money to get him to California and stake himself for months, he estimated as he stepped out into the chilly, moonless night and turned toward the Bratton Hotel whistling "Garry Owen" and glorying in the bulge of money against his skin under his shirt.

Moments later a blow struck behind his right ear and put him out.

When he came to he found himself staring into the face of the long drink of water from the bar.

"The good part is you're alive," said the tall man, "but the bad part is," he went on as he wiggled Morgan's sealskin purse, "they cleaned you out."

Groaning and shoving himself up by the elbows, Morgan said, "Who?"

"The fellas from the poker game, obviously," said the tall man as he bent to help him up. "It's an old trick, lettin' a sucker—sorry! Lettin' a man into a game and judgin' what kind of roll he's carryin' and if it's big enough lettin' him win and then rollin' him afterwards. It's better'n cheatin' and a whole lot safer."

Struggling to steady himself, Morgan mumbled, "Where are the bastards?"

"Long gone."

"Well, I'm damned good at trackin'," Morgan muttered as he shook his head as if the shaking could

148

cast off the ache, "so I reckon I'll hunt them down."

"Yeah, I s'pose you could. But if you go after them, you'll probably jest wind up dead. And you got no real proof they did it. So why not quit while you're ahead? For now all you've lost is a little money."

"A little? Everything! My whole bankroll. Plus my winnings. That money was goin' to take me to California."

"If it's any consolation, boy, I've been to California and in my opinion there ain't nothin' there. Of course, if your mind's set on it, you can always earn new money. But that's to worry about later. For now, how are you feelin'?"

"Don't know what's worse. The headache or the humiliation." Rubbing the bump behind his aching ear, he forced a smile. "Hell, I haven't even expressed my gratitude to you for pickin' me up. My name's Morgan. Who do I have to thank?"

"Charlie Carew's the monicker."

A year later they were still in Abilene, a town that was no longer just a rest stop on the way west but the realization of Joseph McCoy's vision, the terminus of the railroad, the northern end of the Chisholm Trail and known far and wide as the Queen of the Cowtowns—the first of the breed.

After three months on the trail, cowboys proved eager to squander the hard-earned cash in their pockets. "Look at 'em," crowed Charlie as he stood beside Morgan on the porch of Joe McCoy's splendid new hotel, Drover's Cottage, watching carousing cowboys roaring past on their way to the brand new saloons of a brand new street called Texas. "If only I'd a knowed this," Carew said, thumping the floorboards with a big foot, "I'd a been prepared."

"Prepared for what?"

"Shoot, I'd a opened myself a saloon. Put in a few card tables and maybe rounded up a few gals from Junction City to provide a little companionship for all those lonely, horny cowhands. If I'd a been smarter I'd've been ready for this!"

"There's always next year, Charlie!"

"Next year, hell," he exclaimed. "There's no time like the present. I'm gonna open that saloon right now!"

Erected on a prize plot at the head of Texas Street, Long Charlie's had been a well-lighted room on the ground floor entered through emerald-green batwing doors. Occupying the entire space to the right was a mahogany bar with a brass rail. Behind it on a shelf stood a forest of whiskey bottles made to look even more numerous by mirrors interrupted at intervals of five feet by gilt-framed paintings of voluptuous naked women especially chosen during a week he'd spent in St. Louis purchasing the furnishings. To the left, for those who wanted to sit down to drink, were tables and chairs. At the back, larger tables were arranged for the customers who might fancy poker, faro or monte, although a roulette table ordered from the St. Louis supplier had not yet arrived, its space being occupied temporarily by a billiard table.

For those with a yen for women he had enlisted seven from Kansas City brothels on terms that allowed them to keep all their earnings, the saloon's profit flowing from a small fee payable at the bar in advance of going upstairs to three bedrooms on a nightly-rental basis or to a half-dozen curtained cubicles that could be engaged by the half-hour containing a bed, a chair, a lamp, a stand with a porcelain water pitcher, wash bowl and towels and a line of nails in the wall to hang clothing and six-guns.

Being Irish, he was a natural bartender and it was his Gaelic charm as much as the whiskey, the gambling and the women that instantly turned the place into a roaring success.

Soon it became Morgan's custom to go to the saloon late at night and stay until the place emptied out so as to be on hand when Charlie totalled the receipts, put them in a strongbox and then into a safe until they could be deposited in the bank.

Before long he was able to estimate what kind of day it had been simply by glancing at the line of horses hitched in front and by the amount of noise spilling into the street, as flawless a measure of the state of the cattle business as the head-counters and the Fairbanks scales at Joe McCoy's stockyard being the number and the mood of the cowboys.

The year after it opened for trade three men Morgan recognized as the ones who'd rolled and robbed him coming from Josiah Jones's saloon—the Dowd brothers—barged in and, soon thereafter they encountered Death's reaping scythe in the form of a Colt pistol in Morgan's revenging grip.

"That'll sure make this joint famous," declared Charlie, adding, "Maybe I should put up a sign."

That recognition of the value of advertising hadn't diminished, thought Morgan as he crossed Wichita's river into Delano, chuckling with amusement at the memory and the garish red-and-yellow sign

Charlie had erected on the prairie beckoning cowboys to Wichita so that he could harvest a share of the profits of sin.

Competition was plentiful in Delano, Morgan noted as he guided Grulla past the alluring fronts flanking Wichita's version of Texas Street: Rowdy Joe's, the Alamo Beer Garden, Syndicate, Spirit Bank, Gold Room and, in the middle of the excitement, Long Charlie's.

Like its predecessor in Abilene, it was entered through emerald-green batwing doors.

Shoving them open, Morgan again felt catapulted back in time as he encountered a familiar layout — the same gleaming long bar, same bottle-studded shelf, same mirrors, same lewd paintings.

The same roar of baritone voices.

The permeating smell was the same — beer, tobacco smoke, sweat.

Sawdusted plank floors.

The customers: a hundred unleashed cowboys with coins in their pockets and desperate to spend them to find out if it was true that Wichita was boundless.

Rising above everyone and ruling everything, as tall and stately as a sailing ship, Charlie worked his way from the far end to the curved head of it near the batwings.

Quietly, Morgan said, "Hi ya, buddy."

"Morgan," shouted Charlie as loud as a gun going off. Grabbing across the bar, he clutched Morgan's slender shoulders in huge squeezing hands. "Christ on a crutch, when did the cat drag you in?"

Chapter Seventeen

Fueled by whiskey and animated by Charlie's reminiscences of their time in Abilene, the evening spun past midnight and toward dawn as the saloon's clientele dwindled to only two hard drinkers and three iron-butt poker players at an eight-sided table in the rear who prompted Charlie to recall the Dowd brothers and their demise, concluding his reverie with an admiring, "Yeah, you was quite the gunman."

"That's all in the past," said Morgan forcefully. "These days I'm a peaceable man." With a shy smile, he added, "And a married one."

Rearing to his full height, Charlie thundered, "Hitched? You?" Shaking his head, he muttered, "Oh, I know you were always a ladies man. But you with a ball and chain? It's hard to comprehend."

"Gonna be a father, too," grinned Morgan. Thinking fondly of Rebecca and feeling a pang of regret for not being with her, he added, "Any minute now, I expect."

"Well, I wish you good luck, old buddy," said Charlie as he topped yet another jigger of whiskey.

"But to me, you'll always be the hell-bent-for-leather kid I ran into in Abilene."

"Life has to move on, Charles," said Morgan. "You seem to know that better'n anyone, seeing as how you've quit Abilene for Wichita, lock, stock and barrel."

"That ain't life. That's economics. The bottom fell out of Abilene, so I had to move. Besides, what's Wichita but Abilene with a different name? Not that it will stay that way, of course. Pretty soon the reformers will get their way here and this spot will be as lively as a dead dog's tail. Just like what happened in Abilene."

"And what does Charlie Carew do then?"

"He moves on to the next place. All the way to California prob'ly."

"And when the reformers reach California?"

"Then I guess I'll make a jump over the big water to Australia. Or Canada. Maybe Alaska. Wherever the frontier is."

Awakening at eight in the morning after four hours of fitful dreaming about Rebecca as he slept on an iron cot in the back room of the saloon that served as Charlie's office and residence, Morgan surrendered to Charlie's insistence that he have a bit of the hair of the dog that bit him and gulped down a shot of whiskey at the bar.

Later, at a table beside the front window of a restaurant as he devoured a breakfast of steak, eggs, and two mugs of steaming black coffee, he observed Main Street's passing parade of the familiar cowtown characters whose purposes his practiced eye discerned from their varied costumes: checkered outfits worn by eastern sharps, gamblers and confidence men; the somber preacher-like suits of McCoy-like business-minded men; sleek and well dressed speculators with airs of genteel living and stuffed purses; rough-threaded independent drovers; reckless, footloose and carefree paid-off sunburned cowboys straight off the trail in worn jeans, chaps and weathered hats; vaqueros shoulder-draped in serapes under wide and floppy sombreros; buckskin breeches and jackets of a pair of grizzled plainsmen who kindled warm memories of California Joe Milner and his own days scouting for the Seventh Cavalry; the immense dignity of a handful of friendly Indians in brightly colored blanket togas leading paint ponies.

Meeting McCoy at the Harris House at ten o'clock, he was escorted to the Munger Hotel where he was introduced to three men in black suits who bought the entire herd at twenty dollars a head for their Chicago syndicate, bought him lunch at the hotel to celebrate the deal and then accompanied him to a bank to draw a check for the cattle and make arrangements for paying cash to the Colter cowboys who would be coming to town in shifts over the next week to collect their pay and spend them, proving the truthfulness of Charlie Carew's boastful billboard: Everything goes in Wichita.

Especially a cowboy's wages, he thought as he rode out to their camping ground with the good news of the sale.

On Saturday night, Dalgo was arrested.

This news was blurted breathlessly by the caporal's

155

best friend among Colter ranch vaqueros, a spindly youngster named Hector Gonzales, on his first drive. Barging through the green batwing doors of Long Charlie's and immediately grabbing Morgan's arm, he cried, "You gotta come, boss. Dalgo's in a heap of trouble. You gotta help him."

Calmly, Morgan said, "What did he do?"

With a forward jerk of his fist, Hector gasped, "Knifed."

"Dalgo was knifed?"

"No, boss. Dalgo did the knifin'."

"Christ," grunted Morgan. "Where is he?"

"In the calaboose, boss."

Turning to Charlie, Morgan asked, "Where's the marshal's office?"

"Top end of the street," said Charlie with a nod. "His name is Mike Meagher. He's a friend of mine, so mention you know me. And be sure to tell him your name. He'll recognize it."

Hurrying through the batwings, Morgan retorted, "Not sure if that'll help or hurt."

Even seated behind an oak desk that faced the door and bending over a bowl of stew, Meagher was a broad-shouldered, granite-jawed and hard-eyed personal assertion of law and order that made a silver-colored star on his chest needless as he looked up sharply toward the door when Morgan opened it.

"Sorry to interrupt your supper," said Morgan.

Immediately shifting wary eyes to the gun strapped to Morgan's hip, Meagher said, "There's an ordinance about wearin' iron within city limits, mister. Dischargin' a gun in town is punishable by a twenty-five dollar fine."

"I only draw in self-defense," said Morgan as he

156

closed the door.

Pushing aside the stew and tilting back on his chair while his right hand drifted down to his own gun, Meagher said, "So they all say."

"In my case," said Morgan, crossing the room to the desk, "it's true."

"Didn't you see the sign about guns at the bridge? Or can't you read?"

"Only sign I saw was the one put up by my pal Charlie Carew."

Meagher grunted a laugh and uncoiled. "That damned thing," he said, shaking his head ruefully. "It has caused me more trouble than I'd care to think about. Long Charles is a friend of yours, eh?"

"Since way back."

"Way back where?"

"Abilene. M'name's Morgan."

"*The* Morgan?"

"I understand you've got another friend of mine in your lockup. His name is Dalgo. That is, Felipe Hidalgo."

Meagher nodded slowly, turning wary again. "He's here."

"May I know the charge and the bail?"

"He knifed another Mexican in a brawl in the parlor of Ida May's bawdy house down by the bridge."

"Is the man he knifed dead?"

"He ought to be but he ain't."

"So the charge against Dalgo is what? Assault?"

"The charge ain't fixed yet. He's only in on suspicion. Right now there's nobody who's willin' to say exactly what happened. If the victim croaks, then it'll be a murder case and lips will be looser."

157

"Is it likely to become a murder case?"

"Prob'ly not. Truth is, I've tossed him in the pokey just to keep him from being killed by the pals of the Mex he stuck. Protective custody."

"When might I post bail for his release?"

"I understand he's from somewhere down in Texas. Came up here with a herd. May I assume that you're the boss of that outfit?"

"You assume right."

"When are you plannin' on leavin' town?"

"As soon as I tie up some loose ends. In another day or so."

"Stop by here on your way south and I'll spring your man. That is, if the Mexicano he cut doesn't die."

"Can I talk to Dalgo now?"

"Sure," said Meagher, rising behind the desk and reaching for a loop of keys. "The cage is in the next room. But leave that Colt Army iron of yours here on my desk."

Laying the gun on the oak with a heavy thump, Morgan said, "Suspicious soul, aren't you?"

"It's the only life insurance policy I carry."

Satisfied that the marshal was right about keeping Dalgo in protective custody and finally succeeding in getting Dalgo to accept his word that leaving him in jail was the best thing for him, he returned to Meagher. Shifting his eyes from his bowl of stew to the sheathed Bowie knife hanging from Morgan's gunbelt, the marshal said, "Long Charlie tells me you're as handy with a blade as you are with this." His left hand settled atop Morgan's pistol. "Which I do intend to keep right here, as the ordinance requires, unless you're heading out of town?"

"The night's young," Morgan grinned, "and I haven't even started to taste Wichita's plentiful attractions."

"If it's women you'll be wanting," said Meagher, sliding Morgan's gun into a desk drawer, "I'd customarily recommend Ida May's house. But considering tonight's circumstances . . ."

Feigning a shocked look and a chastising tone, Morgan said, "I happen to be a happily married man, marshal."

"Then the place for you," said Meagher, "is Mrs. Hudson's, the finest house in Wichita. One of three places of, shall we say, assignation actually licensed by the city council. It's not here in Delano but in the, uh, respectable part of town. Very sedate. The women are high class. Genteel. The sort who'll be happy to just sit and listen if you'd rather just rhapsodize about the wife you left at home."

Chapter Eighteen

Accompanied by the marshal into the roiling mayhem of Main Street on a muggy Saturday night, Morgan asked, "Isn't it a little peculiar for the lawman of the town to be handing out advice on houses of ill repute?"

"We are not hypocrites here in Wichita, Mr. Morgan," said Meagher as they unhitched and mounted their horses. "I'd be one if I were to pretend that prostitution isn't central in the social and economic life of the city. Now, it is true that the trade is officially illegal and that fines are levied and collected, but I'd be a bald-faced liar if I contended that the fines were a means of suppressing the practice. They're operating fees, plain and simple. All we ask of the women and the houses is that they be discreet. We will draw the line from time to time. Just the other day, for instance, I had to put a stop to the girls of Ida May's establishment from engaging in races from the house to the river completely in the nude and to the accompaniment of cheering from the rowdies who were betting on the outcome. There are limits. After all, nobody likes to feel embarrassed."

"Of course not," chuckled Morgan as they crossed the bridge from Delano to Wichita proper.

"That's the appeal of Mrs. Hudson's, uh, shall we say, boarding house? Very unintrusive."

At the end of a rising, muddy and deeply rutted street paralleling the river, the white clapboard house stood apart from half a dozen similar structures. With its windows ablaze with light against the dark rolling expanse of prairie, it looked like a ship upon a lonely sea.

"Best house in town," said the marshal as he slid from his horse and hitched it to a rail.

"Looks decent," said Morgan, not knowing what else to say.

"It'll be just what the doctor ordered," said Meagher going up steps to the porch, "especially after being, uh, *without* during all that time on the trail, eh?" Opening the door, he said, "And what the little wife don't know won't hurt her, right?"

"Right," said Morgan, following him.

Stepping from a shadowy vestibule, he turned into a large parlor with red-papered walls and scarlet-shaded lamps that cast clusters of scantily clad women in devilish light and struck him with the impression of having stepped into Hell itself.

Wedged among the women were their customers— same mix of men Morgan had found everywhere in Wichita—the same as he'd found in Abilene and Newton. They looked up in shock and terror when Meagher bellowed, "The whole place is pinched."

Looking on in delight as the squealing girls quickly persuaded the men that they were not about to be arrested, he turned to Morgan and said, "I always do that. It's my little joke."

Pushing through the room, the proprietor of the house arrived at Morgan's side. Although she was short and dumpy and her face had gone to jowls, Morgan thought he could discern the remnants of what had been youthful beauty. "Who's this, Mike," she said gaily, "a new deputy? Or is this handsome galoot here to spend money instead of extort it?"

"I'm not a lawman, ma'am," Morgan laughed.

Poking his ribs with an elbow, she said, "Ooo, on top of the good looks, he's polite! With all that goin' for him, I may decide to keep him."

"Sorry, Mabel," said the marshal. "He's already got himself a wife. In fact, I had a devil of a time persuadin' him to visit this lively establishment of yours."

"Don't fret, honey, I won't tell," she said, curling an arm around Morgan's and leading him away. "What sort do you like, doll? Mrs. Hudson's got 'em all. Tell me what kind of gal you're lookin' for, honey."

Rebecca's face formed in his mind. Then Sarah Coffee's. Neither was a whore, he thought, chastising himself for thinking of them and trying to conjure up the whores he'd been with. Only one face appeared. Sue's. Sweet Sue Cantrell, of dubious and questionable memory. Then, quite suddenly, as if he were experiencing a waking dream, he actually saw her.

At the far edge of the crowded room, she stood alone in the shadow of a curving stairway.

It can't be her, he thought. Impossible. After all these years? No.

This was a mirage, he told himself. A trick of the

eyes and the light. Like shimmering heat fooling parched cowboys to see the prairie turned into an ocean, this woman in the reddish shades of Mrs. Hudson's hellish parlor was a cruel twist of reality.

But what an extraordinary resemblance, he thought as he tugged at Mrs. Hudson's sleeve and whispered, "Who's that?"

"Who's who, boy?"

"The girl by the stairs."

"Oh, that's Susanne."

"God no," he sighed. But it was true. She was not a mirage.

At the instant she saw him Sue gasped in panic. "Oh my God."

"Susanne, darling," said Mrs. Hudson gaily, "this handsome thing wants to meet you!"

"Hello," said Morgan.

The years had not been kind to her. Plump and with her hair tinted by henna and cheeks streaked with pink rouge, she looked used and a far cry from his sweetened memory of a slender girl with long brown hair that smelled like rosewater, cat-green eyes, peach-toned cheeks, high breasts, wide hips, long legs, firm arms and fingers as soft as pussywillows.

Alone with him, she threw her soft arms about him. "As handsome as ever," she said, squeezing him hard. "Still as skinny as a hitching post."

"You haven't changed either," he mumbled, a polite lie while he struggled to accept the cruel reality of her.

"You are such a fibber," she giggled, "although you are a sweet-hearted one." Taking his hand, she tugged him toward the stairs. "C'mon, let's get away from the crowd. Upstairs."

Like the drowning waters of a burst dam, memories of her room in Sally Magruder's house swirled in his head and threatened to suffocate him. Frilled, curtained, cushioned, warm and welcoming, it had been an expression of herself and going into it he'd always thought of her as fresh and innocent, a girl for whom this was to be the first time with a man.

Her room in Mrs. Hudson's house was plain.

Except for a white-painted double-sized iron bed, it was as austere as a barracks. Strictly for business, he thought.

Closing the door, she said, "We won't be disturbed here. This is my private room. We can talk first. Or after, if you prefer. We'll catch up." She was talking rapidly; so fast that he suspected she was afraid to let him get a word in. "My, this is a surprise. A bolt from the blue. Like lightning."

"A real jolt for sure," he exclaimed.

Standing before a mirror and beginning to undress, she sighed, "I have put on a few ounces."

"You look great," he said, desperately wishing he had not come to the room and wondering if he ought to tell her about Rebecca.

Considering herself full length in the glass, she pondered whether to tell him that the "ounces" she'd added were the result of a child she'd had several months after leaving Junction City; a blue-eyed and flaxen haired boy who was very lively and good-looking but who'd died in St. Louis of scarlet fever at the age of two—possibly Morgan's son.

"You look naked without a gun in your holster," she said, smiling at him as she saw him reflected in the mirror.

164

"It's a city ordinance," he said absently, slapping a hand against the empty leather.

"Saves a lot of lives, I suppose," she said, turning abruptly.

Whether it was the movement or the perfumed room making his head swim or the weight of the accumulation of years of wondering about her that brought the question exploding into his head he could not have explained, nor did it matter, he realized. His smile abruptly disappeared, his throat tightened and his mouth went dry as he asked, "Why'd you run off, Sue?"

She'd been expecting and fearing the question, but was nonetheless taken aback hearing it. "It, uh, seemed the right thing at the time."

"The right thing?" he moaned, sounding more perplexed and bewildered than hurt. "What in tarnation does that mean?"

Nervously, she sank onto the edge of the bed and said, "Well, after the trouble concerning that man Walters I thought I should leave."

"What the hell's Walters got to do with it? That was strictly self-defense. He drew first. The fact of it was clear." His tone was rising in anger now. "So I don't see why you got it into your head to take off and leave on account of him."

Meekly, she said, "I didn't want to make any more trouble for you."

Striding to her, he begged, "How in blazes could you make trouble for me?"

"I didn't want to cause you trouble with the army."

"Wait a minute!" He turned away, paced the small room and turned again with his fists jammed against his hips, a familiar pose to her, a sign that he wasn't going to let up. "How'd you come by the idea that you'd get me in trouble with the army?"

Lightly dismissing the question with a shrug, she said, "I heard fellas from the fort talk about it."

He advanced a step. "Such as?"

"Well, I can't remember exactly. It was years ago. But I do recall that fellas from Riley was always afraid of landing in hot water for things they did when they came to town. I didn't want anything bad happening to you because of me."

Shaking his head, he said, "How could you get the idea that something bad could happen to me because of you?"

"It just seemed likely," she said edging close to tears and wishing he would stop the questioning.

"Somebody had to put that cockeyed notion in your head."

"No," she sobbed.

Fury darkened his face. "Who was it? Who told you I'd get in trouble because of you?"

"Nobody," she cried.

Suddenly he was looming before her and speaking tenderly. "You never could lie to me, Sue, so don't try now. Tell me who gave you the idea that I'd get in trouble because of you."

Unable to resist him further, she sighed, "That old geezer. California Joe!" A lie.

"Impossible," he exclaimed, bolting away. "Joe was the one who first told me about you. He said you'd take to me like honeysuckle to a porch. Joe approved of you and me together, so it wasn't him. Who then?"

She was in tears now and turning down her head. "What's it matter anyway?"

"It matters to me," he said sharply, grasping her arms and pulling her to him. "So tell me who it was."

Trembling, she muttered, "Major Kimball."

Stunned, he gasped, "Ward Kimball? Why?"

Utterly defeated, she was weeping against his shoulder. "He told me I was all wrong for you. That I'd only spell more trouble. Like the business with Walters. The best thing for you, he said, was for me to clear out of your life. He was really determined about it. You'd've thought he was your father. I mean, he acted like you were something extra special to him. If he wasn't a man I'd've thought he was in love with you. He offered me money to go away. Frankly, I was so confused and scared, I took it."

"Jesus," Morgan groaned.

"Like I said, it seemed like the right thing to do at the time," she said, lifting her eyes pleadingly.

Letting her go, he growled. "You should have thrown the money in his face."

"I loved you and didn't want to hurt you."

"Well you did! Running off. As if I didn't matter to you at all. You broke my heart, Sue."

"We're here now, together," she pleaded, hesitantly touching his sleeve.

She thought back to leaving him. To the puzzle of Major Kimball insisting that she go. Threatening. Frightening her into going. The heartbreak of going, of not seeing Morgan again. The sickening realization that she would never see him again. Dreaming about him and longing for him in Kansas City and then St. Louis. Ridiculously searching the faces of men in the houses where she worked in the foolish hope of finding his. Then discovering she was pregnant and being certain the child was his. Having the baby — that lovely boy. Morgan's son. Naming the boy for him. Morgan. Losing the boy as she had lost his father.

Should she tell him all this? Now? After all these years?

"I shouldn't've come up here with you," said Morgan harshly. "What's past should stay past."

Reaching for him, she sobbed.

"In life you can't go back," he said. "You come to a fork in the road and choose and you can't go back."

She was pressed against him so that her face was close enough to kiss.

Too close, he decided. Backing way, he blurted, "Sue, I'm married now. My wife's having a baby. Possibly at this very minute. So there can't be anything between us now like there was when I wasn't married. It would be wrong. A betrayal."

Suddenly he became sickeningly aware of what a hypocrite he must seem to her as he stood there talking moralistically of a wife and child. If they meant so much to him, she was entitled to ask, why had he come to this house in Wichita quite prepared to forget wife and child for whatever amount of time and money he was willing to spend on a whore?

But she was not thinking that. Instead, a memory of her own baby stabbed into her and for that sharp, piercing, hurtful second she verged on telling him that she'd already had his child. But in the next instant she realized that to do so would be pointless, save for the sheer spite of it. She'd obviously wounded him deeply when she'd fled Junction City thinking she was protecting him. She could not —

and would not—hurt him again. "I guess you'd better go," she said.

"Yeah, I guess so," he muttered.

To his back as he moved toward the door she sighed, "Small world, isn't it?"

Small, cruel world, she thought.

Pausing at the door, he plunged a hand into the pocket of his vest. "About money, I guess I should, uh . . ."

With an affectionate laugh she said, "Never mind that, for God's sake!"

"But don't you have to, uh, share with, uh . . . what's the name of this madam?"

"Mrs. Hudson."

"I recall you always had to share the money with Sally Magruder, so I'd better give you whatever . . ."

"I'll handle Mrs. Hudson, darling," she said, laughing to keep from crying as she shoved him out the door.

Chapter Nineteen

On the night before his father would return from Kansas, Arbuckle Colter Owen Morgan cried, startling his mother awake in the sweltering August heat. Struggling from bed, she muttered, "Will the wailing never cease?"

"What a lovely baby," Migdalia Coffee had cried at the completion of the birth. Singing to him in Spanish, she'd cut and tied the cord and washed him. Then, tenderly placing him naked upon his mother's breast, she'd sighed, "Like Madonna and Jesus."

Roused from a twilight slumber by the weight upon her, Rebecca had heard, "Hay-soos."

"You will have many lovely children," Migdalia had said happily, as if she were reading fortune-telling cards for the drunken and gullible patrons of her cantina.

"No," snapped Rebecca, remembering the pain. "No more."

The whole thing had been a mistake. It seemed to her as she crossed the warm wooden floor in bare feet, that the baby had been screaming the entire two months since he'd been born on a Wednesday dawn. She ought never to have had a baby. Ought never to have married Morgan. She'd been a fool to get involved with him in the first place. She'd been weak when she'd meant to be strong. Abandoning common sense to the itch of flesh, she'd imagined herself to be a female scorpion demanding satisfaction from a male that she'd expected to promptly devour.

Instead of feasting, she was the one who'd been consumed.

Instead of conquering, she'd been vanquished.

Lifting the wailing child from the crib, she muttered, "Wednesday's child is full of woe."

Then with a bitter laugh as she loosened her chemise and the baby began to nurse, she remembered Morgan's taunting poem and recited it, as if it were a nursery rhyme:

"I thought if only I could marry,
I'd sing and dance and live so gaily;
But all the wedded bliss I see
Is rock the cradle, hush the baby."

Early the next morning her slumber was disturbed again, this time by distant voices.

The shrillness of a woman's.

Migdalia's. Overwrought and excited.

And a man's.

Steady and familiar.

Turning her eyes to crib and the baby, peaceful at

last, she drew the bed covers to her neck and muttered, "Morgan's back."

Closing her eyes, she feigned sleep.

A moment later, she heard him come into the room.

"Rebecca? You asleep?"

Breathless and dreading, she waited for the scrape of his heels crossing the floor. Expecting his shadow to darken the pale pink light through her eyelids, she anticipated his touch. But instead she heard the sound of his boots treading softly in the direction of the crib and then his dulcet voice, as adoring as he ever was with her.

"Well, look at you, fella," he said as she opened her eyes a slit to see him gently lifting his son. "Ain't you something!"

"My God," she shouted, "don't set him off crying."

Cradling the boy peacefully in his arms, Morgan turned with a proud grin. "Lordy, Rebecca, isn't he *something?*"

"He most assuredly is," she said.

Then, boastfully, Morgan declared, "Colter, what a fine little Morgan you are!"

Chapter Twenty

Like almost everyone upon the Nueces Strip who knew Rebecca Colter before she married Morgan, Migdalia Coffee would have described Rebecca in glowing terms as a woman of solidity with grit, determination, and purpose while depicting Morgan as being hopelessly self-centered, unstable and quite likely to either disappear for good without warning or explanation or explode with deadly violence. But of all those on the ranch and in Goliad who celebrated and blessed or doubted and mocked the marriage, only Migdalia detected a mystifying reversal in the complex nature of their relationship following the birth of the boy called Colt.

Now Rebecca was the one who swung wildly between not caring and seeming ready to blow up while Morgan was the one with a core of earnestness and reliability. And never more evident than in their attitude toward the boy.

"I don't think she ever wanted that baby," she told her own child two weeks after Morgan's return from the drive, warning Sarah not to breathe a word to anyone of what she was confiding as she bent over

173

the stove in the cookhouse behind the cantina while Sarah rolled tortillas.

Sarah exclaimed, "How could she not want that cute baby?"

"I clearly remember her saying that birthing was God's curse," said Migdalia. " 'Everything will be changed,' she said. Well everything sure has changed! And I think she blames Morgan for it. Oh, it's a scandal the way she treats that young man."

Sarah's dark eyes widened. "How?" she asked eagerly. "How does she treat him?"

"Not like a husband, that's for sure," sighed Migdalia. "More like a ranch hand. As if they never married. Since she had the baby she's become very cold toward him."

Closing her eyes and picturing Morgan, Sarah could not imagine any woman being cold to Morgan.

"It's a scandal," said Migdalia emphatically. "And a tragedy. But what can I do? It's none of my business."

Dalgo, too, sensed trouble but looked for its cause in matters of greater familiarity to him than the intricacies of the affairs of man and woman. Detecting more than the occasional and thoroughly understandable anger of a man who was the boss of a great cattle ranch and responsible for riding herd on a hundred hands who could be as lazy and cantankerous as the cows they were hired to care for, he worried that Morgan's dark mood stemmed from the knifing incident in Wichita.

174

But reason soon told him that Morgan had been in enough saloons and whorehouses in cowtowns to look on a simple knife fight as something to be embarrassed about or to hold a grudge because of it. Nobody'd been killed, after all. If had been a fair fight. And the man he'd cut had been expected to skip town anyway, which is why the whole thing had been settled by the marshal accepting bail, knowing there'd never be a trial because the men involved in the fight weren't likely to come back to face the music. So the bail Morgan had put up was, in effect, a fine which had been repaid to Morgan out of Dalgo's share of the proceeds of the cattle they'd sold.

If that were the case, he told himself, then he had no idea what sort of burr had gotten under his boss's saddle and hoped that Morgan would get over his vexation in his own sweet time for everyone's sake, including Morgan's.

Arriving unexpectedly at the ranch in October as he made his way toward Matagorda and El Rancho Grande from Wichita by way of Houston and San Antonio, the third person to discern something amiss was Shanghai Pierce. "I hope I didn't drop in at an inauspicious moment," he whispered as he and Morgan left Rebecca to the cleaning up after dinner. Filling the commodious chair that had been Buck Colter's favorite place for savoring after-dinner brandy and cigars in the large parlor decorated with the souvenirs of Rebecca Colter's ancestors, he lowered his voice further. "Rebecca seems a little put out."

175

"It's nothing important," said Morgan self-consciously as he held a match under Shanghai's cigar and then lit his own. "She's just not herself yet since she had the baby, I s'pose."

"Yes, that must be it," said Shanghai, knowing a lie when he heard one. Loosening his vest and easing back into the soft chair, he said, "Sorry I missed you up in Wichita. Joe McCoy told me you brought a herd in during the summer. I heard you got excellent money."

"Respectable, yes," said Morgan proudly. Glad for the change of subject, he tilted back his head and watched the slow drift of cigar smoke toward the ceiling timbers. "In times like this," he said dreamily, "there's a poem comes to mind:

What is it comes through the deepening dusk, —
Something sweeter than jasmine scent,
Sweeter than rose and violent blent,
More potent in power than orange or musk?
The scent of a good cigar!"

Shanghai chuckled, "Shakespeare, no doubt."

"Shoot no," laughed Morgan. "I read that on a cigar box."

Appearing suddenly in the arched doorway, Rebecca announced, "I'll leave you two to your smokes. I'm going for a ride."

Bolting upright, Morgan snapped, "Rebecca, we've a guest."

Stroking her long hair, she retorted, "I'm sure Mr. Pierce won't mind."

"Not at all," said Shanghai, rising half-way from

176

the deep chair.

Fixing Morgan with a look of triumph, she said, "There, you see?"

When she was gone, Morgan was red with embarrassment. "I'm sorry, Shang. That was damned rude of her."

"So there is a little trouble between you two."

Rising abruptly, Morgan strode to the fireplace and angrily flung his half-smoked cigar into the fire. "Ever since I got back from Wichita I can't seem to do anything right. Nothing suits her. Anything I say is wrong. I can't get near her."

"Perhaps it's as you said. The lingering effects of bearing the child. It's common, I think, for a child to appear to come between its parents. A man can get the impression that he doesn't count and that his wife doesn't love him anymore."

Turning his back to the fire and facing Shanghai, Morgan jammed his hands into the pockets of his pants and let his head come down until his chin was almost against his chest. "Maybe that's all it is," he said as he saw her out of the corner of his eye flashing past the windows exactly as he'd seen her on his first visit to the ranch. As if pursued by demons, she was flying madly toward the sunset upon her racing-hearted dun.

"It's dismaying to me to see you two troubled," said Shanghai, also observing Rebecca.

"Too bad Buck's not around," said Morgan. "He'd soon settle the issue."

"Yep," said Shanghai. "Turn her over his knee and spank her, most likely. Maybe that's what you should do."

"I never hit a woman in my life," said Morgan

177

soberly. "Too scared to, I guess. Afraid I'd be bettered," he added with a snorted laugh.

Rising, Shanghai left his chair and crossed the room to the fireplace to discard the chewed and soggy remains of his cigar. "The trouble with women is, you can't do anything with 'em and you can't do without 'em."

At that moment, Colt cried, a shout in the distance of the vast house.

"That sounds like a dogie in distress," chuckled Shanghai.

Morgan beamed. "Want to take a gander at him?"

" 'Deed I do!"

As Morgan reached into the crib, the boy's crying subsided and the tiny fingers of his left hand grasped the thumb of Morgan's right.

"Looks like he's gonna be a southpaw," said Shanghai.

"Which side he draws from doesn't matter as long as he shoots true," said Morgan, lifting the boy from the crib. "You remember what your daddy says, Colt."

Crying again, the boy tugged at the front of Morgan's shirt.

"Sounds like he's hungry," said Shanghai.

"Needs his mama," said Morgan — bitterly, Shanghai believed.

Chapter Twenty-one

With no cyclones whipping in from the Gulf, that autumn's weather in the Nueces Strip was placid as Morgan sought solace from Rebecca's sudden and inexplicable storms in the work of the ranch, spending as much time with Dalgo and the hands at the range camps as he did around the big house, although he missed Colt considerably when he was away.

In February the tranquility of the ranch was disturbed by an outbreak of raids by Mexican bandits in the chaparral of the big bend of the Nueces near Artesia Wells.

Everywhere he rode with Dalgo, Morgan came upon the carcasses of Colter cattle slaughtered and left for the feasting of coyotes and wild boar, their stripped and bleaching bones littering the countryside like a field of battle, except that this was a war where the spoils were cowhide and tallow. "If they keep up this Skinning War," said Morgan as he and Dalgo surveyed the aftermath of yet another butchering party, "we won't have a herd to take north come spring. I thought we'd put an end to this when we

179

wiped out the Flores gang down in Las Cuevas."

Shaking his head slowly and tugging at the points of his flowing mustache, Dalgo said, "This is the work of *Cortinistas*."

Sliding back his hat, Morgan said, "Who the blazes is that?"

"Oh, they're bandits, just like the Flores gang, but these go way back," said Dalgo. "Cortina himself was before your time, before the war." With a tone that seemed full of admiration to Morgan, the caporal continued, "His name was Camargo Nepomuceno Cortina. He ruled the Strip for twenty-five years. I knew him a little. In fact, I might have become a *Cortinista* myself if Buck Colter hadn't hired me. Anyways, Cortina was a *huero*. That's a Mexican with reddish skin. They used to call him the Red Robber of the Rio Grande. And the whole border from Brownsville for five hundred miles up the river was known as *Zona Libre*. A rustler could take his cattle into the zone and get paid fifty cents a head. That was a good price. For this service, the Red Robber claimed a *pecho*, which means tax. The tax was every fifth cow."

"Nice set up," sneered Morgan.

"These days the *dinero* is in the hides and the tallow," said Dalgo with a nod at the strewn carcasses, "not the beef."

Staring angrily at the remnants of Colter cattle and resting his hand on the butt of his revolver, Morgan muttered, "Maybe we'll have to organize the ranchers again and see if we can put a stop to this."

"Maybe so, boss," said Dalgo as they rode on, grimly.

Increasingly, when he returned from these tours of the range camps Morgan did not know what to expect from his wife. At times she greeted him warmly and with a torrent of questions and observations relating to all he had to report or railing against the thieves who were plundering Colter property. But just as much he found her aloof, cold, and contentious.

More and more he smelled whiskey on her breath.

Except for the joy he'd found in their son, he began to regret marrying her.

Still, he hoped that she would change and become the Rebecca he'd fallen in love with, although he didn't know it at the time, when he'd first observed her arguing with her father at dinner when she was just sweet sixteen. Desperately he hoped that she would snap out of the sullen and withdrawn moods that had overwhelmed her since the birth of Colt, but as they sat down for one of their last suppers together before he would have to ride out again to the holding range camp where Dalgo was organizing the men for the spring roundup, she asserted, "I want you to stop calling my son Colt."

As stung as if she'd slapped him, he gasped, "Don't be ridiculous."

Rigidly she said, "From now on please call my son Colter."

Shooting up from his chair and leaning on the table with his fists, he snarled, "He's my son, as well, Rebecca."

Unflinchingly, she said, "His name is Colter. I want you to call him Colter."

"Damn *you*," he said, kicking back the chair. "I'll

181

call him anything I want to."

As he stormed from the dining room, she remained at the table listening keenly to the pounding of his furious boots across the stones of the foyer, the slam of the front door, the crunching of the gravel path between the house and the barn, the creak of its double doors and, after a time, a horse galloping in the direction of Goliad.

"Going to see that cantina girl, no doubt," she said at last, contemptuously.

Then, rising serenely from her chair, she gazed at the portraits of her illustrious ancestors—the first Arbuckle Colter, her great-grandfather, the *ladrone* and Hero of Goliad; her grandfather David whose vision of the future was the mastering of the Texas longhorn; and her beloved and lamented father who had had no sons.

At the turn for the Goliad road, Morgan paused and gazed at the sign which Buck Colter had erected:

THIS IS BUCK COLTER'S ROAD,

TAKE THE OTHER ONE.

"A pity I didn't heed that advice long ago," he muttered bitterly as he rode on. Calmer now and with nowhere that he wanted to get to in a hurry except away from the house and the likelihood of a worse fight with Rebecca, he let the horse set the pace under the kind of cool moonlight that made a man feel alone but not lonesome.

The horse beneath him was Grulla, the capable and steadfast steed of roundups and cattle trails, but as Grulla rocked him in the saddle with their noses pointed toward Goliad, fond memories stirred of his first horse, Strawberry, whom he might just as easily have thrown a saddle on if he hadn't had his mind set more on getting away from the house than choosing a horse.

Strawberry!

What a name for a horse! That was what Joe Mc-Coy had cracked way back in Abilene.

Ah, but such a horse!

Bought in Kansas City with the last of the dollars of army mustering out pay, Strawberry'd soon adjusted to the prairie life and had been every damn bit as good a cav horse as any of the army's mounts at Fort Riley. He'd been vetted beside the Platte and in the senseless slaughter along the Washita. Faithful and patient, he'd stood many an hour looped to the hitching post outside Long Charlie's Saloon in Abilene. He'd explored the Chisholm Trail going and coming. Then, like himself, Morgan thought ruefully, Strawberry had gotten sidetracked, winding up in Texas when the aim had been to reach California.

Now old Straw was in a kind of well-deserved and easy retirement, replaced by a gray horse with a Mexican name and temperament better suited to brush popping and longhorn herding.

Picking up the pace now, Grulla's flaring nostrils had caught the scent of Goliad.

At Migdalia Coffee's El Dorado the smell was a pungent stew of Mexican cooking, beer, whiskey, boots, sweat, cigars and the burnt-rope odor of the weed that Dalgo rolled into ragged cigarettes and sucked on when he wasn't working, pronounced marry-wan-uh.

The sounds were cantina too: the same baritone drone of the saloons of Kansas but spiced with the lilt and twist of Mexican tongues, a tinny out-of-tune-piano and the knife-point jab of a girl's lusty laughter — Sarah Coffee's, Morgan recognized as he looped Grulla's reins around the hitching rail.

Clumping across the plank sidewalk in two strides, he ducked beneath the too-low curve of a doorless archway and inside, halting at the near end of the sparsely patronized bar tended by Sarah in her customary inflammatory red, white and black costume of skirt, apron and billowy deep-necked blouse.

"Morgan," she said teasingly as she sauntered with swaying hips to his piece of the bar, "You've sure been a stranger lately."

"Have I?"

"The wife's got you on a tight reata, huh?"

"Who says?"

"Hey, you sure are sour!"

"Is that so?"

"Want me to sing your favorite song to cheer you up? 'Green grow the lilacs all covered . . .' "

"I'm here for the mescal, my sweet muchacha, not the floor show. Where's your mama?"

"Out back in the cookhouse. You want me to fetch her?"

For an instant he'd thought it might be a good idea to talk to Migdalia about his troubles with Rebecca but now he said, "Nah, I was just wonderin' where she was." Letting his eyes penetrate the smoky room he asked, "Who's here tonight?"

Pouring a glass of mescal, at last, Sarah said, "The reg'lars."

"Pretty dull, huh?"

184

"It was," she said, squeezing his arm. "Until you came in."

"Mud in your eye," he said flatly, lifting his glass with that arm and shrugging off her grasp.

"Jesse Bruton was in awhile ago," she said pointedly.

"So? What's that to me?"

"I thought the two of you was enemies."

"Why should we be?"

"Since you ran him off Colter property when he was lookin' for work awhile back, I thought . . ."

"I didn't run Bruton off. It was Dalgo gave him the boot. I don't even know Jesse Bruton, except his reputation as an owlhoot."

"I've heard from people that *you* were an *owlhoot* once upon a time. A reg'lar gunslick."

"Pay no attention to what you hear from people, Sarah."

He knew the look that was coming over her pretty face. Needling. Trying to get a rise out of him.

"How many people did you kill up in Abilene, Morgan?"

"None that didn't try to kill me first."

"I heard . . ."

Riled, he snapped, "Look, Sarah, I don't know what's set you off on this toot about me, but drop it. *Pronto.*"

"You really are soured t'night," she huffed, tilting her head upward in what passed for offense and abruptly turning her back to him to proceed down the bar checking the condition of glasses.

From the card tables in the back through the tobacco haze drifted a familiar voice, "Hey, Morgan you feelin' lucky?"

185

Lurching away from the bar, Morgan shouted, "Is it an honest game, Jasper?"

"As clean as a new suit of longjohns."

One of the regulars and a grizzle-bearded, elderly, and somewhat dimwitted cousin in a notorious family of lawbreakers, owlhoots and other hardcases, his name was Jasper Fulcord and the friendly verbal exchange was a never-varying ritual that Morgan enjoyed as much as the old man.

Pulling up a chair next to him, Morgan said, "What's the game and the ante, Jasp?"

"Usual. Five card stud and two bits."

Morgan whistled, pretending to be shocked; part of the ritual. "Kinda steep for my blood."

At this point Jasper was expected to retort, "You expect me to stake ya?"

Instead, from the front of the cantina someone shouted, "Let him go and beg it from his old lady."

Though he'd heard the voice only once, at a range camp two years earlier where Dalgo had given him the boot when he'd shown up expecting to be hired for the spring roundup, Morgan knew without looking that it was Jesse Bruton.

Now came an instant that was not unfamiliar to Morgan. He'd lived it many times. The first happened in a woods above Willoughby Run back in Gettysburg when he'd suddenly found himself looking down the barrel of a Virginia rifle in the hands of a jittery Reb. He'd known it when he'd awakened beside a stream in Kansas and discovered a young Indian close enough to him to touch him, let alone kill him, and after that in saloons in Abilene when every murdering owlhoot, known gun, and tinhorn with an itchy finger felt the need to test him and his

186

Colt pistol. Like those times past, here was a split-second when everything around him in the cantina seemed to stop—people, the drift of smoke and smells, the tinny piano, the Mexican voices and breathing itself: a moment of decision.

In that frozen bit of eternity, he assayed Bruton's slouching stance, describing it to himself as that of a scarecrow that had stood too many seasons to be of any use except as a source for uninhibited birds seeking a ready supply of straw for their nests. The arms he judged to be too long and the hands too low in relation to the pair of pistols slung from belts that crisscrossed at a level that he estimated to be about where Bruton's belly button was. The X the straps formed was an ideal target to aim for, he noted. The guns that the leather supported, if he discerned them correctly through the tobacco fog, were weighty nine-shot Confederate Army Le Mat revolvers.

Excellent guns, Bruton wore them much too elevated and, quite stupidly, backward, meaning he'd have to form an X with his arms to draw them. By the time those long and lanky arms could yank the big hands high enough to grasp the Le Mats' handles, figured Morgan, five rounds from his six-shooter carried at just the right level for his arms and hands could be blasted when X marked the spot; or six bullets, he supposed, if he didn't have the habit of not loading the top chamber as a guard against accidentally shooting himself.

Rising easily as his gun hand curled comfortably next to his holster, he said, "That's a mighty offensive familiarity, sir, coming from someone I don't believe I ever had the opportunity to be properly introduced to."

"The name's Jesse Bruton."

"I know the name, sir. My point is that you made a comment that I take to be highly offensive. First, because you referred to my wife as my 'old lady' and, second, because you appear to have intended to slander me."

"Wordy bastard, aint'cha?"

"Now, slanders against me I never did pay any mind to—talk being cheap and the lower the talker, the cheaper the talk. But I am bound to call you on the aspersion aimed at my wife. I await your apology, sir."

With that, Bruton's arms twitched upward. "Is that so?"

Drawing his Colt and leveling it with the X, Morgan said flatly, "Don't lift 'em another inch. Lower 'em. Slowly."

As Bruton complied, released held-breaths suddenly stirred the smoke and the passage of time resumed.

"Sarah," said Morgan quietly, "come out from behind the bar and around behind Mr. Bruton, please, and carefully relieve him of his guns. Then pour him a glass of whatever it is he drinks, if he cares for one. I'll pay for it. Then, Mr. Bruton, I and everybody else in this cantina would be obliged to you if you'd leave. You can come back and claim your pistols later. Say, when you've reclaimed your senses?"

"Keep your lousy whiskey," Bruton bellowed. Lightened of the weight of the Le Mats by Sarah's ginger fingers, he turned on his heels and hurried out amidst a silence-shattering explosion of humiliation-engendering laughter that, Morgan expected, would echo for a long time in Jesse Bruton's impetuous young head and heart.

Chapter Twenty-two

Because Rebecca appeared to be asleep in the center of their double bed when he returned from town, Morgan did not disturb her, choosing to curl up on a divan in the parlor. Nor did he attempt to rouse her when he stirred at first light to travel to the camp where Dalgo and a dozen cowhands were organizing a herd of five thousand longhorns and waiting for the word from him to start them across the San Antonio and northward to Kansas.

"Don't come in here to this bed drunk and randy," Rebecca was thinking as she'd lain motionless and pretending slumber when he'd peeped through the bedroom door on his return from Goliad. And in the few minutes it took him to get up, steal into the room to peek at Colter mercifully asleep in his crib, leave the house without breakfast, saddle a horse and ride away, she'd prayed silently, "Lord, let him go and leave me in peace."

Contented in the silence of the house and in dreamy anticipation of the months of quiet that would envelop the ranch during the months of the drive, she drifted to sleep until Colter cried, demanding that she rise and tend him at eight o'clock.

By then Sarah Coffee had been up for more than three hours at the prompting of her tireless mother in preparation for the arrivals of the El Dorado's first customers who swore that they'd never make it through the new day without an El Dorado breakfast, mugs of scalding coffee and chickory, or booze unaccompanied by vittles.

At nine when the cantina was patronized only by a handful of card-playing old men for whom work was a memory and the future a blank, she was free to take off her apron and spend the next three hours on her own. As long as she was back and behind the bar in time to handle the noontime crowd, this was a portion of each day when she enjoyed herself by wandering around town, browsing in the stores and shops, relishing the flirting of the men she passed on the sidewalks or who teased her from the porches and galleries of the hotels and, best of all, gossiping with the girls and women of the town whom she encountered in the markets.

This morning, of course, she had a deliciously juicy tidbit to relate concerning what had transpired last night at the cantina between Jesse Bruton and Morgan. But as she stepped from the cool quiet of the El Dorado into the bustling hot street, questions about the incident arose that, if she could find answers to them, would make her story even better. "Did Rebecca know what had happened?" "Had Morgan told her?" "What might Rebecca have to say about the thrilling way in which Morgan had defended her honor?" "How did Rebecca feel to know that Morgan had risked being shot by standing up for her?" "Was she proud of him?" "Was such a thing

191

a reason for pride?" Or was she, perhaps, embarrassed and feeling humiliated to have been the cause of a row in the cantina?

As these questions formed, Sarah realized that they certainly would be raised by her listeners if she told the story to her friends.

Therefore, she reasoned as she came to an abrupt halt in the middle of the street in front of the cantina, it was only fair and decent to seek those answers directly from Rebecca beforehand.

Turning and hurrying toward the stable behind the El Dorado to fetch her horse, she muttered, "Yes, I must find out. I must go and visit with Rebecca."

When she passed Buck Colter's warning sign and turned into the lane toward the house where the mounting heat shimmered above the orange roof tiles and made them look as if the whole place were on fire, she thought of another question she'd like to ask Rebecca: *"What's it like to make love to Morgan?"*

Chapter Twenty-three

Atop a rise, Morgan bent a leg around the saddle horn, lit a cheroot, nodded toward the milling herd and said to Dalgo, "Look at 'em. People call 'em dumb animals and beasts. But I have to tell you, *amigo,* there are times when I envy their uncomplicated lives. It's not the animals that are dumb, Dalgo. It's us." Exhaling a sigh of smoke, he said, "It's good to be among 'em again. Good to be trailin' once more. And it's damn good to be ridin' with you again, my friend."

"Not as good as havin' you among us," said the caporal.

Barking a laugh, Morgan shot a gentle punch to Dalgo's shoulder. "You've heard about last night at the El Dorado! Forget about it. It was nothin' and it's past."

"That Bruton kid's crazy, boss. You may think it's past, but Jesse won't. He'll be wantin' revenge."

"What's he gonna do? Follow my tracks all the way to Kansas? Bushwhack me on the trail? Jump me in some dark alley up in Wichita? Or be lyin' in wait when I come back to Goliad?"

"That loco kid's known to carry a grudge."

Flipping away his cheroot, Morgan unlimbered his leg from the pommel and chuckled, "Don't be such a worry wart, Dalgo," as he touched spurs to Grulla's sides.

Slowly circling the herd, he paused for as long as it took to talk about all the things that needed addressing with each of the hands selected by Dalgo to go on the drive. Out of the hundred or so who'd taken part in the spring roundup, a dozen had been picked. All had been veterans of previous treks up the Chisholm and devoted to Novillero when he'd been trail boss and now, Morgan noted with pride as he chatted with them, they were as unreservedly dedicated to him and eager to hit the trail once more.

"We'll prob'ly head 'em out first thing tomorrow," he told them as he rolled his eyes to the fair skies, "depending on the weather." Fair like today, they'd go. If the mounting heat turned into a night of lightning storms, as well it might, they'd wait a day to let the herd settle. But by late afternoon the likelihood of tempests diminished as the wind shifted, blowing up hot and dry from Mexico.

Waving his hat and with a hoot, a holler and a grin, he rode up to Dalgo and declared, "Mañana, amigo. Have 'em up and ready to go at first light."

"Bueno, boss," grinned the caporal.

"I'll see you bright and early," Morgan said, clapping on his hat and spurring Grulla homeward.

"Hasta mañana," Dalgo shouted after him.

"I understand you had some trouble in Goliad last

194

night," asserted Rebecca as he sat down for supper.

"No trouble at all," Morgan replied with a puzzled look.

"Oh? I was led to believe there was some sort of ruckus with Jesse Bruton," she said with a smirk.

"It was nothing," he said, wondering who could have told her and then knowing instantly who the culprit was.

It had to have been Sarah Coffee who'd spilled the story. None of the others in the El Dorado would have dared, even if they were familiar enough with Rebecca to do so. Of all who'd witnessed the event, only Sarah qualified by way of personal familiarity and with a known history of being a tattletale.

"My understanding of what occurred," said Rebecca goadingly, "is that Jesse Bruton insulted me."

"Well, in fact, Rebecca, he insulted *me*, not you," he said.

"Why didn't you shoot him?"

"Hell, Rebecca, your daddy only horsewhipped him. And that was for something a damn sight worse. Besides, I did worse than horsewhip or even shoot him. I shamed him."

"It's my understanding that you bought him a drink!"

"Rebecca, stop it," he shouted. "Drop this and let me be. I've got a herd of our cattle to launch up the trail starting tomorrow, you know."

"My cattle," she snapped.

"Honestly, darling, there are times when you make me wish I'd never quit Custer's cavalry. This is one of them."

"Do not mention that man in my presence," she exploded. "You know I despise that horrid, vain,

195

peacock of a man. I truly do not understand your admiration for him when it's plain that he has been nothing but a negative influence upon you. I do not want you infecting my son with your lurid stories of your time with that awful man."

"*Our* son," he said with rising impatience. "Frankly, I can think of nobody better for Colt to emulate."

"I have told you repeatedly that I do not want you to call him that."

Impatience ignited into anger. "Honey, I don't give a damn what you want."

"You are a contemptible cur," she shouted, flinging her napkin at him, jumping to her feet and running from the room.

A part of him wanted desperately to go after her, to catch up with her, to apologize and beg her forgiveness. To hold her. To kiss her. To make things as they were. To love her again. But a core of stubbornness as weighty as lead held him down and his pride argued, "No, let her apologize. What is there that's your fault? She's the one who should be sorry."

A few moments later he saw her through the window astride her favorite dun and fleeing as if she were being chased by demons.

Chapter Twenty-four

Lifting her face into the slap of the wind and toward the last warmthless rays of the setting sun and feeling the surging power of the horse between her thighs, she cried, "Go, go, go," as she spurred the horse into a rage to reach the top of the bluffs before the impending nighttime darkness obscured all that she longed to survey—all the property that was hers.

In the near distance were the cattle Morgan and Dalgo had assembled for the drive. Stretching in every direction of the compass as far as the horizons, she could view her land and know that there was even more of it where she could not look beyond the rim of the earth and encompassing a great part of the Nueces Strip.

This was the land which the first Arbuckle Colter had wrenched unto himself. This was land his son had inherited. This was the land of the empire the second Arbuckle Colter—her father—had built, expanded, cherished, and died defending.

All this land was now hers and a treasure that must remain forever in the Colter name.

Yet her son's name was not Colter. "His name is

Morgan," she said as the excited dun pranced to the top of the bluff and pawed the ground, eager to race farther.

"Arbuckle Colter Owen Morgan," she said, stroking the horse's sweat-flecked neck. "That will never do."

She must find a way to keep the land and the ranch in the Colter name, she thought as the last vestige of sun sank out of sight and darkened her land.

But how?

Divorce?

"That would be a real scandal," she laughed as she addressed the restless dun. "Wouldn't that give the gossips of Goliad something to chew on?"

Divorce would be more than a scandal. It would be a disgrace of the family name.

Straightening in the saddle of the impatient horse, she asked, "What can I do?"

Her dilemma was how to keep the ranch and the land in the name of Colter.

That could happen only through a son.

"I *have* a son," she asserted, tightening the horse's reins around her hand. "But . . . his family name *isn't* Colter. It's Morgan!"

How might she keep the son and make his family name Colter?

"I have to find a way to get Morgan out of the way, to get him to let me have my son," she whispered, flicking the horse with the leather.

What I must do is persuade Morgan to go away, she decided as the dun flew down from the bluffs into the purple flatland. Morgan must be persuaded to leave her. Then, somehow she must make it appear that he'd abandoned her. Once he was gone she could reasonably apply for a legal change of the name of her son from Morgan to Colter.

A splendid idea, she told herself upon the speeding horse.

But would Morgan agree?

Of course he would!

Why shouldn't he go along with her plan?

If he appeared reluctant, she'd offer him lots of money. As much as he wanted.

"I have plenty of money," she asserted as the wind howled past her ears while the horse dashed through the darkness and created a counterpoint to the music of the wind with the thunderous drumbeat of its striving hooves kicking up clods of Colter earth.

"I'll do it," she laughed exultantly as the horse hurtled toward the yellow lamplight of the enticing windows of her house.

In one of them she thought she saw a flicker of movement. Morgan, probably. Waiting for her.

Now was the time to tell him her idea, she thought. Yes, she must tell him tonight, for in the morning he would be leaving for Kansas.

"Tonight, yes," she cried.

Then, in the obscuring darkness of the last hollow before the tableland where the glowing windows of her house beckoned her, the dun stepped into a hole.

Stumbling, the horse pitched like an unbroken mustang, hurling her off and forward as abruptly and ludicrously as Morgan when he'd dared to ride the unbroken mustang Dalgo had called a devil.

Like Morgan on that funny day, she slammed to earth ahead of the horse.

With a cry of pain and terror, the cartwheeling dun fell atop her with crushing weight that snapped her spine.

But by that moment she was already dead from a broken neck.

Part Four
The Morgan Brand

Chapter Twenty-five

Across the leftovers of as fine a supper as Morgan had ever tasted, his host, Shanghai Pierce, said, "You appear to have weathered the tempests in your own life and come out on smooth waters," reminding Morgan that Shanghai had been a sailor in his youth and that it was his running off to sea that had planted him, at last, on the Gulf coast of Texas where through sheer perseverance and savvy he'd come to this stage of his life—owner of El Rancho Grande, the baron of Matagorda Island, one of the richest men in the cattle business and surrounded by the trappings of that wealth in a house that was as grand as his ranch.

"If I am faring better it's thanks in large measure to you," said Morgan, sipping coffee from a blue-and-white cup the likes of which he hadn't seen since his mother last put out her finest china in honor of the visit of the family's preacher.

Shanghai snorted. "What'd I do that was so useful?"

"Nobody was kinder or more caring after Rebecca was killed than Old Shang, believe me."

"It's hard for me to believe she's gone," said Shanghai as quietly as Morgan had ever heard the gregarious giant of a man speak.

"Nearly a year."

"Can't imagine what it has to be for you, though. But what I keep remindin' myself—and you should, too—is that you've still got part of Rebecca in the boy."

"Yeah, there's a lot of her in Colt."

"As long as we're on this subject," said Shanghai, reaching into the deep breast pocket of a blue silk smoking jacket and withdrawing a pair of long black cigars, "I'm bound to say somethin' that's probably way out of line. But it needs sayin' and in the whole hist'ry of my life I've never been one to shy from sayin' what ought to be said."

"That's true," smiled Morgan as Shanghai passed him a cigar. "So fire away."

Lighting up, Shanghai said, "That boy of yours is goin' to need a woman's steadyin' hand. I know it's only been a few months since you lost Rebecca, but I'd hate to see you make the mistake Buck Colter made. 'When there's a child to be raised,' I always said to Buck, 'there needs to be a woman around.' He'd nod his head and say he agreed with me a hunert percent, but he never did get hisself another woman."

Firing his own cigar, Morgan said, "I heard Buck did have himself another woman."

"Oh, there's no question Buck dallied," said Shanghai on a plume of smoke. "But it was the marryin' that he needed, for the sake of Rebecca. If he'd gotten a wife maybe his little girl wouldn't've grown up so wild and . . . troubled."

"She was that," said Morgan sadly.

"I had high hopes you might rope her in. Now I see

that nobody ever could. So don't go blamin' yourself for anythin' that happened. Just don't make Buck's mistake. When sufficient time for mournin' has passed, you rope yourself a woman and give that son of yours some apron strings to hang onto for awhile. Not to mention some brothers and sisters to keep him company. There's nothin' quite so levelin' as siblings. It's a shame Rebecca never had any."

"There's a story I heard that she did."

"You refer to that Mexican girl in Goliad?"

"Is it true that Sarah Coffee is . . ."

"Buck's bastard child?"

"I was going to say 'daughter.' Is she?"

"Some folks say they see a strong resemblance, I never did. Maybe I didn't want to. Maybe I didn't care to admit that Buck could have had a child and not accepted it, claimed it, cared for it." Jabbing the cigar like a spear, he asked, "Has Sarah been makin' any noises about layin' any claims of inheritance to the ranch or anythin' like that?"

"Not that I know of. Do you think she might?"

"Well, Sarah might get ideas like that. After all, she's prob'ly heard the same gossip you heard and might get to thinkin' she's entitled. The thing about that, though, is that her mama wouldn't want any part of it. Migdalia's fiercely proud, so that even if she happened to be the mother of a child by Buck Colter . . . one that Buck never acknowledged . . . she'd never admit to it. So I reckon if Señorita Sarah got it into her head to make a fuss, Señora Migdalia would stomp her the way she would a Texas fire-ant!"

"You know, Dalia took care of Colt while I was trailin' last season. Frankly, I don't know what I'd've done without her. And when I got back she helped me find somebody permanent. A cousin of hers, name of Theresa, about the same age as Dalia. So far she's worked out fine cooking, keeping the house fit, tending to Colt."

"All that's good," asserted Shanghai as the cigar wobbled like the trunk of a shaky tree protruding through the thicket of his luxuriant beard, "but it's a mother the kid needs. And you a wife."

"We'll see," said Morgan with a shrug.

"Now, my boy," declared Shanghai, assuming again the booming voice that was famous everywhere from the Rio Grande to the cattle towns of Kansas and loud enough to provoke all the seabirds between El Rancho Grande and Corpus Christi and send them airborne to arch, wheel, and screech above the beaches, "if you'll step into the game room, I've got a couple of gifts for you."

Astonished, Morgan nearly spilled the last of his coffee. "Gifts? How come?"

"Well, fella," said Shanghai, thrusting the full force of his considerable size against the red-leather back of his chair, "you've had more than your share of grief lately, and I figured it was high time somebody did somethin' to lift your spirits."

"That's very generous of you, Shang, but you've already been such a consolation since Rebecca died, I just couldn't let you . . ."

"Now hold on," bellowed Shanghai with a dismissing flick of an enormous hand sporting a diamond that looked as big as an oyster shell. "You ain't even seen what I got you yet, so just hold your hosses and come on."

Following Shanghai strutting from the dining room into the vaulting chapel-like space whose walls were decked not with religious icons but dozens of taxidermied heads of wild game that were the trophies of

206

Shanghai's hunts and lined with half a dozen glass-fronted gun cases, Morgan saw the justice of this towering, raw-boned, rough-and-ready pioneer cattleman whose bootheels were adorned with huge silver spurs having been nicknamed for a rooster.

"Help yourself," said Shanghai pointing to a long oak table that stretched between a pair of sofas before the hearth.

On the table lay a gleaming mahogany pistol box with silver hinges and hasp and a walnut rifle case.

"Shang, it's beautiful," gasped Morgan as he tenderly lifted out the rifle.

"It's the Winchester Model 1873," said Shanghai. "The company's newest design, just out. This baby's the second one in Texas, mine bein' the first!"

Shouldering it, Morgan sighted between the eyes of an overlording buffalo head at the far end of the room.

"Center-fired cartridge," said Shanghai enthusiastically. "Chambers a .44 caliber bullet and 40 grains of powder. That's some stopping power, eh? Takes a 15-shot magazine. That's mighty quick-firin'. The ideal saddle gun!"

"Javelinas of Matagorda, watch out," laughed Morgan as he lovingly stroked the forged iron frame and butt plate.

"Don't forget the other," said Shanghai, jerking a finger toward the pistol box. "Also somethin' new on the market," he added, beaming with pleasure.

Opening the mahogany lid, Morgan sighed, "Jesus, that is pretty."

"The official name of it is Single Action Army," said Shanghai as Morgan grasped the walnut grip and raised the steel-blue revolver from its bed of red silk, "but Mr. Samuel Colt himself calls it the Peacemaker."

Fondling the gun, Morgan muttered, "Shang, these must've cost a pretty penny. You really shouldn't've, what with the market in cattle bein' so soft lately . . ."

"I done fine last year," blurted Shanghai. "And I expect to do good this year. The panic of last season ain't hurt me a bit. Fact is, the recent trouble is pro-b'ly a beneficial thing in the long term. Maybe the cattlemen will get themselves organized and not be at the mercy of the railroads, the buyers and the banks from now on."

"Well, you always did have a shrewd head for busi-ness," said Morgan, tenderly laying his new gun in its box. Then with a broadening grin that Shanghai hadn't witnessed in the ten months since the death of Rebecca, he said, "Therefore, if you're doing as de-cently as you claim, I accept these outstanding gifts!"

"Excellent," bellowed Shanghai. "You can start breakin' in the Winchester tomorrow, 'cause this here island is just crawlin' with your favorite game. The crafty and cunning Matagorda Island wild boars!"

"May the Good Lord protect 'em," said Morgan, peering admiringly at the gleaming Winchester rifle and longing to try it. "But not too good," he chuckled.

They were up for breakfast an hour before the crack of dawn and tracking through the shallow grass and sandy expanses of the island as the first light flaked the broad watery plain of the Gulf of Mexico on their right.

By noon they'd seen many traces of wild boar but not one in the flesh. "Ain't it just like the ugly beasts to stay out of sight," grumbled Shanghai "when we've got brand-new Winchester '73s!"

At sundown they returned to the rambling house boarless and with their rifles having been tested only on seagulls. Tricky and elusive targets, they'd provided impressive evidence of the effectiveness of the guns, seeming to explode against the pale blue sky like air-burst artillery shells, followed by a snowfall of feathers and the tumbling plummet and splash of the white birds into the turquoise water.

Slouching in a cane chair on the eastern veranda of the big house that rested like a jewel on a crown of land in the heart of El Rancho Grande and with his unbooted feet slanting into a spot of diminishing but drying sunlight, Morgan alternately sipped rye whiskey and savored a Cuban cigar. As relaxed as he'd ever been, he looked sidelong at Shanghai and said contentedly, "This is the life."

Standing and facing the Gulf but with Morgan in the corner of his eyes, Shanghai said, " 'Tis pleasant, isn't it?"

"You're a mighty rich man, Shang."

Turning slightly and puffing on his cigar, Shanghai said, "And so are you, my boy. You've got enough means to be crowned King of the Nueces Strip, that is if you'd care to declare yourself such and the government of Texas permitted it. I'd say that God, or Good Fortune or Luck or whatever you care to call it has smiled on you. With all due deference to Buck and Rebecca, may they rest in peace, I can't help but remark that you find yourself in a remarkable position. You are what age?"

"Twenty-four years."

"Twenty-four and look where you are! The sole owner of the Colter ranch! Son, there have been kings and potentates all through history who've been described as rich and powerful, yet many of those legendary figures couldn't touch you with a ten foot pole when it comes to wealth. Morgan, the world is your oyster."

"Never thought of it quite like that," said Morgan, blushing.

"Then it's time you did! That's what I mean about you givin' some thought to marryin' again. For your son, of course. But also because you've inherited a great and lasting responsibility in the form of the ranch. Until now you've been a kid on a hoot, I expect, and I'll wager you've had plenty of good times. But you've got a son now. And the ranch. And all the things that go along with bein' grown up. You're not a kid anymore, Morgan. You're a man."

After a long and thoughtful pause, Morgan cracked a smile and said, "That's darned scary stuff, Shang."

"Yeah, but I figure you'll measure up."

"As to the ranch, I'm thinkin' of changin' its name."

"Why think about it? It's yours now. Call it whatever you want."

"What I have in mind is calling it the Double M."

"Morgan and Morgan! Has a nice ring to it."

"Sure does."

With a thunderclap of his big hands, Shanghai boomed, "That's settled. Now let's eat."

"Great," cried Morgan, vaulting from his chair. "I'm starved!"

"It'll be roast beef," chuckled Shanghai, looping an arm across Morgan's shoulders as they entered the house, " 'cause you was supposed to bag us a boar and failed miserably!"

Chapter Twenty-six

Shaking out his loop, Dalgo eyed the tawny calf that he deemed worthy of the honor.

Flankers stood by to assist but he was not about to look for help when his boss was watching. And two of the boss's friends, to boot.

With a half-swing of the rope, he made his cast and yelled triumphantly, "Calf on the string!"

Quickly trussed up and thrown, the calf lay still, utterly defeated and bewildered.

"Okay, boss," Dalgo grunted, "Put your stamp on 'im."

The shaft of the iron rod in Morgan's hand was warm from the wood fire but shiny-new. "Brand new," he thought, chuckling at the pun as he pressed the iron to the rump of the calf, rocking the glowing heavy end of the iron a little for a more uniform burn that would prove deep enough to remove hair and the outer skin and leave a brand the color of saddle leather.

Lifting the iron, Morgan let what was scorched into the calf burn into his memory: **MM.**

The first of the Double **M** brand.

No matter how big this calf grew, no matter how far it might range, for as long as it lived, it would bear the mark of its owners. Morgan and Morgan. Father and son.

Handing the iron to one of the flankers while Dalgo let the insulted calf up and booted him free, Morgan proudly envisioned the thousands of long-horn cattle that soon would be bearing the Double **M**.

Clapping dust from his chaps and glancing furtively at the two men who'd been watching, Dalgo declared, "Good job, boss." Then he whispered, "You may become a vaquero yet."

Grinning, Morgan whipped off his hat and fondly slapped the caporal's rump. "Git back to work, you Mexicano fart. There's plenty more where that dogie came from."

Observing the branding approvingly from the back of a snow white horse sturdy enough to accommodate him, Shanghai Pierce shouted, "Congratulations, Morgan!"

Also witnessing the branding of the calf from a coal black horse of military bearing was a frail-looking man whose long, sallow and almost gaunt face was elongated further by chin whiskers that thrust down to nearly obscure a drooping black silk bow tie that at the same time exaggerated his thinness and drew Morgan's attention to an outfit of clothing that was the most peculiar mixture of plainsman, cowboy and military uniform that Morgan had seen since he'd last laid eyes on California Joe Milner. "Allow me to add my felicitations, sir," he said.

"Thank you, Captain McNelly," said Morgan, climbing onto Grulla, who looked like a pony and a dirt-poor relative with his plain brown saddle beside Shanghai's goliath and its gleaming black and silver-studded rigging and McNelly's cavalry-smart mount. "Now, gentlemen, how about a drink to celebrate?

Got me some excellent brandy at the house."

"You know me, Morgan," guffawed Shanghai. "Never been one to turn down drinks on the house. And neither's the cap'n, I expect."

"Indeed so," smiled McNelly.

As the horses turned from the corral where Dalgo and the flankers were rapidly roping and branding calves and scenting the air with burnt smells, Morgan turned slightly toward McNelly. "You armied for the Confederacy I'm told, Captain."

"Quite correct," said McNelly, his eyes sliding toward Shanghai quizzically, undoubtedly Morgan's source for this information.

"And now you're going to scrub the Nueces Strip clean of the Cortinistas," said Morgan.

"Well, not all by myself, of course," McNelly replied with a self-deprecating shrug that Morgan was pleased to see. "I'll have the help of the Special Battalion of the Texas Rangers." After a lengthy pause, he added, "And you, I trust."

Morgan barked a laugh. "Me?"

"Well, I heard you've had some experience."

With his questioning eyes sliding now in the direction of Shanghai, Morgan muttered, "I hope what you were told wasn't embroidered."

"A successful raid in which many of the outlaws were killed hardly needs embroidering, I think," said McNelly.

The brandy Morgan poured generously into two-handed snifters had been Buck Colter's, the graceful glasses a wedding gift to Morgan and Rebecca from Shanghai.

"Let there be no false modesty about what you, the late Mr. Colter, Mr. Pierce, and the others did in attacking the Flores gang," said McNelly. "It was a singularly brave and audacious act that stands out in

213

contrast to the attitude I've encountered from many ranchers. The ones I've visited lately don't have nerve enough to take an active, decided stand, either by giving information or personal assistance."

"Well, I can't rightly blame them," said Morgan. "It's been the history of the region that when any man, Mexican or American, has made himself prominent in hunting down the raiders, he's been forced to move from his ranch or been killed. And many of them believe that it's the job of the government to put an end to the lawlessness. It is from Mexico that they come. So why doesn't the army clean 'em out?"

Swirling his brandy, McNelly replied, "The government fears another war with Mexico. That's it in a nutshell."

"Don't see how these bandits can be wiped out unless somebody goes after 'em where they hole up," said Morgan.

"Exactly," said McNelly as he lifted his snifter to his lips.

"Do I take that to mean you and your Rangers are prepared to cross the river?"

Setting aside his brandy and loosely linking his long fingers, McNelly leaned urgently toward Morgan. "What I am about to say must not go beyond this room. Understood?"

"Of course," said Morgan with a nod.

"I intend to ignore orders and go after the bastards and hit them hard."

Morgan lurched forward. "Great! I'll go with you!"

"I admire your bravery and patriotic fervor, sir, but I'm afraid I couldn't permit that."

Jerking back, Morgan exclaimed, "Why the hell not?"

"You're a man with responsibilities, among them a young son, I believe. No, you can't go with us to

Mexico."

"If that's the case what in tarnation are you talkin' to me for?"

"I have a pair of purposes. First, I've come to seek the hospitality of your ranch for my Rangers. We'll be needing a staging area and, as much of your land is ideally situated for that purpose . . ."

"Certainly, your Rangers are welcome on the Double **M**, Captain."

"There is also that matter of provisions."

"No problem. I'd sooner give your Rangers my cattle than have them stolen by the Cortinistas."

"Thank you."

"And what was your second purpose in visiting me?"

"I understand from Shanghai that you've had a good deal of experience as a scout and tracker with Custer's Seventh Cavalry. Because of that, combined with your familiarity with your land between the Nueces and the Rio Grande, I'd like to ask you to volunteer as a scout for our little mission."

"It's a deal."

"But you must understand that you'll not be riding with us across the river."

"Captain McNelly, I'll do whatever you ask if it'll help you to put an end to the Cortinistas."

"You're a true Texan, sir."

"Transplanted."

Raising his brandy, McNelly smiled, "Aren't we all?"

Chapter Twenty-seven

At four in the morning on Friday, November 19, 1875 while he stood beside the horse named Strawberry and gazed at a waning moon above the bluffs of the Rio Grande, Morgan was silent as thirty Texas Rangers gathered their horses from the cattle corral of a Double **M** range camp five miles from the river. They'd been camped for two days and three nights. Now they were listening intently while Captain McNelly described what awaited them in Mexico. "The layout's been thoroughly reconnoitered," the slender, bearded figure in his half-civilian, half-soldierly clothes was saying from the saddle of his coal-black military-minded horse. In a rasping voice broken by coughs, he continued, "What we know is that the Cortinistas' hideout is in a bottle-neck canyon three miles the other side of the river. The trail going into their lair is picketed in with high posts set in the ground with bars for a gate. We will march single file, as the trail is not wide enough for you to go in twos. An advance party on foot will let the bars down. At that point, we all head in. We hit 'em at daylight when they're still asleep.

Sensing the encroaching ghosts of cavalry raids on slumbering Indian villages at the Platte and the

216

Washita, Morgan shuddered as he watched the Rangers mount and ride out in a column of twos.

Seeing the shiver, Shanghai Pierce whispered, "Feelin' the cold?"

"A bit," said Morgan, lifting the fur collar of his hide jacket to validate the lie. As brisk as the morning was, it was not the temperature that chilled him but what he knew to be the true nature of the mission of the Rangers.

"I have no authorization for this raid," Captain McNelly had revealed to Morgan and Shanghai Pierce in the firelight of a range shack only moments before he rode into the corral to address his men. "You might even say that I have orders to the contrary," he went on, adding with a frown, "There's a good chance I could be hanged for all this. That is, if I get out of Mexico with my skin intact."

As startled as Morgan, Shanghai bellowed, "What the devil are you sayin'?"

"Well, you see, when I first talked with the U.S. Government officials at Fort Brown about the Rangers moving against the bandits, I was given assurances that United States forces would go with us. But somewhere up the chain of command things got fouled up. Delayed. Maybe it was just the way things work in the government. Or maybe somebody just decided to scuttle the enterprise. The upshot was no action. Nobody said, 'Very good, McNelly. Go in and hit 'em hard and we'll be with you.' So I just decided the hell with it and told the army that I was going in anyway. I informed them that I would raid the hideout, take up a defensive position and wait for the troops to come over and extricate us. I told them flat out that none of us could get back alive without the aid of the troops."

"But that's madness," gasped Morgan. "A suicide mission."

"The army will come," McNelly retorted smugly.

"It's crazy," muttered Morgan as the last pair of Rangers topped a small rise and rocked out of sight behind it. "Nothing in all my experience in the cavalry comes anywhere near it for foolhardiness. If I'd've known this when McNelly first asked for my assistance, I wouldn't've gone along with it."

"Which is prob'ly why he didn't tell you then," said Shanghai with a mischievous smile. "And why he made it plain at the outset that you couldn't go along across the river, though it was obvious from the look in your eyes at the time that you hungered to."

Staring at the spot where he'd watched the last of the Rangers dip out of view, Morgan shook his head in dismay. "They'll never make it back, you know. And Captain McNelly will go down in Texas history in disgrace and ignominy."

"That may prove true," said Shanghai, stroking his beard, "but if he pulls it off, he'll be so big a hero that even Texas might not be able to contain him. Why, if this works, Captain Lee H. McNelly of the Rangers could turn out to be as glorious in the mem'ry of Texans as the defenders of the Alamo."

Two years later Morgan would admit that Shanghai's view was the one that was bound to prevail when it came time for someone to write McNelly's story.

Asked to speak at the funeral of McNelly, dead at the age of 33 of consumption, Morgan noted that in the short span of time since his raid into Mexico

McNelly already had become a hero.

"But only by the skin of his teeth," Morgan insisted as he spoke at McNelly's grave.

Truth and fairness demanded that he relate how close the Rangers had come to disaster. First of all, he pointed out, they'd attacked the wrong spot, hitting the peaceful settlement of Las Curchas a mile away from their target of Las Cuevas. "They'd lost the element of surprise." Then at Las Cuevas they'd found themselves outnumbered 250-to-30 and had had to retreat to the river. "They got out by the skin of their teeth," he said, looking down into McNelly's grave. "But it's fair to say that a good deal of history has been skin-of-the-teeth stuff," he continued, looking up. "What Captain McNelly did was downright crazy. I'll never say the contrary. But what he did taught the Cortinistas a lesson, for after that mad attack by McNelly's Rangers those Mexican bandits have realized they are no longer safe behind the Rio Grande. They know that they will be pursued and punished. Therefore, they've reduced their desire to cross the border lookin' to swipe Texas cattle and pretty much have stayed on their side of the Rio Grande." Raising a salute, he concluded, "So here's to you, Captain McNelly, from all the grateful ranchers of the Nueces Strip."

Chapter Twenty-eight

March 1876 in Goliad came in on a note of sharp violence, dark tragedy and high drama.

It started on the third, a Friday night, when Jesse Bruton swaggered into the El Dorado already drunk and promptly insisted on harassing Jasper Fulcord, goading the grizzly old loner about cheating at cards. Had this poking come from Morgan, everybody agreed later, Jasper would have taken it in stride.

Whether Morgan was the reason for Jesse turning on Jasper on that particular night would be the bone of considerable contention in the days that followed, but those who recalled the previous incident which had involved Jasper and Morgan and a slur on Rebecca leading to the humiliation of Jesse were convinced that Jesse had come in boozed up and hungering for revenge.

Expecting to find Morgan at the cantina as usual on a Friday night, he found only Jasper and picked on him instead. "You got the ugliest face and crookedest hand in Texas," he needled from the bar. Striding to the back of the room, he went on tormentingly, "You never dealt honest poker in your stinkin' life." Looming above the old man, he sneered, "A card sharp, that's what you are." Ripping the worthless hand of cards Jasper was holding, he mumbled, "You snake, you never took a card from the top of the deck in your whole miserable existence."

Then, impressing the onlookers with the clue that Jesse was really thirsting for Morgan's blood, he snarled, "You're just a crooked licker of Yankee boots, ain'tcha?"

At last, the old man asserted, "Leave me be, boy."

Snorting and flinging down all the cards, Jesse snapped, "Don't call me a boy, you old coot."

Bridling, Jasper grumbled, "Don't you talk to me that way!"

Silent as a graveyard, the El Dorado waited.

Giving Jasper's chair a kick, Jesse laughed, "And just what are you goin' to do about it, coot?"

In the quiet as Jasper calmly gathered up the strewn deck, his reply carried to every pair of ears. "Guess I'll have to turn you on my knee and spank the livin' daylights outta yuh."

The cantina erupted in hoots and laughs.

Witnessing all of this from behind the bar, Sarah Coffee did not join the hilarity. Instead, she was seized with fear as Jesse Bruton's shamed eyes narrowed to slits and his hand dipped to his gun. "Jesse, don't," she screamed — too late.

He fired once, point-blank and dead center into Jasper's chest, then twice more as warning shots into the ceiling while he scrambled to escape through terrified customers who weren't about to try to stop him as they dove for cover, overturning chairs and upsetting tables.

Less than half an hour later a posse roared out of town with lynching in mind, but when it came to knowing the wild country to the west of the San Antonio there'd never been anybody to beat Jesse Bruton. There, in the Spanish dagger thickets, cactus

221

and brush he knew so well he vanished in the direction of Atascosa County and, presumably, beyond to Frio and Dimmit and then into Mexico, legendary haven of outlaws.

At the burial of Jasper Fulcord, Morgan spoke a line from Shakespeare's *Julius Caesar,* "O judgment! thou art fled to brutish beasts, and men have lost their reason."

Ordinarily, such excitement would have kept the people of Goliad buzzing for months, but two weeks after Jesse Bruton's trail went cold, Goliad forgot all about him in the explosion of a grand commemoration of the 40th anniversary of the Goliad Declaration of Independence and the martyrdom of the heroes of Goliad. Being recalled were executions on March 26, 1836 of 417 of the rebels who had battled General Urrea's Mexican forces in a series of engagements following the first proclamation of Texas Independence issued at Goliad the previous December, one of Rebecca Colter's ancestors counted among them.

Although Sarah Coffee considered herself Mexican, she nonetheless looked forward excitedly to the festivities, primarily because the schedule of events was to climax in an entertainment on Saturday night in the town plaza where she had been invited to sing, followed by a dance that the organizers of the event promised would last until the ringing of the Mission La Bahia bells for the first mass on Sunday morning.

When it came to the dancing, Sarah had decided, Morgan was going to be her partner. That he'd attend was never a doubt in her mind. There were three causes for him to be there, she reasoned. First was his obligation as the inheritor of the Colter ranch to demonstrate that he appreciated that much of Goliad's prosperity depended on the ranch and, therefore, on him. More significant to her, however, was her reckoning that the passing of sufficient time would allow him to emerge from mourning Rebecca. And because she knew him to be a young man brimming with all the normal needs and desires, she was certain that by now he must be longing for some fun and itching to break loose.

She had picked out the song she was going to sing before the dance and practiced it over and over.

'Neath the yellow moon
   We would meet and part too soon,
We'd converse in tones so low
   So the *madre* wouldn't know.
Oft I kissed his lips so tender,
   Little stars blinked on in wonder,
While the gentle breeze would moan,
   "Mi amor, mi corazón."

As the town racketed with the hammering and sawing of wood for a dance platform rather than the gallows most of the folks of Goliad had wished they'd observe being built for the hanging of Jesse Bruton, Sarah sauntered through the plaza during her morning walks, letting her mind construct vivid fantasies of dancing with Morgan. So sharply honed were these imaginings that she already felt the warm gusts of his breath and the prickle of his whiskers as his cheek brushed hers, the squeeze of his arms around her, the pressing of him against her, the sway of his body, the thrust of it.

Oblivious to the noise and lost in her dreaming, she sang to herself, *"Mi amor, mi corazón,"* and when the night of the dance arrived at last there he was wearing a linen duster coat and riding his favorite strawberry roan into Goliad at the head of what looked like a cavalry troop of Double **M** ranch cowboys all duded up.

At the edge of the dance floor, he looked nervous in a brown suit with a frock coat, the first she'd ever seen him wear, and new brown boots and Dakota hat, so spiffed up and shiny that she could not take her eyes off his handsome face streaked by the yellow and red light glowing from the pretty paper lanterns strung like a sky above the dance floor. When she sang, *"Mi amor, mi corazón,"* directly at him, he blushed so much that even the light from the lanterns couldn't hide it.

Square dancing was next and she bounded toward him, hooking her arm around him and claiming him.

Soon the floor was shaking beneath stomping boots that thundered like downpouring rain as the caller twanged,

"Whet up your axe and whistle up your dog,
Whet up your axe and whistle up your dog,
We're off to the woods to hunt ground hog."

"Oh, this is so much fun," she cried as she whirled into Morgan's arms. Spun out of them, she kept her eyes turned to him. Back in his embrace at the end of the dance and smiling into his sweat-beaded face, she looped an arm around his waist under his coat and felt his heat through his damp shirt.

Two more spritely dances followed before the winded dancers were allowed to rest.

Shanghai Pierce had come from Matagorda decked out in finery and glittery jewelry and now he was singing in a voice more raspy than lovely but sweeter than anyone expected.

"Come all you Missouri gals, and listen to my noise,

224

Don't you go trust those Texian boys,
'Cause if you do, your fortune will be
Johnny-cake and venison and sassafras tea.
When they come courtin' I'll tell you what they
wear,
An old leather coat all patched and bare."

"You've got a fine suit," Sarah whispered, stroking
Morgan's sleeve.

When Shanghai ended his song, the dance music
began again, this time a waltz.

"I'm no good at this, Sarah," objected Morgan.

Tugging him to the center of the tremulous floor
amidst the swirling of the long colorful skirts of grace-
fully gliding women, she laughed, "C'mon, it's easy."

Reluctantly he followed her lead and promptly discovered as his legs became lost in the billows of her
red dress that he had a knack for the waltz, the prettiest of dances, he'd always thought, although his
mother had disdained all dancing as un-Christian.

When the music stopped and a Mexican boy Sarah
knew from the cantina stepped up and shyly asked for
the next dance, she was curt. "I've promised all the
dances to my partner."

Surprised but flattered, Morgan said, "Possessive
creature, ain't you?"

Looking as hurt as a chastised puppy, she muttered, "Of course if you don't want to dance all the
dances with me . . ."

"Of course I do," he laughed, grabbing her.

He'd arrived in dread of being invited to dance,
having been warned by Dalgo to expect that single
women and girls he barely knew would be swarming
to get near to the rich young widower daring his first
public appearance since the loss of his wife. "The
maidens of Goliad are goin' to be lickin' their chops

and inspectin' you like an eagle-eyed Cheyenne Indian itchin' to hang a new scalp on his belt," the caporal had declared, only half teasingly. But now, thanks to Sarah claiming him, Morgan felt relaxed and exhilarated and welcomed as many dances as the band had to offer and Sarah wished to have.

In interludes he helped himself to a viciously spiked fruit punch sloshing in a huge crystal bowl at the side of the dance floor as the platform trembled with the impatient stomp of the waiting dancers, and while he drank he chatted with as many well-wishers and condolence-offering Goliadans who cared to approach him.

Because so many approached and because they seemed so genuine toward him, for the first time since he'd come to Texas, he felt that he could rightly call himself one of them.

This parade of people to his side did not pass unnoticed by Shanghai Pierce. "You seem to be the man of the hour," he said, sidling up to Morgan in a lull between dancing in which Sarah had excused herself for the moment to greet her mother, arriving late after finally closing the El Dorado with the realization that there would be few paying customers at the cantina when there was so much free liquor at the celebration.

"It's a nice party," said Morgan to Shanghai, "considering that it marks a massacre."

"It's freedom that these folks is hurrahin', my boy. The freedom of Texas, for which a blow was struck right here."

Rising on the lift of several glasses of the punch, Morgan smiled lopsidedly and slapped Shanghai in the back. "Well put, as usual, Shang!"

"It's a day of freedom for you, too," Shanghai said, measuring Morgan to see how drunk he might be and welcoming it as a mark of healing. "Your first venture out since . . ."

Tipsy, Morgan said, "Say it, Shang. Shince Rebecca died."

"That's an encouragin' sign, Morgan. When you can say it, you're on your way back. Only go easy on that punch."

"I'm doin' fine, my friend. And I'm just about set for headin' out a fresh herd to Kansas. Six thousand head. Leavin' in a few days."

"Where to this year?"

"Dodge City seems to be the new spot. What about you?"

"I'll be sendin' a herd but not goin' myself," said Shanghai as his eyes drifted toward Sarah threading her way through the crowd. "Pardon me for sayin' this, Morg," he said nodding toward her, "but for a moment there I thought that was Rebecca. I haven't seen Sarah Coffee for awhile. I told you I never found any resemblance to her and Rebecca, but tonight I have to admit the similarity is strikin'."

"In some ways, yes," said Morgan guardedly. "But in lots of other ways, no."

"Mr. Pierce," exclaimed Sarah as she came up to them, "I had no idea you could sing so good!"

"That's very nice of you to say, my dear," he said "but the truth of it is, what I lack in talent I make up with sheer gumption."

"I hope you sing again," she said as the band tuned its instruments in preparation for resuming the dancing.

"May I have this one, young lady?" said Morgan, opening his arms to her.

"No," Sarah declared, turning to Shanghai, who towered above her. "You've had too much to drink. You need to rest. I'll have this one with Mr. Pierce."

227

When they returned from a waltz in which their grace in one another's arms overshadowed the difference in their heights, Morgan clapped his hands. "Was it as delightful for you two as it was for me watching?"

"My dear boy," guffawed Shanghai as he placed Sarah's tiny hand in Morgan's as delicately as he might place a flower, "all she did was talk about *you!*"

Twanging his fiddle, the leader of the band announced, "Choose your podners for *Ducks in the River,*" and a moment later his and four other fiddles were sawing as he called,

"Ducks in the river, goin' to the ford,
Coffee in a little rag, sugar in a gourd."

During the next dance, slow enough for holding, Morgan was more keenly aware of Sarah than in previous dances. Of the smell of her hair; a sweet scent of prairie flowers. Of her closeness. Of her sliding against him. Of her softness. And of her being a woman in his arms now and not the fresh girl teasing him from behind the bar at the Eldorado.

Dancing with her, he began to wonder if there might have been more to her than the teasing. And as he thought about that goading girl in the cantina and this spirited woman in his arms, he suddenly felt weak in the knees and light in the head. Was it the punch, he wondered, or the effects of her that he was experiencing? What was happening here? What was going on? How come she wanted to dance only with him?

The question popped from his mouth. "Sarah, why'd you only want to dance with me?"

Suddenly as taut as rawhide in his arms, she did not answer.

"C'mon, Sarah," he insisted, "tell me how come."

"Well, you are the handsomest fella here," she said, an intended joke from the old tease, though true.

Pouting, he said, "What's the real reason? On account of feelin' sorry for me, the pinin' widower?"

Lurching hard against him with hip and thigh, she sighed, "Don't be silly."

"If that's silly, tell me somethin' that isn't."

"Such as?"

"That maybe you, uh, like me?"

"Sure I like you," she said, trembling slightly against him.

Drawing her closer, he suddenly appreciated what this night was about. Holding her and feeling her quiver in his embrace, he understood what had been going on since he'd arrived. Why she'd claimed him for every dance. She wanted him! Knowing it, he now wanted her. Desperately. With a need and hunger that was frighteningly real and fresh to him, he desired her.

"That was a darn pretty song you sang, you know," he whispered. "Specially the part that went, *'Mi amor, mi corazón.'* That's Spanish, you know. You see, I happen to understand a little Spanish. Those words mean, 'My love, my heart.' "

"Si, señor," she said mockingly. "I know you know Spanish. *Yo entenderé.*"

"So how come you were singin' those words direct to me?"

"Was I?"

"It sure seemed that way to me."

Suddenly it was an interlude again and Shanghai was bellowing,

"Oh brandy is brandy any way you mix it,
But a Texian is a Texian any way you fix it.

229

When other folks have all gone to bed
The Devil is a-workin' in the Texian's head."

Rising on her toes, Sarah whispered in Morgan's ear. "And what's in that Texian head of yours?"

Suddenly tangling his fingers in hers, Morgan blurted, "Honey, let's you and me get the hell out of here and go off by ourselves."

"But what about the dancin'?"

"Hang the dancin'."

"But where to?"

"Out to the Double **M**, of course," he said urgently. "Out to . . . my . . . place."

Chapter Twenty-nine

Astride the 100th meridian and on the Arkansas River five miles west of the military post of Fort Dodge, Buffalo City had been nothing more than a small whiskey peddler's camp and buffalo hunters' trading spot consisting of a handful of sod huts until the officers of the Atchison, Topeka and Santa Fe Railroad found themselves pressed by circumstances to look for a new cattle shipping site.

Animated by the choking off of the Chisholm Trail by rural settlement and impending extensions of Kansas cattle quarantine laws, they sought a more western location to erect a new cattle center wholly free from the difficulties being encountered elsewhere. "The country about Wichita is becoming so well settled," they'd reported to the railway's stockholders in 1874, "that the tendency will be to drive more cattle to the Great Bend of the Arkansas; and it may be necessary, the coming season, to prepare a point of shipment still farther west in a site where the citizens are full of that vim and pluck that knows no such word as fail and who appear determined through their genuine energy and enterprise to make their town the leading city of Western Kansas."

Thus was Dodge City put on the map along with a

pledge that its citizens would adopt wholesome measures whereby the cattlemen could be treated upon general principles of equity and reciprocity. Trustworthy men would be in readiness to assist the Texans in finding the best pasturage, where water and other amenities could be found. The town's businessmen would reduce the prices of liquors, cigars and tobacco, they promised, for the especial trade of the cattlemen. Reductions would be made in prices generally. Accommodations for a large influx of Texans would be made by the hotels and restaurants. All with a view to the adage of "live and let live."

Morgan arrived at Dodge in the second week of July 1876 at the point of a herd of six thousand bearing the **MM** brand.

Not surprisingly, along with the Green Front, the Junction, the Old Horse, the Alhambra, the Opera House, and the Long Branch saloons south of the railroad tracks, he discovered beneath a yellow-and-red sign the emerald-green batwings of Long Charlie Carew's traveling drink emporium. Called the Old Dodge, it was the latest incarnation of the same saloon Charlie had operated in Abilene, Newton, and Wichita.

"Still workin' your way west, I see," said Morgan, hooking his right boot heel on the same brass rail at the front end of the long bar he'd propped his foot on in all those cow towns.

Looking up from polishing the far end of the bar, Charlie laughed, "Well, look what the wind blew in," and dashed forward.

Beaming, Morgan said, "How the hell are you, Charlie?"

"I'm good. Damned good. And you?"

"Thrivin' but parched."

"Rye whiskey?"

"Got any mescal?"

Reaching for a full bottle of it from the shelf behind the bar, Charlie said, "I forgot you'd gone Texas."

Watching the pouring, Morgan said, "So what's new?"

Jerking upright, Charlie blurted, "You ain't heard?"

Blankly, Morgan said, "Heard what?"

"About Custer!"

"What about him?"

Resuming the pouring Charlie muttered, "He's dead."

"Dead?"

"Massacred by redskins."

With a shaking hand Morgan lifted the mescal and gulped it. "Holy Jesus."

"Someplace up in the Montana Territory," said Charlie, refilling Morgan's glass. "It happened a couple a Sundays ago. On June twenty-fifth, I think. Word is he and six or seven hundred of his men were on their way to destroy a band of trouble-makin' redskins along a stream called the Little Big Horn and was ambushed."

"They wiped out the entire Seventh?"

"About a third, looks like," said Charlie grimly as Morgan downed the second mescal.

Closing his eyes and imagining the horror, Morgan whispered, "So that's the last we'll hear *Garry Owen in Glory.*"

"Huh?"

"Nothin'."

"Needless to say, Morg, the news has put the whole frontier on edge. There's been a sizeable Indian scare since the word came in with the mail hack a few days ago."

"I wonder if old California Joe was with them."

Grinning, Charlie said, "He wasn't."

"How do you know?"

"The old coon drifted through here not long ago on his way east, not north. He said he was headin' for Nebraska. Weren't your ears burnin'? They shoulda been 'cause Joe and I spent practically a whole night swappin' yarns about you. When you're bein' talked about your ears burn. Yours didn't?"

"Not so as I noticed."

"Well we sure gabbed at length about you."

"How was the old fart?"

"Full of piss and vinegar as usual."

Morgan laughed. "That's what he used to say about himself. The first day I laid eyes on him, he said to me, 'I mix my whiskey with tarantulas and vinegaroons for flavor and add wolf's piss and rat poison for bite.'"

"Sounds like a recipe for this stuff," cackled Charlie, pouring mescal again.

"I learned a lot from old Joe," said Morgan fondly, toying with the glass. "And plenty from Custer."

"Whatever they taught you appears to have served you well."

"What they taught me," Morgan said, raising the mescal to his lips, "was the most important thing a young man needed to know on the frontier. How to survive. Because of them I survived long enough to learn the next lesson."

"That being?"

"What's worth livin' *for*."

"Maybe you could let me know what that is sometime," said Charlie, wiping away the little wet circles Morgan's glass had left on the bar.

"I can't speak for you, Charlie, but for me, what's worth livin' for can be said in a name: Colt."

With a look of puzzled amazement, Charlie blurted, "Your gun?"

"For cripes sake, no," groaned Morgan. "Colt is my son. Colter Morgan! My kid!"

"You've got a kid?"

"Goin' on four years."

"Well, hoot and holler, Morg, that's terrific."

"You should see him. He's somethin'."

"To think I knew you when you was still wet behind the ears and here you are a papa. I guess before long he'll be ridin' the trail with you and tearin' up cow towns like this one."

"Oh no, my friend. Colt's goin' to get the best. He's goin' to grow up right. There'll be no cow college for him. Colt will go to a real college. He's goin' to get the education I never did."

"You allus seemed mighty educated to me, Morg. Allus recitin' Shakespeare! I was allus mighty impressed by that."

"My son is goin' to learn to survive with his brains," said Morgan as his hand drifted to Shanghai Pierce's gift, "not with a gun. The reputation he'll have will spring from him havin' an upright and righteous character." Resting his hand on the butt on the Colt Peacemaker, he went on, "It won't come from his fast draw and the number of men he's gunned down."

"Now hold on, Morgan. I think you're bein' unfair to yourself. You never gunned anybody who wasn't tryin' to gun you first and that didn't deserve it."

In the instant needed for Charlie to pour another mescal, Morgan's mind raced back, summoning the faces of those who'd died since his army boots had hit the planks of the docks of the Kansas City riverfront. A peaceable Kaw Indian named Daniel Lonetree who'd died in the raid on a Cheyenne village by the Platte because he was wearing cavalry blue. A kid at

Fort Riley named Mickey Ludlum who held a dream of going to California with his barracks buddy Morgan but died in a bloody ravine because a green lieutenant named Gordon had been suckered into a trap. How many red Indians? A woman-beater by the name of Walters in a saloon in Junction City. The Dowd brothers in an Abilene alley and all the too-slow six-shooting fools and cocky owlhoots who'd dreamed of making a rep by burying the kid the newspapers called the Gunman of Abilene. Grudge-carrying John Redus. Buck Colter and the scurvy bandits who'd killed him. A cattle thief who'd died in the shrinking agony of being wrapped in rawhide and left in the sun by Novillero. The Anderson boy, who wanted to live life fast but was too slow to survive one minute inside Perry Tuttle's Dance Hall and Saloon in Newton. Major Ward Kimball, a victim of George Armstrong Custer's mistake in the valley of the Washita.

Now, Custer himself was dead up in Montana where, Morgan would have bet, he'd probably followed his usual tactics of dividing his forces and ridden blithely into disaster at the Little Big Horn, wherever that was.

Then there was Rebecca, the most heart-breaking death of all.

As Charlie Carew's steady hand filled Morgan's glass to the top, Morgan looked at his old friend through eyes that were just as brimming and said, "I've had my fill of people I know dying."

Over the next week while Morgan sold off the herd, two trains arrived at Dodge City bringing newspapers filled with the slowly emerging details of Custer's defeat. Among them was his friend Henry

Kidder's Abilene *Herald* with an editorial under the banner headline:

CUSTER'S LAST STAND.

Settling into a cane chair on the gallery of his hotel, Morgan read:

The tragedy that befell Custer and his soldiers at the Little Big Horn in the Montana Territory clearly demonstrates the cruel fact that the conduct of the U.S. Government toward the Indians of the Plains has not been very kindly nor wise.

The history of our dealings with these Indian tribes from the very beginning is a record of fraud, and perjury, and uninterrupted injustice. We have made treaties, binding ourselves to the most solemn promises in the name of God, intending at that very time to hold these treaties as light as air whenever our convenience should require them to be broken.

To any student of this lamentable story it must now seem inevitable that there will soon be an outcry from the populace demanding that these Indians be driven backward to death or to yet more distant and barren reservations.

As this transpires, many will rise to proclaim that Custer's death was not in vain.

What a calamity it will be for the entire nation if this vain, egotistical and cruel man is enshrined in the pantheon of genuine American heroism.

Uttering a bitter laugh and tossing aside the paper, Morgan muttered, "Hank never did think much of Custer."

Moments later as he rode Grulla across the railroad tracks that separated the respectable part of town from Dodge City's version of the Abilene's Devil's Half Acre, Newton's Hide Park and Wichita's Delano, he paused to turn and read a sign that greeted anyone going the other way:

DEADLINE!
Persons Intending
To Discharge Firearms
Are Not Allowed
North Of This Sign.
Violators Will Be Arrested
Larry Deger, City Marshal

Lightly fingering his Peacemaker, Morgan chuckled, "Grulla, this fella Deger sounds tough."

Any anger over the massacre or mourning for Custer and the dead of the Seventh Cavalry that citizens, businessmen, and cowboys may have been feeling did not dim the excitement of roiling and raucus Front Street, Morgan discovered as he dismounted at Charlie's Old Dodge Saloon.

With the warning sign still on his mind he said to Charlie, "This Marshal Deger sounds like a hard case."

"Deger's nothin' but a figurehead," said Charlie disdainfully. "The real law in Dodge is Wyatt Earp, the assistant city marshal. And backin' him up is a deputy, name of Jim Masterson." Snorting a laugh, he said, "Why's it matter? You plannin' on shootin' up the town?"

"Those days are done for me, pal."

"I reckon Earp and Masterson will be glad to hear that."

Scoffingly, Morgan said, "They wouldn't know me

from a prairie dog hole."

"Don't be so sure. The name Morgan's still respected in Kansas."

"Even so, I'll be pullin' out tomorrow."

Setting up a mescal, Charlie cracked, "Hightailin' it back to the arms of the little woman, eh?"

With a pang of regret for Rebecca and a twinge of guilt concerning Sarah Coffee, Morgan said, "My wife's dead, Charlie."

"Oh geez, Morgan," groaned Charlie. "I'm sorry, I didn't know."

"How could you know? I'm the one should be apologizin'. I should've told you when I was in earlier."

"Well, at least you've got your kid to go home to."

Breaking into a grin that lit up Charlie's saloon as only his ever could, in Charlie's estimation, Morgan said, "Yeah, I've always got Colt to go back to!"

Chapter Thirty

With one quick fist banged on the rough plank door, Dalgo barged in. "Boss, looks like a *problema* comin' up the lane."

It was a sultry Sunday afternoon late in August four days after their return from Dodge City and Morgan was kicked back in his desk chair with his feet crossed at the ankles and his spurless boots resting on a half-open drawer of a tall oak file cabinet in the converted tack room that had been Novillero's office when he ran the ranch for Buck Colter and which Morgan had continued to use for that purpose. He'd been leafing lackadaisically through a sheaf of feed and lumber invoices and checking them against ledgers to see if they'd been paid. In the process he'd been struggling to keep from dozing off. Now he was wide awake. *"Que problema, amigo?"*

"Two-legged, wearin' a skirt."

Swinging his feet to the floor, Morgan sighed, "Dalgo, you've got a twisted outlook."

"Yes, boss."

Tossing the invoices on the desk, Morgan took on the tone of a chiding schoolmarm. "Just 'cause a female of the species is comin' up the lane it doesn't have to spell trouble."

"*Sí, señor,*" said Dalgo in mock apology.

Standing and tucking his sweat dampened shirttail into his Levis, Morgan asked, "Who is it?"

"A Mexican songbird," the caporal responded with a smirk.

Lurching to a yellowed tobacco-smoked and dirt-streaked window, Morgan saw Sarah Coffee on a piebald pony turning from the lane toward the office. "What the hell's she doin' here?"

With the smacking of puckered lips and a raspy singsong'd "*Mi amor, mi corazón,*" Dalgo ducked out, then was heard on the other side of the door dripping sweet politeness. "*Buenos días, señorita! Bienvenido al rancho* Double **M.** How nice to see you."

Emerging squinting out of the soft half-light of the cool office into the blunt shock of the glare of daylight as Dalgo scurried away, Morgan blared, "Howdy, Sarah."

"You've been back from Kansas four days," she said witheringly. "How come you didn't come see me?"

Rearing back as if he'd been slapped, Morgan leaned against the office door and waited for his eyes to adjust and then he saw her clearly in her enticing white blouse and red skirt flowing over the black-and-white pony. "I haven't been in touch with anybody since I got back."

"Is that so," she said, jumping off the horse. "Well, I sort of reckoned I was more than just anybody . . . considerin'."

"Considerin'?"

Glancing furtively around them, she whispered, "Considerin' what happened the night of the dance."

A smile curled up the corners of his mouth and he quickly lifted a hand as if to smooth his sparse cornsilk mustache, a fruitless effort to try to conceal the tell-tale evidence of a pleasantly stirred lewd memory of that

241

night. "Well, now, Sarah," he alibi'd from behind the shielding fingers, "what happened was that I got a little drunk and . . ."

Cutting him off, she lashed out like a bullwhacker. "Don't you say you got so drunk you didn't know what you were doin'!"

Staggered, he stammered, "Of . . . of . . . c-c-course I knew, but . . ."

"And not so drunk you didn't enjoy it," she cut in, pawing the ground with the pointed toe of a scuffed black boot and gouging a slash in the gravel that recalled his drawing such a dare-line in schoolyard dirt a lifetime ago in Pennsylvania; "Step across that line and get your block knocked off!"

"Hell, yes, I enjoyed what we did that night," he said, gingerly, drawing close to the line she'd carved between them as surely as the one she'd made on the ground. "But so did you," he said, crossing over daringly. "Didn't you? Admit it."

Now she was knocked off balance, abruptly looking down and leaving him wondering if her turning her eyes away was because of shame and starting to feel sorry for her. But then she looked up as abruptly as she'd glanced away, drilling her dark eyes into him defiantly. "Sure I liked it!"

Sensing a turn but not sure to whose favor, he pressed on hopefully. "And as long as you're bein' honest today, you have to admit that you were after me that night as much as I was hungerin' for you. Singin' that song straight at me. *'Mi amor, mi corazón.'* Then latchin' onto me. Claimin' every dance."

Limply, she sighed, "I'll not lie to you. I did all that."

"So the fact is we both knew what we were doin'," he crowed triumphantly, "and we both got a kick out of it." Feeling victorious only a moment, he was overwhelmed with a need to turn gentler. "But it was just that night,

Sarah," he said cautiously. "It didn't mean anythin' beyond that night." Having made that clear, he thought what was required now was firmness and a bit of chastisement. "So, if that's the case, I don't see why you're here all of a sudden and jumpin' on my back about me not comin' to see you the minute I got back from the drive. Like I said, I haven't seen any . . . uh, folks. There hasn't been time. No offense intended. But you've got to get it clear in your head that what happened that night was just that night and it doesn't mean either of us is beholden. It was a good time and nothin' more. It's all over and done with."

She fell silent so long that suddenly a dagger of suspicion stabbed him. "Ain't that right?"

A tear glistened at the outside corner of each of her eyes then rolled down her cheeks as she shook her head, clutched at the folds of her red skirt and sobbed, "No, honey, it ain't over and done with."

"Course it is!"

"Not for me."

"Look, Sarah, honey," he said, reaching for her. "Listen to me."

"No," she shouted, "you listen to me!"

Backing off, he raised his hands in surrender. "I'm listening!"

"Morgan, I love you and . . ."

"Sarah, let's be reasonable," he said, reaching out and stroking her cheek.

"And," she shouted, brushing away his hand, "I got your child in me."

Chapter Thirty-one

"Given the fact that she's a cantina girl," said Shanghai Pierce, "how can you possibly be sure that the child she's carryin', *if* she's carryin' one, is yours? She could be concoctin' this whole tale, you know."

Shaking his head in bewilderment, Morgan exclaimed, "Why on earth would she do that?"

"You're a rich man, Morgan! Some people would do anythin' to get their clutches on what you got. You wouldn't be the first fella to be wrecked on the shoals of a fictitious paternity. Don't forget that this is a girl who's been hearin' all her life that she was born on the wrong side of Buck Colter's blanket, so why wouldn't she see in you a way to get what she might be thinkin' she's entitled to in her own right?"

"That's bein' pretty rough on her."

"Don't toy with me, boy," Shanghai thundered, loud enough, it seemed to Morgan, to shake the timbers of every building on El Rancho Grande. "Did you come to me for blunt talk or sympathy?"

"It just sounded so heartless, is all."

"Heart . . . and somethin' else . . . is what got you into this pickle. It's a clear head, an unblinkin' eye, a steady hand on the tiller and the abandonment of sentiment that you'll be needin' to steer you into a snug harbor."

"Yes, sir."

Within minutes of Morgan's unexpected arrival at El Rancho Grande they had settled into cane chairs on the veranda of Shanghai's house fortified with cigars and the scotch whiskey that Shanghai bought by the case and had shipped by sea and reserved for extraordinary moments, such as Morgan showing up on his doorstep in the plainest and most severe case of agitation he'd witnessed since the early days of Abilene when it appeared that the railroad was going to renege on its promises to Joe McCoy. "Colt pistol to the temple moments," he called them. Fine scotch, Cuban cigars and calm deliberation were their infallible remedy.

"As I see it, you've got these choices," he said, between a sip of the whiskey and a puff of the cigar. "One, you can marry the girl, which is what she wants."

Stabbing the air with his cigar, Morgan exclaimed, "She never said that, Shang."

"Two," said Shanghai as he inserted his cigar into the thicket of his luxuriant beard, "you can disown any responsibility for her bein' with child."

Sullenly, Morgan snapped, "It's mine."

"Oh, how do you know that?"

"The night it happened is a right fresh memory."

"Yeah? And what about the nights when you were trailin' up to Dodge City?" Shanghai was waving his cigar like an orchestra conductor's baton now, setting the tempo for what quickly approached the dimensions of a crescendo. "What was the little lady doin' on those nights? How many rolls in the hay did she take with how many Goliad muchachos in your absence? Who's to say that she didn't find herself in this condition on account of one of them? Or maybe she got in a family way the night before she decided to commemorate the Goliad Massacre by trystin' with you. I heard she was

245

always flirtin'. I even heard-tell that she might be tumblin' for that scoundrel Jesse Bruton. Maybe this is Bruton's seed she'd nurturin'."

"She says I was the only one."

"And if I said I was the King of Timbuktu, that javelinas can fly and that the South whipped the Yankees in the war," roared Shanghai as he bolted from his chair to pace the veranda, "would you believe me?"

"As to Sarah, what are my other choices besides marryin' her and disclaimin' the kid?"

"If you are convinced it is your child and you feel an obligation that falls short of legally admitting parentage you can provide for the child; lump sum payment to the mother or over the years until the child comes of age. Bear in mind that paying to support the kid would be admitting it's yours, which would be a risky thing for a man in your position because at some point the offspring in question may seek relief in court."

Over a long silence Morgan sipped scotch and smoked the cigar and pondered the question that was burning to be asked, then asked it, nervously. "What did Buck Colter do?"

Spinning around to face Morgan, Shanghai snapped, "I wasn't aware Buck had to do anything."

"C'mon, Shang," Morgan shouted. "Sarah Coffee is Buck's kid and you know it. God, all you have to do is look at her and you see Rebecca. They were Buck's daughters."

"I'll not debate the point," Shanghai said, turning his back again. "Not with the only man I know of who went to bed with each of them."

Sighing hurt and disappointment, Morgan said, "That was uncalled for, Shang."

"Indeed so," he said, turning. "I apologize, *amigo*."

With a forgiving smile, Morgan said, "Now tell me what arrangement Buck made."

Shanghai returned to his chair and his scotch. "He provided Migdalia with a generous lump sum, which she used to establish that cantina of hers. And he afforded monies at regular intervals. All very discreetly."

Frowning in puzzlement, Morgan said, "Why didn't he just own up to it?"

"For Migdalia's sake. At her request. You see, she knew Buck couldn't marry her because, well, he was a descendant of the Colters who'd fought Mexicans all their lives and she's Mexican. Texans would disown him and Mexicans would turn on her. She was a very wise woman. Plus she didn't want to do anything to hurt Rebecca. She loved Rebecca as if she were her own. Migdalia's a sweet big-hearted lady. And very proud. Take it from me, she's not going to step forward and make trouble for you over this forthcoming child. Pride and that big heart will forbid it. Her daughter apparently is different."

"So what's your advice to me?"

"From all that I've seen of you, I'd say that you're a man of conscience."

"Thank you. I hope I am."

"Therefore, you must do what your conscience dictates. But for God's sake don't play Hamlet! You've got to be as decisive as you were with those bandits in the Flores gang. Either claim the kid or don't. Examine your conscience and follow it. There is one thing that I haven't asked you."

"What's that?"

"Could it possibly be that you're in love with this girl?"

"I like her."

"That wasn't the question."

"What's it matter now if I love her or not?"

"It matters because sooner or later you're goin' to have to face up to her child. My guess is that once you lay eyes on the child you're apt to want to lay claim to it. Before you can, Sarah may insist that you make her your wife. If you love her, that wouldn't be a problem. If you love her and marry her, your son Colt will get the mother he ought to have. If you don't love her, marryin' her will be hell on earth. When's the child due?"

"December. Just in time for Christmas."

"Perhaps, like Joseph in the nativity story, the Angel of the Lord will appear to you in a dream and tell you what to do," said Shanghai, stroking his long beard and looking like a Biblical figure himself, except for a long column of exhaled cigar smoke that caught up in the wind and swirled toward the water.

Chapter Thirty-two

It was not the Angel of the Lord who appeared but Migdalia Coffee in Sunday finery befitting the seriousness of her purpose, bouncing up the lane of the Double **M** ranch in a smart and still-shiny 33-year-old black Dearborn gig with a red leather seat and a red-fringed top that had been presented with great fanfare and assertions of his undying love by her husband the week before he absconded to California in 1849 to seek his fortune in the California gold fields. Drawn by a blue-eyed skewbald horse which she'd obtained from a customer in payment of a long-standing liquor bill after she'd threatened to put the law on him, the carriage was usually taken out of the barn behind the El Dorado and hitched to the pampered black-and-white horse only for Sunday mass at the Mission la Bahia, weddings and funerals. But this day was exceptional.

It was a sultry September morning marked by the ragged slate-gray skies and sea-scented gusts that were signs of an impending cyclone and she found the handsome young owner of the ranch shooing horses from their stables into a vast fenced pasture.

"Howdy, Migdalia," he said, shirtless and sweating as he lifted his hat both as a greeting and to blot the band of sweat it made around his head. Tugging at his matted-down long blond hair, he said, "Seems like there's a storm comin', so I thought I'd best get the horses out. This barn fell down once in a blow."

"I remember it," she said, reining up.

"First hurricane I ever saw," he said, reaching to assist her down from the rig. "But I expect it's not the weather you've come to talk about, is it?"

"No, Morgan, it ain't."

"You want to know my intentions regarding Sarah."

"Your intentions are a matter to be settled between you and God," she said. "If you believe in Him."

"I do, Migdalia. I surely do."

"I figured such, judging by how you cite the Holy Scriptures from time to time in your conversations."

"My ma was strong for the Bible and believed people should know it, 'specially her son."

"Then I expect you're familiar with the story of Jezebel."

"A determined woman out to get what she wanted."

"And you know what happened to her."

"She was killed. The Lord said, 'The dogs shall eat Jezebel by the wall of Jezreel' and that's what happened."

Clutching his arm, Migdalia exclaimed, "Morgan, I'm worried that my daughter's turnin' into a Jezebel. I know that just because you was with her once she's tryin' to pressure you into marryin' her on account of her bein' in a family way. Right?"

"Migdalia, this is more than a little embarrassin'."

"I've known you a few years, Morgan, and I never saw anythin' in you that ever led me to believe that you're a man who wouldn't want to do the right thing. But I also know my daughter. So what I'm sayin' to you is that you oughtn't take her word for it that the child she's carryin' is yours."

Unable to suppress a grin, Morgan said, "Migdalia, you're a surprisin' lady. By all rights, you ought to be comin' out here totin' a shotgun."

"Now I'm not sayin' you're blameless in this. It still takes two to make a baby. But I know my girl. She's got a heap of me in her character. And she's a lot like her father." She paused, pondering and chewing her lower lip, then blurted, "Buck Colter. No use denyin' it. Buck and me had too much hot blood for our own good. Buck had an eye for a good-lookin' woman, which I was then."

"You still are," grinned Morgan.

"And I knew a man when I saw one," she said. Drifting back a pace, she raked him with her eyes starting from his matted locks and progressing down to his sweat-slicked chest, nearly threadbare jeans and scuffed squared-toed boots that gave him the appearance of a penniless cowhand. "The truth is, Morgan," she chuckled, "if I was twenty years younger I could feel mighty warm toward you myself. So I don't blame Sarah on that account." With vanishing smile, she said, "Only I don't care to see her usin' the situation the way she is. Like a Jezebel. That's why I expect you to do what you believe is right for yourself and hang what anybody else thinks, includin' Sarah."

"I truly appreciate the consideration, Migdalia."

Climbing into her gig, she said, "In the meantime Sarah will be visitin' relatives up in San Antonio."

Astonished, he could only gasp, "She's goin' away?"

"She's startin' to show and there's no way I'm goin' to permit her to be seen in that condition traipsin' around and workin' in the cantina."

"Yep, I can see the wisdom of that."

"And her bein' away will allow you the time for whatever contemplation you need to decide what's best accordin' to your conscience."

251

"For that I'm in your debt, Migdalia."

Stinging the horse with the reins, she snapped. "No you ain't."

Chapter Thirty-three

Dressed to the nines and with a veneer of cheerful pretense that she was off for a spell with cousins and that it was her idea, Sarah was gone with the next mail-and-passenger coach that snaked its way up from Corpus Christi with stops at Refugio, Beeville and Goliad and then Karnes City and Saspamico before its terminus in the city of the Alamo.

A coach reversing the route a week later brought Morgan a letter written on foolscap from Buck Colter's favorite hotel.

THE MENGER
San Antonio, Texas

Dearest lov Morgan,

I wanted to see you before I left Goliad but mama wouldn't let me. I'm no good at ritin so all I can say as I take this pen in hand is the words of the song I sang just for you that nite at the big danse. *Mi amor, mi corazón.* I pray that our baby will be a boy and that you will lov him as feerce as I lov you.

I miss you and wish you were here so I cud give you all my love and kisses,

X X X
Sarah Coffee

"X's for kisses," he said with a chuckle as he folded the letter and placed it with his personal papers that he kept separate from those of the ranch in a locked drawer of his desk in the tack room.

Among these were two big-handed but sparse letters he'd received from Charlie Carew over the years and a string-bound sizeable bundle of wordy letters sent by Henry Kidder from Abilene. Often containing clippings or entire pages from his newspaper, Hank's letters amounted to a running history of the place Morgan would always think of as the Queen of the Cowtowns and the one he'd name if he ever had to return to the place that most folks thought of as a hometown, meaning the spot that shaped them and left its mark more than any other, for neither the Gettysburg of his innocent boyhood, nor the cavalry years of his hell-bent-for-leather youth nor the brush-popping and trail herding Texas of his settled manhood had shaped him as much as Abilene.

Loosening the string from the Kidder letters, he thumbed through the date-ordered envelopes, pausing here and there to recall without opening any letter what it said, until he came to the one that had come long after the attack by Custer's Seventh on Chief Black Kettle's village along the Washita in which Ward Kimball had been killed. Propping himself with the heels of his boots bracketing the lip of the edge of the desk, he tilted back on his chair and opened the four sheet letter to the last page.

As you know, I had never held Major Kimball in

high regard, considering him to be a vain and dangerous martinet cut from the same block of granite conceit as the officer he most admired, namely George Armstrong Custer.

In light of the fact that you were Major Kimball's abiding friend and admirer I've been plumbing my memory for what you'd obviously discerned and I had missed in the man but I remain as perplexed as before. Perhaps one day you will explain what you found so compelling in this man whose only saving grace, in my opinion, was that you were his friend.

Lest you think me cruel and unfeeling in saying this, I hasten to add that because I have always been flattered and grateful to have had your friendship I have no hesitation in admitting that the same can be said for me; that the most redeeming feature in my life has been knowing you.

Perhaps, one day, I'll write a book about you.

"That'd be something to read," Morgan laughed as he returned the pack of letters to the drawer, closed it and locked the desk.

Chapter Thirty-four

Shouldering a bag of oats from a Studebaker wagon stacked with them, Dalgo decided to come right out with what was on his mind. "Boss? You all right?"

With a snort, Morgan said, "Certainly, *amigo*. Why?"

"You sure seem off your feed lately."

Hefting a bag, Morgan grunted, "Just worry about this wagonload of grain and never mind mine."

"Well, I'm not the only one's noticed it," said the caporal on his way into the barn.

Following him, Morgan heaved the oats on a chest-high criss-crossed pile of similar bags. "Such as who?"

"The hands at Range Camp Three thought you was a bit snappy with 'em when you was out there last week."

"Just 'cause I booted their asses for bein' slow comin' up with a head count?"

"They had the feelin' they was gettin' cussed when somebody else deserved it."

"Did they say who?"

"They had no idea."

"Do you?"

"All I know is there's a burr under your saddle and it warn't put there by no hand workin' on this here ranch of yours."

"Okay, out with it, *amigo*," sighed Morgan, leaning

against the bags. "It's nothin' the hands said, is it? You were in the cantinas when you went in town for this feed and you heard somethin'. Correct?"

"That's about the shape of it, boss."

"When are you goin' to learn not to listen to cantina lizards gossipin'?"

"There wasn't no way not to listen, boss."

"You could've left the place."

"Wouldn't a done no good, 'cause anywhere I went it was the same. People comin' up to me and wantin' to know was it true what they'd heard."

"And what had they heard? C'mon, I'm a big boy. There's nothin' anybody could say about me that hasn't been said a thousand times over, I expect. More horse manure about what I did before I landed in Goliad? About my bein' a pistoleer up in Abilene?"

"This was about somethin', uh, more recent."

"For cryin' out loud, Dalgo, spit it out!"

In a burst, Dalgo said, "The word all over Goliad is that you're the papa of the kid that Sarah Coffee went to San Antonio to have."

"And what's your opinion on the subject, *amigo?*"

"Well, Sarah's a pretty *señorita* and it's never been a secret that she always had her eyes set on you, so . . ."

"So you believe that Sarah's havin' my kid."

"What I believe don't matter, boss. I just thought you ought to know what's bein' said in town and that the widely held opinion is that you're not doin' right by Sarah in not makin' her an honest woman and givin' the kid its due."

"Thank you, Dalgo. I'm deeply grateful for you keepin' me up to date on the court of public opinion on a subject that's no one's damn business but mine," Morgan said, striding from the barn.

So there it was, he said to himself as he stormed into his house. In the court of public opinion that Henry

257

Kidder was so fond of praising in his civic-minded newspaper editorials the upstanding citizens of Goliad had judged him exactly as they'd rendered a verdict on Buck Colter as being the father of Sarah Coffee. "Damned busybodies" he growled as he threw himself into Buck's favorite chair facing the portraits of all the Colters who'd been illustrious rather than scandalous in the history of Goliad.

With a worried look on her face, the housekeeper peered at him through the kitchen doorway. "Is there something wrong, *Señor* Morgan?"

"No, Theresa. Sorry if I troubled you comin' in like that, makin' all the noise."

"No trouble, *señor,*" she said, her smiling face a painful reminder to him that this woman taking care of his son Colt was a cousin of Migdalia and Sarah's aunt and soon would be kin of a child that might be Colt's half-brother. Or half-sister, he thought. Then he wondered if Theresa knew all this as she disappeared again into the kitchen brimming with the savory smells of the supper she was cooking for him.

Perhaps I should ask her, he thought, bolting from the chair.

As he stepped into the kitchen, Theresa looked more puzzled than worried as she asked, "Something I can get you, *señor?*"

"No, uh, nothing, thanks. I was just, uh, wonderin', that is, I wanted to ask . . . how's Colt?"

"Your little buckaroo's sleeping, *señor.*"

On his belly with a thumb in his mouth, the boy was Rebecca in all aspects except his hair—the same soft gold as his father's. Smiling down at this son that he knew was his, Morgan fingered a strand of the boy's hair while stroking the wispy mustache he'd never been able to cultivate satisfactorily over a span of eleven years. "Better luck with yours, Colt," he whispered, "should you ever try to sprout one."

As if he'd understood, Colt stirred, opened his eyes and gurgled a laugh.

Whisking him into his arms, Morgan bounced him. "This is just like ridin' a horse, fella," he said, kissing the boy's cheek and exulting in his weight. "Soon you'll be big enough for that, won't you? Soon you'll have a horse of your own."

Carefully placing Colt in his crib, he admired the boy's blue eyes and yellow hair and wondered if this was how a baby named Hugh Morgan had looked to his father and if this was how his father had felt — so pleased and proud to see himself in his son's eyes, so thrilled to know that he had achieved a kind of immortality, that something of him would go on living in the form of this boy and in the boy's sons and their sons.

Then, as sudden and illuminating as a lightning bolt, the boy he was looking at changed to another child, one that soon would be coming into the world.

Whose child would it be?

Would that child have a father to hold it and bounce it like the ride of a horse?

Would there be a father to peer into that baby's crib and dream about immortality?

Or would Sarah's baby be born disavowed and disowned and left like a maverick calf — stray and unbranded?

Loud enough to startle Colt and make him blink, he said, "No!"

Half an hour later he stomped into the cookhouse behind the El Dorado and frightened Migdalia into dropping a skillet by declaring, "Damn it, Dalia, I mean to do right by this situation between your daughter and me and marry her."

Chapter Thirty-five

Away in a manger, no crib for a bed,
The little Lord Jesus laid down His sweet head . . .

Untouched since Rebecca last played it, the piano in the parlor was not so out of kilter that Morgan didn't recognize the tune that Theresa played from Rebecca's book of carols, coaxing the old favorite from the piano's stiff and tinny keys while behind the closed door of the bedroom Sarah labored.

When her painful moans had started around noon Dalgo had been sent to Goliad to fetch Doctor Rickards, *pronto*.

At dusk when there were increasingly agonized cries Morgan barged into the bedroom shouting, "Is it happenin'?"

"Not yet," said the tall, spare doctor calmly.

"You just go about your business and keep outta the way," said Migdalia brusquely as she shoved Morgan out the door. "I'll let you know when."

Fidgety and smoking cheroots, he had not risen from a chair in a corner since, although the doctor had taken time for a leisurely but silent supper prepared by

Theresa.

Now, nearing the stroke of midnight and Christmas day, the house was silent except for the piano.

To break that stillness, if for no other reason, he blurted at Theresa, "Why's it take so long?"

Lifting her fingers from the keyboard, Theresa shrugged. "The child will come in the Lord's good time," she said, adjusting the drape of a lace shawl. "And in the child's," she added, abruptly abandoning the piano and striding into the bedroom, leaving a quiet worse than before.

With the first gray glimmer of daylight there came a piercing scream from Sarah that was worse than any Morgan ever had heard on a battlefield.

A moment later he heard a baby cry.

Bolting into the bedroom he yelled, "Is that it? The baby?"

With his arched back to Morgan and blocking him from seeing the bed, Sarah or the baby, the doctor abruptly said, "A boy, sir."

After a joyous yelp, Morgan said, "I was prayin' it'd be."

"Theresa," said the doctor urgently, "fetch towels, clean rags, a shirt, anythin'."

As she brushed past him, Morgan demanded. "What's the matter?"

Sobbing, she uttered, "She's bleedin' real bad."

"Somethin' musta tore," said Migdalia grimly as the doctor worked feverishly to stem a soaking pool of scarlet blood and Morgan stared in wordless disbelief as it spread quickly across the white covering sheets like bottom mud in a stirred creek.

At last, the doctor's shoulders lifted then sagged as he whispered, "There's nothing I can do."

Making the sign of the cross, Migdalia turned to Morgan, and sobbed, "She's goin' to die, son."

261

Furiously, Morgan seized the doctor. "That's impossible!"

"It was a difficult delivery," said the doctor calmly. "It's what's known as a breech birth. The baby gets turned around."

Loosening his painful grip, Morgan cried, "What about the kid?"

"He's fine," said the doctor, turning slightly and pointing to a yellow-haired baby sound asleep in a cocoon of pale blue blanket in an oak cradle.

Part Five
Morgan's Road

Chapter Thirty Six

At the turnoff from the Goliad road into the long graveled lane in the year 1889 stood a weathering sign.

> This is Morgan's Road.
> Take the Other One.

The sign had stood there for thirteen years, put up by Morgan the day after Christmas 1876, which was the birthdate of his second son, whom he'd named Owen in memory of his own father.

Commencing that same day, the brands on the thousands of cattle on Morgan's ranges and the hundreds of horses in his remuda had been changed from MM to MMM, spoken thereafter as the Triple M. Or simply, Morgan's brand.

Should anyone ignore the admonition against taking Morgan's road, as many did because Morgan was a likeable man as well as an important and powerful one, the traveler would find at the end of the lane a sprawling old adobe hacienda with orange roof tiles that shimmered like fire in the glare of the sun.

Morgan had added rooms to the house, turning it into what everyone who lived and worked on the Nueces Strip called a mansion and a showplace befitting the centerpiece and crown jewel of the cattle empire Morgan had built during a baker's dozen of annums.

Of course, he would say to people, the credit for all that happened belonged to Rebecca and he'd talk about her so vividly that they could almost see her, pretty and perky, and hear her as plain as yesterday, full of prophecy and promises:

"I mean to match my father and to better him. I'm not being disrespectful or irreverent in saying this, believe me! I merely want you to understand that I do not intend to simply go along as things are on this ranch. I want to build on what my father created from what he inherited. Daddy built an important enterprise and no one can ever detract from that achievement. But there are going to be enormous changes in the years ahead, changes that this ranch must be able to meet head on. For example, I am looking toward the day when the railroads reach Texas. It is simply a matter of time. That will revolutionize the way we'll conduct the livestock business. I mean to be ready for that day. And when it comes, I want the Colter ranch to be the largest and mightiest there is. When people all over the country eat beef, I want it to come from the Colter ranch. I can even say that I'm looking forward to the day when no one will think of beef without thinking simultaneously of Texas and of Texas without thinking of the Colter brand. I envision the day coming — sooner rather than later — in which we not only breed and raise cattle but handle the slaughtering, packing and shipping!"

Now, not quite twenty years later, he'd turned her vision into a reality.

Except it was not the Colter brand. It was Triple M.

The Triple M ranch, largest of the Nueces Strip and second-largest in Texas.

The Triple M Livestock Shipping Company with holding pens and loading chutes and platforms built on an exclusive spur of the Missouri, Kansas and Texas Railroad.

The Triple M Slaughtering and Packing Company.

But none of this was as important or satisfying to Morgan as his two sons, the second and third M of the ranch's famous brand: sixteen-year-old Colt and Owen, almost thirteen.

So the story of Morgan continues on a warm Sunday evening late in April 1889 when he laid aside a newspaper and came to the table for a Mexican-style supper cooked by Theresa for him and the boys with their sun-bleached straw-yellow hair combed and big blue eyes shining out of faces fresh-scrubbed after an afternoon of riding instead of doing their schoolwork.

The keener observer of the two, Owen decided his father looked unusually grim-faced and, never one to hold back his thoughts, asked, "Is there anything wrong, dad? You mad about something?"

Morgan flashed a reassuring smile. "I was just thinking about something I was reading in the paper."

"Something bad?"

"Nothing to concern you, Owen. Merely an article about the opening of the Indian Territory to settlers."

Pausing over his plate of corn-pepper soup, Colt spoke up. "Nobody lived there before?"

"Indians lived there."

"Where'd they go?"

"Out."

With his face crinkled by a frown Owen persisted. "How come that's got you upset?"

"Well, I guess you could say it's the closing of a pretty meaningful chapter in my life. You see, it's through the Indian Territory that I used to drive cattle up to the markets in Abilene, Newton, Wichita, and Dodge City. These days all those wide open spaces are long-settled. Now they're populatin' the Indian Territory. It's just another proof of how much things have changed. How they are changin'. How fast they're changin'. And it's a reminder that a good many fine men I knew back then are gone."

With a wondering look Owen asked, "Such as?"

"Such as Shanghai Pierce!"

"I remember him," said Colt brightly. "Of course, I was little then. Where'd he go?"

"He sold his ranch and all his holdings and retired from the cattle business."

Owen said, "How come?"

"Well, of course he was very rich and able to quit workin', but I think it just wasn't fun for him anymore. Shang was in it for the fun more than the money."

"He must've been a character," said Owen.

Morgan nodded. "Yeah, I've known some characters in my time."

"Name another one," said Owen excitedly.

"Well, there was California Joe, for instance," said Morgan, going on to relate the memories of Joe as they stirred; first seeing him at the end of a long gun barrel in the Kaw Valley in 1865 when a wrong move would have spelled the end of Morgan, learning scouting from him at Fort Riley, listening to his tall tales of Texas cattle with horns as wide as the spread of a man's arms, being taught the art of hunting buffalo. "There's so many stories of California Joe I could go on all night."

Thrilled, Owen said, "Can I meet him?"

"Well, Owen, I'm sad to say that Old Joe's gone. Shot in the back at Fort Robinson up in the Nebraska Territory in '76, the year you were born."

"Who shot him?"

"A dastardly coward by the name of Tom Newcomb."

"Why?"

"I don't know. Somethin' senseless, prob'ly."

Hank Kidder had written him about it, he remembered, but hadn't cited the cause of the shooting, not that it mattered. He still had Hank's letter, bundled up and in a drawer in the desk in the old tack room and office with so many others from Hank over a span of at least twenty-five years. The last had come in 1880, not from Hank but from his widow. "I regret to inform you that my beloved husband

268

Henry has passed away as the result of a chronic heart ailment," wrote Amelia Kidder, whom Morgan had never met.

Shivering with the sudden reality that he'd known Hank Kidder since the opening shots of the Battle of Gettysburg, Morgan joked to his sons, "All this talk about my past makes me feel downright ancient."

Colt looked at him in the same measuring way of his mother. "How old are you, dad?"

"Two score years."

"Forty," exclaimed Owen, making a face that was as teasing as his mother's. "Boy, that is old."

"You won't say that when you're forty," Morgan laughed, ruffling Owen's golden hair. "Which you will be before you know it. Because time flies, my boy. And the more years you get under your belt the faster they go by and add up. But that's enough hot air out of me. Eat your supper and let this decrepit old man enjoy his in peace."

Because he believed the years had been good to him, Morgan found joking about himself easy. Only five pounds heavier than the day he stepped from a Missouri River steamer onto the boisterous docks of Kansas City in 1865, he could still hitch his oldest gunbelt to the same notch where he'd hitched it when he'd bought it in Abilene. Shirts, pants and hats were the same sizes as when they'd been government-issued at Fort Riley.

Peering past his sons at a mirror on the wall behind them, his cornflower blue eyes discovered in his lean and angular face not so much the passage of years as the work of the wind, rain and sun that had burnished, polished and etched his skin to the luster of fine leather.

Stroking a sparse mustache as silky as cornsilk, he found it to be the only disappointment in the man he saw reflected behind his sons. Not since he'd grown it in a hospital while recuperating from a Reb bullet that hit him in the chest and dehorsed him at Jetersville, Virginia, had he

269

ever been satisfied with it. Only his hope and optimism that it would one day flourish had kept it there. Now it was just too familiar a part of him to shave it off.

Lowering his eyes from his reflection to his sons' whiskerless faces and mindful of what he'd said to them about how fast time went by, he knew that before long they'd be trying out their own mustaches and beards, Colt being the first, of course, because he was nearly at the razoring age. Of the two, he thought, Colt would let nature take its course.

Already as tall as Morgan, Colt was as lean, hard and lithesome as his father and so quick and decisive and precise in movements that Morgan saw reflections of himself and heard the faint echoes of the guns of Abilene. Tense and wary, Colt brimmed with rambunctious zest and thirsted for all that ranch life offered, loving horses and riding them as Rebecca had, all devil-may-care and recklessness.

Overshadowed by and worshipping his brother, Owen was quieter; a reminder to Morgan of himself when his mother worked to chip away her boy's hard edges with passages from her tiny library of civilizing books. In Owen he foresaw a clean-shaven youth who might come to possess an appreciation of books if his brother would allow it and not tease him for being a sissy.

"Owen, if you really want to know all about how the cattle business got started," Morgan said as Theresa brought a heaping plate of roast beef to the table, "there's a book in my library that'll tell you all about it. Written by the man that started it all, Joseph Geiting McCoy. It's called *Historic Sketches of the Cattle Trade of the West and Southwest.* Mighty interestin' readin'."

With a permission-seeking glance at Colt, Owen asked, "Are you in it, dad?"

"Read it yourself and find out."

Suddenly Colt spoke up with the bragging tone of the

older brother who has known for a long time something his younger brother hasn't. "There's two books in the library up on the top shelf that are all about dad."

Rising halfway out of his chair, Owen begged, "Can I see 'em, dad?"

Pleased that Owen was interested, but surprised that Colt knew about the books, Morgan overrode an urge to rush with them into the library, letting the responsibility of being an instructive and civilizing father prevail. "You must finish your supper first."

Titled *Morgan of Abilene, Kansas,* Hank Kidder's biographical book had been sent by his widow along with the letter about Hank's dying. "So you insist on getting in the last word, eh, Henry? Albeit posthumously," Morgan recalled thinking with both sadness and great amusement at the time.

Speedily leafing through the dusty morocco-bound volume, Owen asked, "Is this a true story, dad?"

"A lot truer than this one," Morgan said, reaching for a slim, cheaply made volume entitled *Morgan, deadly gunman of the Western cattle towns.*

A sensational dime novel published by Beadle and Adams, a New York City firm, it had been written by one Harry Singleton, Morgan explained as Owen thumbed it. "I only met the fella one time up in Abilene. He'd just come out to Kansas lookin' for stories to write. If Harry didn't find any or if the facts didn't suit him, he embellished 'em."

"Is what's in this one embellished?"

Morgan laughed, "Greatly."

Settling into a chair with the book, Owen declared, "I'm going to read the whole thing right now."

"Well, only until bedtime," said Morgan, placing Hank Kidder's preferable book back on the shelf. "There's school tomorrow, you know."

Chapter Thirty-seven

Because they described only Morgan's experiences as a gunman in the cowtowns of Kansas, neither Harry Singleton's fanciful, sensationally lurid but adoringly flattering dime novel version nor Hank Kidder's thoughtful, analytical and judgmental book included any mention of Jesse Bruton of Goliad and the owlhoot renegade trail he'd followed since he'd murdered old Jasper Fulcord in the El Dorado in March 1876.

On the run, Bruton had joined a gang of rustlers bossed by King Fisher, another Goliad boy who'd crossed to the wrong side of the law and executed his depredations in Maverick County and elsewhere while based in the hideout canyons and caves of Mexico across from Eagle Pass. Soon, Bruton's name appeared high on the lists beside Fisher's in a gray, paper-backed booklet known as "the Book of Knaves" that was carried in the back pockets of Texas Rangers as they tried to clean out the lawless elements along the Rio Grande.

It was five years before Bruton was arrested, not on the Fulcord murder charge but for the killing of an innocent, slender fair-haired young cowhand in an Eagle Pass saloon. Bleary-eyed from drink, Bruton had peered through the thick fog of tobacco smoke and mistaken the youth for Morgan, drawing his gun and firing twice with deadly accuracy for a man as drunk as he was. Although testimony from a lying ally who swore that the youth had gone for his gun first had kept Bruton from the gallows, the close call obviously had not dimmed the fervor of his hatred of Morgan as evidenced by his shouting at the judge who'd just sentenced him to twenty years, "If this fella I shot had been the man I thought he was, namely Morgan, I'd be happy to swing, knowin' I'd killed him."

For the next eight years he was as unrepentant as any inmate in the history of the Maverick County prison.

Then he escaped.

Three days later in the dawning of a damp Monday late in April of 1889 he brazenly rode a stolen horse past eye-popping and gaping early risers in Goliad.

Heedless of the stares and strapped with the gunbelt and pistol of the hapless rider he'd jumped and knifed to death to get the mount, he took the east road from town, a direction that would take him by Morgan's road. There he waited.

The early spring sun was up and warming when Morgan paused a moment in the shade of the porch to watch pridefully as Colt and Owen Morgan threw their schoolbook-stuffed saddlebags over their ponies.

"No racin'," he shouted as they mounted, swung past the house, waved back at their grinning father and rocked down the lane, waiting until they were out of Morgan's line of sight before booting the knowing horses into a mad dash toward the Goliad road.

An easy winner, Colt was first to encounter the stranger at the end of the lane, jerk reins and halt. "Mornin' mister."

"Howdy," nodded Jesse Bruton. "That was quite a spirited competition."

"We always make a race of it," said Colt, boasting, "even though I always win."

As Owen rode up, Bruton smiled, "You good-lookin' fellas must be the Morgan boys."

" 'Deed so," said Colt.

"And what's your name, son?"

"Colt. And this is my brother Owen."

Remembering what he'd read the previous evening in the dime novel about his father having been in Custer's cavalry, Owen snapped a hand smartly to the brim of his hat in salute.

Colt asked, "Are you a friend of dad's, mister?"

"Yeah, an old friend," snickered Bruton as he slowly drew his gun. "We go way back," he said, leveling it.

Astonished and rigid with fear, Colt gasped, "Say, mister, what's . . ."

The bullet drilled into his chest dead center and exploded through the middle of the back of his vest, flinging Colt backward and splattering the horses and his brother with blood and guts.

An instant later as Owen desperately jerked the reins to make his horse turn and furiously booted its ribs to make him run, a bullet burned into him from the left side, barreling through his heart and killing him instantly, then exploded from his right side under his armpit and spun him like a cartwheel out of the saddle and onto the graveled road beside his dead brother.

Chapter Thirty-eight

Drawing up a blue-patterned coverlet to the chins of the peaceful and angelic-looking boys he'd delivered and doctored through all the childhood sicknesses and who now looked as if they were merely sleeping side by side on their father's big bed, Doctor Hezekiah Rickards, who was also Goliad's mortician, muttered, "It has to be Jesse Bruton that done this."

"C'mon, doc, that's impossible," groaned Morgan as he blotted pools of tears from beneath his eyes with his sleeve and then lowered a hand to pinch a driplet of snot dangling above his sparse mustache. "Jesse Bruton's doin' life in the prison down in Maverick County."

" 'Tain't so," said the black-coated lanky doctor, his tone as flinty as his expression. "Jesse was seen ridin' through town at sunup this mornin' headin' out this way."

Stiffening as hard and cold as iron, Morgan whispered, "Who seen him?"

"Half the people that was up that early. It's been the talk of the place ever since."

Brittle-voiced, Morgan said, "They're sure it was him?"

"He rode through as brazen as brass like he wanted to be noticed. If it warn't him it must've been the spittin' image."

As if tucking in his sons, Morgan bent slightly to tenderly adjust the lie of the coverlet. "Doc, you're a man who knows as much about the human spirit as you do about a man's anatomy, so I'd appreciate it if you'd explain to me why in God's good earth anybody, even Jesse Bruton, would want to murder these two fine boys."

"Sick as it sounds," said the doctor, scratching his curly black whiskers, "I figure it was to get at their father."

"That's a piss-ant scum of a coward that'd do that."

"Jesse Bruton always was the scum of the earth," said the doctor. "I have cursed the day I helped him into this life."

"Well, Doctor Rickards," said Morgan icily as his cold blue eyes narrowed and his gunhand dropped from the coverlet to his side and a holster heavy with the Peacemaker Shanghai Pierce had given to him, "I guess I'm gonna have to help him out of it, ain't I?"

"Bear in mind, Morgan," cautioned the doctor, "Jesse could be layin' for you."

Drawing the gun and chambering a sixth round into the top chamber which as a rule he'd always kept empty for safety's sake, Morgan hissed, "Sneakin' snake that he is, it'd be just like him to be skulkin' in the grass."

"Leave this to the town marshal," urged the doctor. "Or the Rangers. Take somebody with you. Fetch Dalgo and a bunch of your hands. Don't go it alone."

Pausing in the doorway with the streaming glare of the morning sun making him a black cutout, Morgan declared, "These are my *sons,* doc. They were what I lived for these past years. They were my future. They're dead; so's my future. A man can't be any more alone than that."

Chapter Thirty-nine

As certainly as they could smell an impending Gulf-born cyclone in the air, the people of Goliad had sniffed what was coming and acted in accord with their different but settled natures. For most this meant getting off the streets and out of the way. Those with children in school collected them and rushed them home. The devout gathered at the Mission for the saving solace of prayer. The curious, of which there were many, selected the best vantage points along the route Morgan had to take between the road into town and the El Dorado where Jesse Bruton made no secret that he was daring Morgan to appear.

"Because there is no direct evidence that Jesse Bruton's the one who killed the Morgan boys," pointed out Acting-Sheriff William Ragland, "there's no cause for me to arrest Bruton for murder." Neither had he yet been notified that Bruton had escaped from prison, as everyone assumed, nor that he was wanted on any charge, insisted the lean youngster known to everyone in town since boyhood as Rags. "With no warrants I got no legal reason to go into the cantina after Jesse," he pointed out to a delegation of incensed citizens who demanded Jesse's instant incarceration. Forlornly, Ragland said, "All I can do is post myself at the entrance to town and warn Morgan."

To which an especially agitated Goliadan demanded, "Warn him about what?"

"Why, that Bruton is layin' for him!"

"For crissakes, Rags," thundered the citizen, "don't ya think Morgan already knows that?"

Unpersuaded and undaunted, Ragland posted himself on the road and dutifully halted Morgan a mile short of town, raising a hand and maneuvering his horse in the path of Morgan's to assert, "As the law in Goliad I order you to turn around."

Shifting impatiently in the saddle, Morgan growled, "Why's that, Rags?"

"Don't want you causin' no trouble, Mr. Morgan."

Abruptly, Morgan said, "Just what makes you think there's to be trouble and that I might be the cause of it?"

"I know about your boys, Mr. Morgan. I'm deeply sorry about what happened. But I can't let you go after Jesse Bruton on the suspicion that he done it. I have to insist that you leave Jesse Bruton to the law."

Cracking a grin and stroking his thin mustache, Morgan said, "Jesse Bruton! A name outta the past! Is he back?"

"He is, sir. He's at the El Dorado. Waitin' for you."

"Then I best not keep him," said Morgan crisply, coaxing his horse forward and bumping Ragland's.

"Mr. Morgan," beseeched Ragland, "I can't let you proceed."

"I've lost my two sons this mornin', Rags," snapped Morgan as he blatantly fingered the sleek walnut butt of the Peacemaker. "Don't make me lose a friend as well."

Wisely dancing his horse aside, Ragland warned, "If you kill Jesse I'll come after you with the full weight of the law."

"Then it looks like this is a day for me to do what I must and you to do what you have to," said Morgan, swinging past him at a trot.

A few minutes later, those who had a window or doorway to cautiously peek through saw him enter town. Proceeding down the middle of deserted Main Street, he appeared as mysterious and calm as the slender young man they'd been wondering about for years. As they watched him pass, they thought the old thoughts, pondered the same questions: who was he, really? what fires had forged him? what searing memories smoldered behind those smoky blue eyes? what secrets lurked in that brain that was so quick to deliver an apt saying from Shakespeare or an instructive verse from the Holy Writ? what about him so engaged and charmed yet scared them?

Rocking past them, he was a solitary horseman wearing a seasoned Stetson hat, a cavalry-yellow neckerchief dangling down the front of a sweat-stained blue workshirt, nearly threadbare jeans, weathered and water-blanched boots with wide-heel spurs and a forty-loop gunbelt and holster supporting a Colt six-gun.

If there was one thing indelible in their memories of Morgan it was the gun, and it was to the gun that all eyes turned as he rode by their overseeing windows and made the turn that led to the El Dorado.

Migdalia Coffee was in front and to the right of the arched doorway seated in her Dearborn buggy with meaty hands holding the reins and her knowing face frozen in grim resignation to the impossibility of stopping him. Reining up, Morgan said, "Dalia, your grandchild is dead."

"I know all about it, son. Jesse Bruton done it."

"How do you know that?"

"He told me. Said he done it to make you come

279

after him. To settle things between you and him at last." Tapping her head with a stubby finger, she said, "He's loco."

Swinging from the saddle, Morgan asked, "Is he in there?"

"Yes."

"Anyone else?"

"They all cleared out hours ago."

"You clear out, too, Dalia," he said firmly.

"When you're done, I'll be out at the ranch seein' the boys," she said, flicking leather to the rump of her horse.

Stepping lightly onto the planked sidewalk and drawing the Colt level as he flattened his back against the adobe wall to the left of the arch, he yelled, "Howdy, Jesse!"

Shouting from the back of the cantina at the same table where he'd shot Jasper Fulcord, Bruton sounded as far away and as deeply distant as Hell. "Hi ya, Morgan. Long time no see."

"Thought they had you locked up, Jesse."

"They did once. Now they don't."

"Jesse, I gotta ask you somethin'."

"What'd that be, Morgan?"

"Did you murder my boys?"

"Sure did."

"Why'd you do that, Jesse?"

"Seemed like the proper thing."

"What in hell's proper about gunnin' down two kids you never saw in your life?"

"Oh, hell, Morgan, they was just the bait."

"Bait," whispered Morgan in revulsion as he sank to a hunker.

Bruton yelled, "They was my way of, shall we say, gettin' your undivided attention."

Easing left on his knee for a gunbelt-high peek

around the corner, Morgan shouted, "I'm gonna kill you, Jesse."

Unseen in the dim light of the back of the cantina, Jesse cackled a taunting laugh. "Not if I kill you first."

Drawing his head back, Morgan yelled, "Care to step out into the light?"

"And get bushwhacked? No thanks."

"No bushwhackin', Jesse," said Morgan as he came forward onto his belly. "Fair fight," he yelled, creeping on hands and knees with his head low and his rump high like a stalking bobcat approaching the doorway. "We pace off ten steps, count to ten and draw."

"You plug me as I come out, you mean," bellowed Jesse as he curled out of the creaking chair and under the table. Kneeling with the top of his head pressing the underside of it, he peered through a tangled forest of furniture legs toward the curve-topped doorway admitting a slanting shaft of dust-swarmed and blinding daylight that glared off the cantina's old, footworn and boot-polished floor planks just inside.

Hearing the creak of the chair as Bruton slid out of it, Morgan gambled. Poised like a preying cat, he sensed that his quarry's movement afforded him a chance to move safely. Springing, he dove through the doorway, hit the floor so hard with his right shoulder that he nearly lost his grip on the Colt and rolled toward the shadow of the bar.

In that instant, seeing the shadow of Morgan if not Morgan himself, Bruton fired blindly and too high into the light.

Out of his eyes' need to adjust from the brightness outdoors to the darkness of the cantina Morgan also found himself sightless as he slammed to a jolting stop against the bar's brass foot rail. Lying still, he waited, relying on his ears to pick out Bruton's movements.

After a moment's silence under the table after firing, Bruton at last eased down out of his cramping crouch to the sawdust floor on hands and knees and gently lowered himself onto his belly. Prone and barely breathing, he extended his shooting arm and followed a searching arc being traced by his squinting eyes from the right side of the cluttered room, quickly through the corridor of light cast by the doorway and then leftward toward the stretch of the long bar where seeing was difficult because of the floor glare and the shadows cast by the bar itself and a clutter of stools.

Lying still, Bruton thought he saw something close to the bar that might be Morgan and, squint-eyed, gunned it.

Simultaneously, it seemed, Morgan heard the explosion, the snap of the bullet buzzing like a riled wasp past his right ear and the splintering of wood as the slug slammed into the bar.

In that same instant he saw the muzzle flash.

Flat on his belly with his Colt Peacemaker nestled at the point of his triangulated arms, he aimed for the flash spot, firing one shot that drilled through Jesse Bruton's left eye and emerged tearing a gaping hole at the back of his head.

That night in the El Dorado with the blood and brains left where they'd splattered for the ogling of the curious, nobody could recall having witnessed or read about any shootout wherein both contestants had dueled from the prone position.

Within two days a hastily convened grand jury probed the incident and concluded that in as much as there'd been two shots discharged by Jesse Bruton, whereas Morgan had fired only once, it was evident that Jesse had to have fired first. Ruling it a clear case of self-defense, they returned no indictment.

Within a week, Morgan was gone and not since he'd first appeared mysteriously amongst them almost two decades ago did the folks of Goliad have so much cause to gossip concerning him.

"He's sold the Triple M spread lock, stock, and barrel to Dalgo," they soon were saying all over town.

This would eventually be proved true, although no one could believe it possible that the sale was accomplished with a handshake and Dalgo paying Morgan the sum of one silver dollar.

"He gave the bulk of what he had in the bank to Migdalia Coffee so she could get out of the cantina business and retire in luxury," they whispered next.

This was also true, as a loose-tongued bank clerk soon attested. "What he didn't sign over to her, he took with him," the agog clerk revealed. "A hundred thousand dollars! *In cash.*"

"Why had he done all this?" Goliad asked.

The considered verdict of the talk of the sidewalks, the lobby of the Case hotel, restaurants, livery stables, barber shop, the Maetze and Brothers staples and grocery emporium, hardware stores, supper tables, church socials and quilting bees, the school recess, the dance hall, saloons and, of course, the under-new-ownership El Dorado cantina was, "The loss of those boys just broke his heart."

Heartbreak. Yes, that had to be it.

The killing of the boys was the last straw, they decided.

Which was accurate. But not all.

Dalgo knew the rest.

"Why are you doin' this, boss?" he'd asked as Morgan made up a pack and bedroll as if he were cattle driving again.

"Because," said Morgan, "I'm sick of all the killin'."

Goliad's next question was, "Where'd he go?"

"As rich as he left here he could go anywhere in the world," observed the bank clerk.

Someone recalled hearing him speak once of a long-held dream of settling in California. Someone else ventured, "He's returned to Pennsylvania. Back where he hailed from. He was a Yankee, you'll recall."

Not even Dalgo and Migdalia knew the destination he had in mind as he saddled up. "I don't want anybody followin' me or trackin' me down," he said to them. "I'm just gonna disappear for a time. When I'm settled, I'll let you know where."

As he rocked down the road, Migdalia brushed tears from her cheeks and turned a sidelong glance to Dalgo. "Where do you think he's headin'?"

After a moment of thoughtful twisting of his splendidly full and drooping black mustache that his boss had always envied, the little caporal replied, "Prob'ly someplace where he was happy."

Chapter Forty

Squinting out from the shade of the porch of the rambling white clapboard house through the sear high prairie grass at the ungainly figure of a boy loping from the direction of Mud Creek, Morgan thought for a moment that the boy he saw loping toward him was himself, that somehow the ghost of his boyhood had materialized in the shimmer of the sun. Then he thought it might be Colt or Owen but that was impossible. Jesse Bruton had killed them in 1889.

This was 1902. A new century but the old heartbreak, he thought as he recognized that this big-eared, tow-headed boy ambling his way was one of the Eisenhower sons, the fellow called Little Ike by his pals. "Howdy, Mr. Morgan," he said, stepping out onto the porch and sitting uninvited and never considering that he wouldn't be.

Coming down flat in the chair he'd been tilting back on, planting his brush-scuffed high-heeled brown boots on the freshly painted gray floor, Morgan asked, "Whatcha up to today, Eisenhower? Swimming? Or going fishing in Mud Creek?"

"Neither, Mr. Morgan," said the boy. Staring into the blaze of the long rolling sweep of that part of the prairie, his heart was not set on the pleasures of a blindingly hot Kansas afternoon when skinny dipping in Mud Creek was a proper thing for a boy to do but on the Abilene of a third of a century ago, on the "Old Days" when Texas Street had been lined with gaudy saloons named Alamo, Bull's Head, Elkhorn, Pearl, and Old Fruit and, of course, Long Charlie Carew's, bawdy houses, dance halls, and gambling dens peopled with painted women and trail-dusted cowboys quick to draw blazing six-guns, a bare-knuckled God-forsaken spot that finally came to need the likes of Wild Bill Hickock to tame it, the Abilene Ike Eisenhower'd been born too late to know first-hand and so had to ask old geezers like Morgan about it. "Is it true what they say about you, Mr. Morgan?" the boy asked hopefully.

"What've you heard?"

Ike shrugged. "Stuff."

"Stuff?" Morgan laughed scornfully at the lack of respect in the word. "What . . . *stuff?*"

"About you being a gunslinger. And about you fighting with the Colt and a Bowie knife. About the men you killed. About . . . you know!"

Fixing his eyes on Ike's, Morgan recognized he had the boy in the palm of his hand, appreciated that Ike was eager to while away the afternoon with all the stories — true and false — about the rowdy years after J.G. McCoy came from Illinois to Kansas to put a no-account prairie hamlet by the name of Abilene on the map as the Queen of the Cowtowns, but he aimed to set an instructive tone for the benefit of young Eisenhower and in that voice that men take on when they are about to deliver a story with a moral began by saying, "I can't help remarking that if I had heeded the advice of a friend of mine and high-tailed it back to Pennsylvania . . ."

Disappointment clouded Ike's eyes and Morgan left

dangling in the hot air the lesson he might have taught, how he might have gone on to be a fine writer of the likes of Bret Harte or Mark Twain or Richard Henry Dana or Henry Kidder instead of winding up being written about in the lore of the West as Morgan the knife-and-gun street-fighter, Morgan the flinty cowhand of the Chisholm Trail and Morgan the ruthless Nueces Strip cattle baron.

"Yes, I was a gunman," he sighed.

"I thought so," Ike said with a vindicated jerk of the head. "I've heard that you were the best gunslinger of all, that you killed more'n a hundred men."

"Not quite that many."

"More than a hundred's what I heard," the boy insisted.

Studying the boy's worried face, Morgan said, "It could have been a hundred. I didn't exactly keep count."

Ike grinned—and what a grin!—as if his lips were made of elastic, a winning stretch of smile brimming with boyish pleasure and relief to hear that, yes, Morgan had been a gunslinger.

As Ike's unspoiled eyes widened in anticipation of the retelling of familiar tales, Morgan cocked back in his chair and propped his boots on the railing to unwind the stories that would be replete with all the fanciful embroidering that had become part of the Morgan legend down through the years, yarns that this boy named Ike had tramped across a field where Joe McCoy's Texas longhorn cattle used to gather to hear all about it from someone who'd been present in the rough-and-tumble shoot-em-up heyday of Kansas and Abilene and all the other trail towns when Morgan had been in his prime—of George Armstrong Custer, the Seventh Cavalry, California Joe, Major Ward Kimball, Long Charlie, and Bad John Redus, of gals and guns, of Cheyennes, of buffalo and Texas longhorns and Texas Rangers, of a man called Novillero and a caporal called Dalgo, of a woman called Rebecca and one named Sarah, of Buck Colter, of Shanghai Pierce and of a sweet horse called Strawberry and one named Grulla, of two boys named Daniel Lonetree and Mickey Ludlum and one way back in the Battle of Gettysburg whose name he never knew and boys named Colt and Owen who'd died way before their time — but presently it got to be a dusky hour when twelve-year-old boys have chores to do and, having stirred the embers of recollection into flame, leave an old man with nothing but echoes of memories to fill the long and lonesome night.